ROAD TRIP

Tania Park

National Library of Australia Cataloguing-in-Publication entry
Creator: Park, Tania, author.
Title: Road Trip / Tania Park.
ISBN: 978-0-9942847-6-1 (Paperback)
ISBN: 978-0-9942847-7-8 (Ebook)
Target Audience: For young adults.
Subjects: Friendship--Juvenile fiction. Automobile travel--Australia--
          Juvenile fiction. Adventure stories. Young adult fiction
          Suspense fiction.
Dewey Number: A823.4

Printed & Channel Distribution
Cover Designed—Laila Savolainen
Publishing Consultants/Interior Design—Pickawoowoo Publishing Group
Publisher
Tania Park Publishing
For enquiries, write to: rights and permissions via publisher.
Lightning Source | Ingram (USA/UK/EUROPE/AUS)

Also by Tania Park

Mistaken

'He never got around to telling me why he wanted me dead.'

When Bella's new boss whacked her across the head and dropped her over a cliff, her life changed in an instant. She became a naïve pawn caught in a very dangerous game.

Retribution

Living with a new identity in a different state on the other side of the country, Amy Masters is stunned and terrified when her ex-husband turns up at her place of work. After almost killing her, he is supposed to be still in jail.

Blind justice

"Panic turned to terror at the sudden onrush of two sets of feet. A rough hand clamped over her mouth to silence her."

Piano bar pianist, Christine Mears, becomes involved in a murder investigation when she meets Detective Ben Somers. She unwittingly becomes the main target of an unscrupulous gang of drug dealers. To them she is worth two million dollars and the gang goes to extreme lengths to snatch Christine to use as ransom.

This book is dedicated to my dear friend, Maria Antonas. She gave me the idea for this book several years ago. She wanted young protagonists. When I began writing, Maria, a former English teacher, read many of my manuscripts in their early stages and is a master of encouragement.

Thank you to members of my writers' group for reading and editing separate chapters of this book. Your input and suggestions are much appreciated. You always manage to find the tiniest of errors. A special thank you to Jodie, whose constant emails of encouragement gave me the impetus to knuckle down and get the final few chapters completed after a too long hiatus of writer's block. Life and other projects kept getting in the way and taking precedence.

As always, thank you to my husband, James, for your constant support.

Chapter One

'Did you hear that?' squeaked Gemma.

Hot breath filled Maddie's ear from the mouth plastered against the side of her face. The vice-like grip on her arm and long nails eating into her flesh sent her a distinct message: Gemma was feeling just as petrified as Maddie. Without making a noise, Maddie gave the hand an encouraging pat then prised the rigid fingers from her arm. Her stomach was in knots as she lay back in her sleeping bag, waiting… and listening… her body on full alert. Oppressive heat pressed against her skin, melding with the tension of waiting for another noise from outside.

Thud. Oh, God, was that a tree branch dropping to the ground?

A spurt of adrenaline surged through her veins. When a whimper forced its way from the back of her throat, she clenched her lips tight together to prevent any more sounds escaping. But Gemma didn't have the same resilience. When high pitched oohs escaped Gemma's mouth Maddie reached over and placed a hand over her friend's mouth.

It wasn't usual for an almost moonless night to bother Maddie but she wished she could see through the thin layer of nylon, the only barrier between them and whoever was roaming around their secluded camping spot. Even more, she wished she hadn't agreed to this hair-brained plan of Gemma's. Why hadn't she gone with her initial gut instincts when Gemma first suggested the idea? It wasn't as if she didn't like camping – she did. Maddie had spent her entire childhood on camping trips with her family, but their normal choice of place to erect a tent was in camping grounds with at least some basic facilities and lots of people around. Not in some forsaken outback place off the main highway. The only times they had roughed it out in the bush, Dad and her older brother, Paul, had been there to protect her.

Thud… thud… snap! That wasn't a branch. It sounded more like someone tossing heavy rocks at them.

Maddie sucked in her breath, holding it in until she had to either breathe or pass out. With passing out not a viable option, the air whooshed from her mouth, the sudden noise causing Gemma to jump beside her. The jolt further inflamed Maddie's nerves, which were already stretched so taut she felt as though they would snap then rebound around the sides of the tent like a ricocheting bullet. A bullet – now that would be rather useful right now, along with the gun to fire it. Not that either of them had ever handled a real gun, let alone knew how to use one. But still, it would be a handy thing to have, even if they only waved it around in the air while threatening all sorts of dire consequences. Anything would be better than this terrifying wait.

Gripping Gemma's hand, Maddie attuned her ears to the slightest sound, undecided on what was better; the uncanny eerie silence or the occasional muffled noises. With silence, they didn't know how close their attackers were. Maybe they were standing right in front of the zippered flap waiting for the girls to emerge. At the thought, Maddie rolled her eyes towards her feet: towards the flap. Even the slightest shadow would give her a clue but it was so darn dark now that the moon, which had been brighter earlier, had all but disappeared beyond the horizon.

With her free hand, Maddie groped around above her head for the torch. She knew it was there, somewhere. Her fingers sidled under the edge of her pillow then crept along the plastic groundsheet until they reached the side of the tent. She felt something hard, cold and circular, wrapped her fingers around then lifted it, but it didn't feel right – not heavy enough. Easing her fingers from Gemma's clenched grip, she brought both hands together then felt along the entire length. Too short, she decided as she lowered it to her nose then sniffed. Deodorant! She dropped it onto her chest in disgust before continuing her search for the torch.

Thud… snap.

Maddie froze and felt Gemma stiffen. The noise seemed so much closer and it definitely sounded like the cracking of a dry stick underneath a heavy boot.

Apart from rapid breathing from Gemma, silence ensued; the sort of silence that was so intense it was downright scary. And Maddie was beyond being scared.

After what seemed like an interminable pause, Maddie continued on her quest, biting hard on her tongue when she almost yelled out in triumph as her hand curled around the cold metal shaft of the torch. Right weight, right length but did she dare switch it on? Decisions, decisions! No. Whoever was out there scaring the living daylights out of them, didn't know they were awake. The element of surprise was their only defence – well, that and the torch. Maddie scoured the recesses of her brain to recall what else they had with them in the tent to use as a battering ram. If only she hadn't insisted on stowing most of their possessions on the back seat of the car. Thongs, toiletries and a roll of toilet tissue were not the ideal weapons. Toilet, now there's another weapon.

Tucking the torch into the waistband of her short pyjama bottoms, Maddie began to wriggle her way out of her sleeping bag, shoving the dense padded fabric downwards as she eased her knees up towards her chest. The slithering fabric sounded like a sonic boom in the maudlin silence.

Thud… thud… thud. Far out, was that their belongings being tossed onto the ground? Was someone going to steal their car and leave them here out in the middle of no-where?

Gemma's indrawn breath was way too audible as she groped for Maddie, her long fingernail catching the tender flesh on the inside of Maddie's thigh. Maddie gritted her teeth together as she grabbed Gemma's hand and tore it away from her leg, hoping Gemma hadn't drawn blood. Heaven help me, but Gemma was going to pay for tonight. Her and her stupid, foolish, dumb ideas!

It felt like forever with no more noises before Maddie dared to slide her legs the final few centimetres out of the confines of the single sleeping bag then crawled on her knees towards the opening, seeking out the only other possible weapon they had within reach. They hadn't had to use it yet but she was certain they would before they left in the morning. While she searched around in the dark for the short handled shovel, she grinned as she recalled the look of horror on Gemma's face when Maddie had explained what it was for. It was at that precise moment when Maddie had known for sure, despite Gemma's very verbose denials, Gemma had never, ever, roughed it before. If she had then Gemma's definition of roughing it was way different from Maddie's. After explaining how one used the shovel to dig a hole in the dirt, squat to do the necessary, then cover over the evidence, Maddie felt certain she was going to live to regret the very second she had agreed to drive across Australia with her friend and living under the stars to save money. She hadn't expected the crunch to come so soon – on their very first night. Maybe it wasn't too late to turn around and return home. They'd only driven five hundred odd kilometres: five hundred and sixty six to be exact. Turning into the first back-road after Coolgardie, they had continued driving until they found a patch of dense bush off the beaten track. It had sounded like a brilliant idea at the time. The place appeared to be completely deserted. She hadn't reckoned on having to share the place with unknown, scary visitors.

At last, Maddie found the shovel leant up in the corner of the tent and recalled how they'd laughed earlier at the way the bulky weight had made such a strange looking bulge from the outside. She felt a lot more confident now she had a fairly decent weapon that could actually do some damage to an attacker. With a sharp rectangular blade and a pointy pick on the other end for the particularly hard ground, the shovel could be a lethal weapon if wielded correctly, but she figured that trying to attack from a flimsy tent at ground level was not all that advantageous.

Shuffling sideways, Maddie felt with her free hand for the tent zipper. Settling the shovel on the ground by her leg, she hunched forwards, pausing to whip the torch from its temporary home as it bit into her stomach muscles. As she eased the zipper upwards she cringed at the noise every time a tooth opened. To her stretched nerves, the sound seemed to echo through the night.

While Maddie worked, she felt Gemma extricating her body from the rumpled confines of her sleeping bag, suppressing her whimpers each time one of them made too much noise. Maddie paused when she heard the snapping of a dry twig, followed closely by two thuds that sounded a lot like someone trying their best to muffle footsteps. This time the sound appeared to be a little further away but she wasn't sure if it was only an illusion because of the increased tension from inside the tiny tent.

When her feet were grabbed, Maddie's heart skipped and bounced in fear and she had to cease trying to free the zipper until her palpitations eased a bit but the extra spurt of adrenaline had her nerves more on edge. Reaching to one side she picked up the torch, twisted then felt around until she had one of Gemma's hands in her fingers, physically wrapping Gemma's fingers around the torch, followed by the motions of lifting her arm in the air as though to hit someone over the head.

Gemma's free hand grabbed Maddie's arm, indicating she understood the intention, and then Gemma shuffled sideways before inching her way forwards until they were side-by-side.

Bending towards the flap once again, Maddie restarted the task of easing the zipper, notch by notch, until it was high enough for her to fit her head through. Leaning right down to the ground, she groped for the shovel, tucked it close to her body then kept her finger and thumb on the zipper tab, ready to whizz it up in one quick action. With her chin on the ground, she peered through the hole, her heart lodged in her throat. She saw nothing, heard nothing. She flashed her eyes in all directions, then spying nothing she ventured further, daring to poke her head outside.

Thud.

Maddie collapsed onto the ground, burying her exposed face into her free hand. Her body convulsed.

Trying to gain control, Maddie wriggled backwards until she was inside then she whooped the zipper higher, her body shaking so hard she had trouble keeping a grip on the tiny tab. Once the flap was open, she reached for Gemma, grabbed the torch and flicked the switch. In one foul swoop she shoved Gemma forwards, the top part of her body shooting out into the night air. Maddie aimed the light outside, waving it around until the beam shone on the culprit. Unable to hold still a moment longer, she dropped the torch on the dew dampened ground then fell back on her foam mattress doubled up in laughter while waiting until Gemma computed the source of the noise. She didn't have to wait very long.

'Kangaroos! Kangaroos! I almost peed myself I was so petrified of… darn stupid kangaroos!' Gemma's loud outburst had the mob bound away in a scurry of thuds.

Still contorted with laughter, Maddie rolled around the floor of the tent unable to find control. She felt Gemma crawl all the way outside while she shouted at the top of her voice to the long-gone animals.

'Vamoose and stay vamoosed!' she yelled into the darkness before stomping around the small clearing, releasing all her angst in a tirade of abuse at the poor defenceless creatures.

'Crap!' Gemma yelled, halting Maddie's laughter in an instant. She shot out of the tent to see the beam of light from the torch shining towards the ground. Little jellybean-shaped pellets coloured in a cross between lime green and aniseed black covered the area beneath where Gemma was standing. 'Oh, yuck!' hissed from Gemma's mouth.

'That's five dollars you owe me,' Maddie called out.

'What for?' Gemma wrinkled her nose in distaste while she searched the ground for a clear spot so she could move to where there were no fresh kangaroo droppings.

'You swore.' Maddie reached back inside the flap to retrieve her rubber thongs.

'Sorry.' Gemma sounded mollified but Maddie knew it was nothing more than an apology of appeasement. Swearing was second nature to Gemma, something they were working on to overcome at Gemma's insistence. After being dumped by a boy she really liked because of her constant use of four letter words, Gemma had begged Maddie to help her overcome the bad habit. The fine system worked well, more so when Gemma agreed to up the ante to five dollars for each word. One dollar hadn't worked so well. She came from a well-off family and a single dollar barely made a dent in her allowance.

After slipping her feet into the thongs, Maddie crawled from the tent and stood then slowly spun around, her eyes following the trail of the light beam until she could make out the outline of Gemma squirming on the one spot. It was a shade lighter outside making it easier to discern shapes and shadows. 'What on earth is wrong with you?' Maddie said as she neared the writhing form.

'Roo poo. It's all over my feet. Can you get my thongs for me?'

Maddie was unable to swallow the giggle that erupted from her throat as she turned back to the tent, reached in then groped around until she had the second pair of thongs in her hands. 'You might want to wash your feet before you put them on.' The words came out accompanied by another giggle as Maddie passed the shoes over.

'It's not funny.'

'It is from where I'm standing and you still owe me five dollars.' Maddie retrieved a fold-up canvas chair from against the tree trunk they had stashed it before going to bed and opened it out next to Gemma. 'Sit here. I'll find some tissues and water.' After disappearing back into the tent, she emerged triumphant with the car keys in her hand.

'Nobody heard me and its extenuating circumstances,' Gemma pleaded as she sank onto the nylon webbing of the chair, lifting her feet from the ground.

'I heard you and we have a pact. We don't swear – ever.' Her voice faded as she leant into the rear seat of the car, switching on the internal light before rummaging around amongst their belongings.

'It's not really a swear word.'

'It's still unladylike and not the type of word we use if we want to be shown respect from the really nice guys we're looking for. This was your idea remember.' Maddie dropped the plastic container of moisturised wipes into Gemma's lap. It was difficult to not let loose with another giggle when she spied the dobs of squashed manure on the soles of Gemma's feet as she inspected them under the glare of the torch.

'Oh, this is disgusting.' Gemma scrubbed away with one wipe after another, scrunching each soiled one up into a ball, her nose wrinkling as she systematically cleaned away gunge from between her toes, ensuring she scraped every last skerrick from her skin, going over and over again with clean wipes. 'I'll never feel clean again. What do I do with these?' She held up the ball of wipes in one hand.

'I guess the best thing is to dig a hole and bury them. I'll get you the shovel.'

There were several moans and groans from the site where Gemma hacked away at the hard, red dirt before she emerged from the darkness. After gulping down half a bottle of water each, they crawled back into their sleeping bags. But sleep eluded them so they lay chatting quietly, interspersed with fits of giggles at the absurdity of the happenings of the night.

Chapter Two

Even so early in the morning the summer sun beat down in a relentless tattoo, turning the inside of the skimpy nylon tent into an oven. Erecting the tent under the shade of a gum tree late the previous afternoon had been a great idea at the time. But it was now shadeless with the already hot morning sun's rays having no barrier. Unable to stand the cloying humidity a moment longer, Maddie searched around for her rubber thongs and wriggled her toes to the end before crawling through the flap. She sucked in a lung full of fresh, cooler air, a grin splitting her face as she recalled the results of Gemma's forgetfulness during the night.

Not bothering to cover her mouth, Maddie yawned, her loud groan stilling the native insects and birds into sudden silence. A few seconds later they continued their morning chirps and twitters. Maddie stretched her arms wide to ease the chinks in her body before wandering away from their camping spot to seek out the privacy of a dense bush to relieve a full bladder. She searched the ground around her for the presence of unwelcome critters, such as snakes, scorpions or ants, before lowering her bare backside towards the earth. The sounds of birds busy foraging for seeds and insects didn't bother her, but the chorus of cicadas so early in the morning indicated the day was going to be very hot. The air already smelt stifling.

Back at the car, Maddie stripped off then pulled on some underclothes, a tank top and a pair of running shorts before retrieving two small bottles of cold water from the icebox along with muesli bars and fruit for their breakfast, setting them out on the chair still unfurled from the night before.

'Rise and shine, Gem, it's much cooler out here,' she called as she thumped the side of the tent.

'Any furry visitors?' Gemma's response came out as a groan, which had Maddie figuring Gemma hadn't had much sleep either.

'They'll be too scared to ever come back here after you screeching at them like a banshee. There are only birds and cicadas to keep us company this morning.'

A sleepy-eyed face, crowned with short, dark spiky hair emerged from the flap of the tent. 'How can you be so bright and upbeat? I hardly slept. I was too scared.'

Maddie laughed as she bent to haul her friend from the tent, pointing towards Gemma's thongs next to the flap with a wry grimace.

Before sliding her feet into the flimsy footwear, Gemma inspected the sole of each foot with avid scrutiny to ensure they were clean. There was a definite shudder down her body. She wandered away with an over-exaggerated air of nonchalance to find a suitable bush.

Feeling devilish, Maddie waited until Gemma's head disappeared below the leafy growth before calling out. 'Watch out for scorpions or snakes.' Her laugh turned wicked when Gemma shrieked out in alarm, her head shooting up above the foliage then dropping from sight again, mumbling very audible derogatory comments when she realised Maddie was teasing.

Maddie couldn't suppress a smile when she noticed Gemma was inspecting every centimetre of the soil for some critter before placing each foot on the red dirt during her return journey.

'I'm going for a quick run,' said Maddie as Gemma approached.

'Why?'

'Because I get antsy sitting cooped up in a car all day and after a night with not enough sleep my head feels a bit woolly.' She headed towards the car, searched around for her sneakers and withdrew clean socks from her clothes bag. Running a few kilometres had been a morning ritual since beginning secondary school when she'd taken outdoor education as one of her major studies. It had become a habit and something she enjoyed, especially when she ran as the sun was rising. That time of the morning when the birds and animals were waking and most of the human population were still tucked under the blankets had become something magical. Maybe not so magical in the dead of winter when it was freezing but even when it rained, she rarely missed her early morning run.

Perching on the edge of the fold-up chair, she brushed the soles of her feet with the back of her hand before donning socks and shoes. 'I'll only be about ten minutes,' she said as she stood. 'How about boiling the kettle on the gas burner so we can have a mug of tea with our breakfast?'

Maddie hadn't expected pounding red dirt in the middle of nowhere could be so interesting. What she'd envisaged was for the bush to be boring but an amazing number of birds of so many different descriptions flittered amongst the low scraggly bushes, giving her heart a jolt when they suddenly flapped their wings, startling her as much as she probably startled them. She slowed to a walk when a speckled tan and black blue-tongue lizard waddled across her path. She didn't mind them especially when she believed the old saying that if there was a goanna then there probably weren't any snakes. Snakes, she wasn't so fond of although they were shy creatures and would only attack if threatened. But then again, what animal didn't try to defend itself if it was threatened – including the human variety. Only most Australian animals didn't pack a punch of deadly poison in their fangs like the venomous snakes.

A bush with the most amazing brilliant vermillion flowers drew her to a stand-still. She crouched down and gently wrapped her fingers around the puffball feathery bloom. Miniscule bright yellow stamens decorated each fluffy flower. It wasn't a native plant she was familiar with but it was gorgeous. She sniffed, jerking back when she discovered she was sharing the blossom with a bee. There was no strong perfume from the flowers but the spiky leaves smelt – bushy was the only word she could think of.

Continuing on at a steady trot she only glanced at foliage of the bushes as she passed. There were very few blooms left but she bet they'd been spectacular a few months earlier in the flush of spring. Western Australia had an amazing variety of native flora but not enough locals appreciated the natural beauty. They seemed to take it for granted. It was mostly tourists from other states and countries that came in droves during the wildflower season to marvel and photograph the unique native flowers.

A sudden whiff hit her nostrils. Maddie stopped dead and sniffed the air. Smoke? Couldn't be. She sniffed again and spun in a slow circle to see which direction the smoke was coming from while glancing along the horizon seeking out a rising swirl of grey cloud. She was almost one hundred and eighty degrees when a shriek filled the air.

'Maddie!'

At the same time she saw the twirling plume of white – right where their camp was. No way! Oh, God! What had Gemma done? How could she have smoke? Had she blown up the gas burner? Adrenaline spurted and Maddie took off running frantically, her feet pounding the dry dirt and sending up puff balls of red dust that swirled around her ankles at each step.

'Gemma!' she yelled then to save her breath snapped her mouth shut and increased her speed, pumping her arms and willing her legs to move faster. Within seconds, perspiration that had only hinted at falling on the steady outward leg, erupted from her pores and began pooling into large droplets before dripping from her face. It seemed to take forever to make progress. Just how far had she run?

'Maddie, help!' came a panicked scream.

To shorten the distance Maddie leapt over a low shrub and into the bush, veering away from the gravel along the edge of the road. Zigzagging, she dodged the larger shrubs and few spindly trees and jumped over the lower plants. Too bad if there was any wildlife sheltering behind rocks or bushes, she didn't have the mindset to seek out then evade any bities.

'Maddie!' Gemma screeched again just as Maddie came close enough to see the source of the smoke.

Far out! Flames flickered in an ever increasing circle around a pathetic ring of small stones. Why oh why did Gemma light an open fire? Unbelievable!

'Grab some bottles of water and something to beat the flames out with,' Maddie yelled as she began stamping on burning leaves and fallen tree litter. She scuffed and kicked, sending loose soil scattering over the flames, working from the outside towards the source of the flames. Burning eucalyptus leaves had a unique smell that usually brought forth pleasant memories of feeling at home. But not now. Here the smell was terrifying for if they didn't get this fire under control very soon it would be a raging inferno within minutes. They could lose everything, including the car. In this weather fire could spread so rapidly and devastate an enormous swathe of countryside.

Maddie pummelled the ground with her feet, sending up blackened ash, red dust and smoke – so much smoke. 'Hurry up, Gemma,' she yelled as she ripped off her tank-top and began beating at the outer edge of the flames. As she beat, she sidled around the circle that seemed to be growing bigger and bigger by the second. The strong eucalyptus tainted smoke invaded her nostrils and seemed to loosen every ounce of mucous stored in her body. Her nose felt like it was a tap turned full on and was accompanied by tears flooding across her eyes in attempt to cleanse the surface of the cloying ash and foreign bodies before streaming down her face.

'Here,' called Gemma from behind before she dissolved into a bout of coughing.

Maddie felt something nudge her back and spun around, spied a bleary image of a two litre bottle of their emergency water. She grabbed it from Gemma's hands then shoved her shirt into the waistband of her shorts before twisting the top off. She jammed one thumb over the top of the bottle and gave it a vigorous shake to create a spray of water.

'Spray water on the outside of the flames. Water down the leaves so they can't catch alight,' Maddie panted as she began spurting water at the same time as she stomped on the burning tinder. She swore under her breath when she noticed Gemma following in her wake and dousing what Maddie had already doused 'Go the other way,' yelled Maddie, 'and hurry. Stamp your feet on the flames. We have to stop this.'

'I've run out of water,' called Gemma, 'what do I do now?'

'Oh, Lord, give me strength,' muttered Maddie under her breath. Doesn't the girl have any brains? 'Grab something to beat at the flames,' she bit out as she emptied the last of her water onto a seriously burning length of dry wood. It hissed and spat before Maddie kicked it into an already burned area then jumped back at the flying red coals and flickering splinters. With no more fuel it would burn itself out. Then an idea struck and she bolted towards the tent, noticing how close it was to the flames. Far out, they could lose all their bedding as well. She grabbed the small shovel and pounded back to the edge of the fire nearest the tent, put her back to the flames and, bent over at the waist, began scraping the dirt and anything else that was in her path, back onto the already singed earth, hoping to smother the orange and yellow flames.

Sidling as she went, Maddie kept up at a frantic pace: hit, scrape, fling, hit, scrape and fling. Her heart seemed to be pumping in rhythm as did the gasps being forced from her tortured lungs. She dared a glance around. The blackened patch seemed enormous. Gemma was still beating at licking flames that seemed to go underground then emerge several centimetres further away, starting up numerous spot fires.

Finally reaching her starting point, Maddie paused to take stock. She scanned the area and leapt towards a river of flame that had escaped and was flickering bright orange at an alarming rate under and along each side of a fallen dead branch. The way the wood and twigs burst into flame indicated just how tinder dry the bush was. She stomped on the highest flares with her feet then yanked out her shirt and pummelled the area, not stopping until she was certain she'd beaten the flames into submission. 'Grab two more bottles of water,' she called to Gemma then stomped on a few glowing embers before shovelling them back into an already burnt area.

Gemma ran back with four bottles of water in her arms. 'Here,' she said as she handed two over.

'Okay, it's nearly out but don't waste the water. We have to drown any glowing coals so they can't flare up again and work from the outside, dampening down the leaves and twigs so they can't catch alight. Then work your way into the centre. Put your thumb over the spout and spray the water like you do with a hose.'

It only took a couple of seconds to ensure Gemma was doing the right thing then Maddie worked her way around the circle again, being careful to spurt and spray only where needed. Blackened ash turned white as hissing steam rose in curling tendrils. Steam was good, smoke wasn't so welcome and flames were a definite no-no.

Before opening her final bottle, Maddie stepped back and studied the entire area with deep scrutiny, casting her eyes over each section several times then widening her line of sight to ensure flames hadn't escaped to flare up elsewhere. Flying embers could land anywhere and catch hold, especially in such hot dry conditions. Finally satisfied they'd managed to get the fire out, Maddie walked over the burnt area, scuffing at anything that looked even remotely like it would flare up again. Man, oh, man, such a large patch had burnt to a crisp. She huffed out a long sigh of disbelief.

'I think it's out,' she said to Gemma as she tipped off breakfast items they hadn't had a chance to eat and flopped into the chair that was less than metre from the singed soil. Only then did she feel the ache in her muscles and notice the sweat that was still poring from overheated flesh. She felt exhausted. But she settled her eyes on Gemma, who had her chin on her chest and just stood to one side, pretending to be a statue or maybe hoping she could disappear from the face of the earth in a split second.

'You want to tell me how this fire started?' Maddie asked. She didn't move, couldn't move. Her jellified legs were stretched out and spread apart. Her arms flopped over the side of the seat, a still full bottle of water swinging from two fingers. She dropped the bottle onto the ground.

'You wanted me to boil the kettle.'

'Yes, and… that didn't require a full-blown bushfire. We have a portable gas ring. You light the gas and put the kettle on top.' Maddie knew she was being sarcastic but couldn't help it.

'I couldn't get the gas to light so I made a fire.'

'What?' Disbelief punched into Maddie. 'You lit a fire in the middle of the bush in the middle of the day in the middle of summer?' Maddie jerked upright. 'How could you be so stupid? You know the rules about fires; no naked flames during the fire restriction times and December is right slap bang in the middle of the friggin' restriction season.'

'But I put stones around it.' Even though Gemma sounded a tad chastened, there was a defiant tinge to her voice.

'Stones!' Maddie yelled. 'Even in winter you HAVE to have a three metre cleared area around a fire. Do you know how far three metres is?' Beyond angry, Maddie stormed from her seat, paced out three very long strides from the edge of the fire and using the heel of her shoe, dragged a circle all the way around then flapped her arms from side-to-side indicating the ten foot wide area. 'This is how much has to be cleared of all flammable material around a fire. A miniscule little ring of stones is about as much use as boobs on a bull.' She didn't care about her language, she was beyond caring.

Then she noticed the item hanging from Gemma's hands: the garment she had used to beat out the flames. Maddie's eyes boggled as she stared. 'My jeans! You used my brand new pair of jeans!' She grabbed them and shook them out. Apart from being filthy they had black ringed holes all the way down the front of the legs. At some stage the flames had caught the lower hem and burned a slash upwards. 'I don't believe this.'

'Sorry,' Gemma mumbled in such a meek little voice. 'I'll buy you a new pair.'

'Darn right you will,' Maddie spat as she flung the jeans into the middle of what had been the fire. They were useless; beyond repair. At the same time she noticed Gemma wince and pull back as though she thought she was going to be belted with the ruined pants. Good, let her suffer. Belting her over the head sounded such a wonderful idea but she doubted if it would knock any sense into Gemma.

Feeling as if she wanted to burst with anger and frustration, Maddie sucked in several very long breaths as she stalked away. Remaining angry was going to serve no purpose but trying to calm felt impossible. What was done was done. There'd been a fire that had almost gotten away from them. They managed to put it out with no real harm done. They'd used up all but one bottle of their emergency supply of drinking water. Thank goodness they'd had plenty of water. It was something both sets of parents had insisted upon before they'd left. Maddie was now the proud owner of a ruined tank top, which was no real loss since it was old, and a pair of ruined brand new jeans that had cost her way too much only a week ago and now they were worthless. She snorted and shook her head. Really, it was a small price to pay. She buried her head in her hands as she counted to ten slowly. Okay, she could live with this but Gemma was definitely going to replace the jeans. She spun around and swept at the wild tendrils of hair that were sticking to her face. She felt like a salt encrusted starched shirt that had been dragged through the dirt then a wringer.

'Okay, let's get cleaned up and have something to eat. There's enough water to wash off the worst of the grime if we use a flannel.' Saying nothing else because she didn't trust herself to not let loose with another tirade, Maddie began collecting their scattered belongings. She snatched and grabbed to work off some of the adrenaline still flooding through her arteries and veins. An uncanny tension had her turn around. Moisture was glistening on the edge of Gemma's eyelids and she looked pale and drawn.

'Are you all right?' Maddie asked as she hugged three empty plastic bottles against her chest.

Gemma began shaking her head then paused and gulped. She looked about ready to burst. Then the tears she'd so obviously been holding back, leaked from her eyes and tumbled down her pale cheeks. Gemma hated anyone seeing her cry so for her to not be able to keep the tears in check meant she was more than distressed.

'I was only trying to please you and… and now…' she sniffed and swiped at her eyes, leaving behind a dark streak of soot. 'And now you're mad at me. I'm sorry.' She sucked in a gasp and sniffed very unladylike before tugging the bottom of her shirt and rubbing it against her wet face. Smut was transferred from shirt to face and face to shirt leaving both looking clown-like. 'I didn't mean to set the place alight. I only wanted to make you a cup of tea to please you.' She turned away and curled up, squatting on her haunches and burying her face in her hands.

Maddie dropped the bottles and ran to Gemma. Falling to her knees she slung her arms around Gemma's shoulders and held her tight. 'I'm sorry I yelled. I guess I was so scared we'd lose everything and wouldn't be able to get the fire out. I shouldn't blame you, I'm sorry. It was an accident and I appreciate you wanting to please me.' She tugged Gemma tighter causing them to both tumble to the ground in a tangle of limbs. It was a tremendous relief when Gemma snorted then giggled then they both began laughing as they rolled on the ground.

When Maddie managed to sit up with her legs bent at the knees she studied them both. They were filthy and looked as though they'd been dragged through a mud spattered obstacle course. 'We look ridiculous,' she said as she stood and held out a helping hand before hauling a grinning Gemma to her feet.

'Yeah, and we're only twenty-four hours into our journey. Let's hope nothing else goes wrong. I'm hungry, let's eat.'

Chapter Three

After their brief breakfast, followed by a quick routine of teeth cleaning and dampening a flannel to wash the dirt and sweat from their faces and grimier body parts, they packed away their camping gear. Maddie found a clean set of clothes and bundled her ruined top and jeans into a plastic bag ready for the nearest rubbish bin. Relatively clean, they set off, headed for Kalgoorlie. Even though it was a fifty kilometre detour, they'd agreed they couldn't miss the opportunity to at least drive through the historical and now booming gold mining town. Besides it was the best place to purchase fuel and supplies, especially water.

First stop was the local grocery store where they bought eight two litre bottles of water and stowed them in the car. Then after visiting the local tourist bureau, they sat by the statue of Paddy Hannan whilst sipping on small bottles of iced tea as Gemma read passages from a pamphlet about the local history. 'It says, "*Kal,* as the locals call the place, was discovered in 1893. This main street is called Hannan Street after Paddy Hannan." This fellow here.' She patted the bronze statue on the head. 'He was the miner who found gold around here and started the gold rush. It says some of these buildings are over a hundred years old. Let's go and have a look.'

They headed down one side of the street then crossed the wide road to return up the other side. Satisfied they'd seen enough, they returned to the car then Gemma pulled into a service station that was so busy she had to queue behind another car. While Gemma waited her turn to fuel up, Maddie wandered inside, making full use of the ladies' room. If there had been a shower she would have taken the time to wash away the lingering dried sweat and stench of smoke. She stunk and knew it but so did Gemma. She bought two take-away mugs of frothy coffee, paying for the petrol out of their kitty at the same time.

When she emerged, a dark sedan stood in the bay where Gemma had been parked. Maddie felt uncomfortable at the way a tall, sandy haired man busy filling the car, stared at her. It was more than a stare, causing her to feel as though he was stripping her naked. She was creeped out when he began making lewd gestures. It didn't take any imagination to understand what one finger of one hand sliding in and out of the circle he had formed with the thumb and first finger on his other hand, meant. Especially when he pointed directly at her, then back down at his groin.

With a shudder, Maddie flipped a finger at him then instantly regretted her action when a look of anger swept across the man's face. Dumb move, provoking him like that, Madison Brown! She eyed the number plate and sighed in relief when she recognised the letters as local. Confident there would be no retribution for her rude gesture she swung her eyes around searching for their own vehicle. The creep deserved it in any case.

'Maddie, over here.'

Following the sound of Gemma's yell, Maddie twisted around then strode towards the scrawny mallee tree close to the road where Gemma had parked. There was so little shade from the bare branches it was hardly worth the while parking beneath it. Maddie sucked in the rich aroma as she handed over a mug. She settled into the passenger seat then lifted the lid of the console to place her coffee in the circular recess as Gemma started the engine.

'Cute, eh?' Gemma pulled her door closed, slamming it the second time when it hadn't clicked shut at her first attempt.

'Who? Where?' Maddie cast her eyes around, wondering whom the heck Gemma was talking about.

'The blue car. Three guys. I prefer the darker one in the back seat. Tall with lots of muscle.'

Maddie snorted in derision then wondered if she should tell her friend what the driver had done to her. Since they were leaving and they'd probably never see the men again, she decided to keep the incident to herself. 'Yeah, and by the look of the driver, way too old. What does that tell you? Three guys travelling together. They must be at least thirty, which means they aren't married, which means there must be something wrong with them. Not what we want. By the number plate they are locals. They're probably miners looking for a good time on their day off. Let's go. We've got a long hot drive ahead of us.'

The never-ending, shimmering heat haze rising from the blue-metal encrusted bitumen was an omnipotent presence, drawing them, sucking them into a supernatural vortex. The unceasing slash – slash – slash of the broken central white line added to the hypnotic effect. To ease the pull of the lines, Maddie centred her concentration on the passing scenery, wondering how many accidents happened when drivers lost concentration due to becoming mesmerised.

The low smoky underbrush was denser than she'd imagined it would be way out here. Mallee trees with glistening olive leaves were abundant, creating a jagged line in front of the blue-grey of far off hills. The Kalgoorlie pipeline, built a century ago to bring much needed water from the city to the prosperous gold town, snaked along the side of the road as it had done since leaving Mundaring in the Perth hills. She hadn't realised it went beyond Kalgoorlie but figured it had been added later to service Kambalda. Old miner's mullock heaps dotted through the bush, each one having Maddie wonder if the poor miner had found the elusive vein of gold or if he had perished in his quest. Were his bleached bones lying hidden down some long forgotten shaft? She shuddered at the thought. She wouldn't want to be roaming around the area in the dead of night. You'd never see the holes and could vanish from the face of the earth in an instant.

Even driving at the maximum speed limit they were forever being passed by other vehicles, temporarily blocking out the intense light of the still rising sun that was blaring into their eyes since they were driving due east. Each time they spotted a road train heading towards them, Gemma sucked in a breath, holding it in her lungs as she gripped the steering wheel until the massive truck had passed them by. Then she let the held air whoosh out in a wheeze. The vacuum created as the huge triple-trailered behemoths passed seemed to suck all the air from around them. Even not driving, Maddie felt their car veer towards the monsters until Gemma gripped the steering wheel to keep it steady. It was nerve-racking being the passenger and she imagined Gemma felt it more so, especially since she'd only had her driver's licence for a few months. Maddie felt more than relieved when they reached the next town, two hundred kilometres later.

Knowing Norseman was a regular rest spot for all travellers driving across the Nullarbor Plain, Maddie suggested they have a short rest to stretch their legs. It was the last decent town for the next thousand kilometres.

Pulling into the shade afforded by an iron clad lean-to at the first service station, Gemma sat back in her seat, her eyes closed, before reaching over to turn off the engine. There was an air of tension radiating from her.

'Are you all right, Gem?' Maddie asked.

'Yeah, I didn't realise it would be so intense driving. Miles of open road and yet it's so scary when those huge trucks pass you. I feel exhausted.' Gemma sighed then straightened before smiling; a smile that looked forced.

Maddie was concerned as she slid the catch up to open her door. Gemma wasn't all that experienced in driving. She'd thought the long stretches would have given Gemma much-needed practise but now she was having second thoughts. She hadn't reckoned on the pressure of passing so many big rigs. Resolving to take on a bigger share, she slid from the car, eager to stretch her body out and ease the tension in cramped muscles. The moment she stood on the ground, the intense heat hit, causing her to gasp. The air she breathed in felt as though someone had opened the door to a fiery furnace.

She squealed when the burning concrete singed her bare foot and immediately dropped back inside the car and slipped her thongs on her feet. She swiped at the sweat that oozed from the pores on her brow before she reached the main door to the café attached to the roadhouse.

'I can't believe it's so hot,' she said as Gemma joined her. It was much hotter than she'd anticipated. They rushed inside together, seeking the relief of overworked humming air-conditioners.

As they gravitated towards the glassed display of ready-prepared hot and cold food, they didn't need to discuss whether or not they would prepare their own lunch from the supplies in their icebox and plastic food bin. They reached for the cold cabinet door at the same time, grinning at each other as their hands clashed then selected the same pack of salad sandwiches.

'Juice?' asked Gemma as she turned towards the glass-fronted refrigerator.

'Apple for me, please,' said Maddie.

Settling at a table, they lingered over their meal before taking turns to make use of the facilities.

Maddie stared at the shower recess. A cold shower would be wonderful but the sign asking for money to pay for the water deterred her from taking a quick dip. But she promised herself, regardless of the cost, a long shower was on the agenda before the day was over. There were only so many days she would go without a proper shower even for the sake of economy.

Outside they ambled down the street. Norseman was a dinky little town serving a vast area. Many buildings looked old with weatherboard walls and corrugated iron roofs. There were wide verandas in front of some giving the shop fronts much needed shade.

Taking her turn at the wheel, Maddie settled back into her seat for the next long leg, almost two hundred kilometres to Balladonia. The map they read said it consisted of no more than a hotel/motel and a service station – the basic necessities required for outback travellers – food, water, fuel and shelter.

With the torrid mid-day sun beating down relentlessly, the shimmering heat turned into mirages of water on the horizon. Dark images of boats floating in the distance soon turned into enormous truck rigs as they neared – some measuring fifty-five metres long according to the warning signs plastered on the rear of each. Tension rose in the car whenever another vehicle approached. The gush of eddying wind being suctioned from around them sent Maddie's nerves into feeling like taut piano strings, followed by a release of held breath and obvious relaxation of muscles the moment she knew they were safe from being bulldozed over – the trailing dust cloud almost a welcome relief. Then the mesmerising white line drew her along until the next vehicle loomed.

To break the monotony of white lines on grey bitumen, Maddie kept glancing either side of the road. The terrain was flat with the occasional low curved line of purple hills in the distance. Dark red soil fed smaller and sparser Mallee trees interspersed with blue saltbush and feathery Quondong shrubs. The contrast in colours was awe-inspiring and something she hadn't expected. She'd heard people tell of the gorgeous colours of the outback, had seen them herself but certainly hadn't appreciated the sheer beauty until now. In the bright light, the new bark of the Mallee trees shone almost orange with a bronze pearlescent sheen; between silver strips of old bark peeling off. Young, smoky green saplings were growing from seeds that Maddie knew were only opened after a bushfire and there were definite signs that fire had been recent with skeletal remains of older burnt trees, which had khaki new growth covering the red dirt like large puffballs. She shuddered. They had so nearly caused another fire.

There were not so many cars passing them now, so the arrival of a vaguely familiar blue sedan, which sped right up to the tailgate of her car, caused Maddie's heart to start hammering. With frequent glances into the rear vision mirrors, Maddie recognised the light hair of the man filling the car back in Kalgoorlie. What really alarmed her was how close the car was, especially at the speed they were travelling. She guessed there couldn't have been more than two metres between the cars – probably less because she could only make out half the length of the bonnet. Adrenaline filled her veins, apprehension causing her heart to begin pounding.

All of a sudden the slumbering Gemma bolted upright from her reclining position and turned to Maddie.

'What's up?'

'Don't turn around. Use the side mirror to look. We've got company.' Maddie eased back on the accelerator, wincing when the car behind raced closer. Her heart shot up into her mouth then she dropped her hunched shoulders as the car matched her slower speed without the expected bump of car hitting car.

'Aren't those the hunks from Kalgoorlie?' Gemma twisted her head around to gain a better view then wriggled around in her seat, peering through the rear window. In her peripheral vision Maddie caught sight of Gemma actually waving at the hoons. She couldn't believe Gemma would be so stupid.

'I asked you not to turn around. Now they know they have our attention. Why did you do that?' Irritation grated at Gemma's impulsive action as Maddie sped up a fraction to see what the car behind would do. It matched her speed again.

'Sorry, but I wanted to make sure it was them. Maybe they want something. Maybe we should stop to talk to them.' Gemma plonked back into her seat but remained half twisted and kept shooting quick glances out of the back window.

'Are you out of your mind? I already know what they want – to make my life a misery. What they are doing is dangerous. If I stop suddenly they'll ram right into us then we'll be stuck out in the middle of no-where, defenceless against three crazy men. If I speed up they do the same and I'm not driving any faster, it's too dangerous. I told you there was something wrong with them. If they were decent guys they wouldn't be sitting in the boot of our car trying to kill us.

'You don't know that.' Gemma had a petulant pout on her lips.

'Yes, I do! Now let me concentrate. I'm going to slow down a bit more to see what happens.'

Maddie drew in a deep breath, releasing it very slowly in an attempt to force her tense muscles to relax before slackening off the accelerator even more. She'd already dropped from one hundred and ten to ninety and now she was down to eighty kilometres per hour. For a brief moment she closed her eyes when she spied the blue sedan close the gap, sure it was going to bump into them and force them off the road. She waited for the nudge and grind of metal.

It didn't happen.

She glanced back into the mirror. The car had copied her speed but was still so darn close.

The speedometer turned over. Another kilometre of terror. Maddie slowed even more, forcing the car to either pass or slow.

It slowed.

Maddie maintained speed for another kilometre then eased back again. Maybe if she decelerated enough they would tire of their little game give up and pass. Then what? Would they sit just in front of them or perhaps play silly buggers and force them off the road in some sick game?

She glanced ahead, searching for another vehicle for help. The road was clear as far as she could see, which was a long way with the land being so flat and the road virtually straight. Where were all the other drivers when you needed them? Even though she detested the big road trains, one right now would be more than welcome. Maddie searched the rear vision mirror for cars behind them then once again scanned the horizon for vehicles coming from the other direction.

There was nothing.

Maddie felt her nerves tighten even more as the blue sedan played cat and mouse games for the next fifty nerve-shattering kilometres. She was so tense that it felt as though the slightest noise would see her body ping apart and splatter into trillions of particles.

Then, thank goodness, she spied road trains from both directions. The one behind the two small cars was forced to slow right down rapidly as it couldn't pass with another big rig coming in the opposite direction. Even though she could hear the many sudden gear changes the poor driver had to make to slow the massive vehicle, Maddie refused to increase her speed. She was well aware she was travelling almost forty kilometres slower than the limit but she didn't really care.

A blast from the big rig. Both girls jumped. The noise was so loud. Maddie's already surging adrenaline gave another super shot to her heart. She could feel it palpitating madly.

Noticing a rest bay up ahead gave Maddie an idea. She waited until the very last moment then veered off without braking, sending up a scattering of gravel pebbles and billowing dust. She fought to maintain control of the steering wheel, her heart in her mouth as the car fishtailed in the loose dirt. She sent a silent message of thanks to her father for teaching her how to handle it.

Gemma screamed as she was tossed sideways against the door.

Since Maddie hadn't indicated her intentions, the driver of the blue sedan had no idea what she planned and was forced to drive on when it missed the entry to the bay for if it braked suddenly it would have been crushed like a stomped on aluminium can by the big rig. Thank goodness for small mercies, was all Maddie could think of as she fought the car back under control. Her muscles felt as though they had constricted into rigor mortis before a wave of shivering beset her.

Another long blast from the rig sounded as it passed. Maddie couldn't blame the driver. What she had done was almost suicidal. It was a wonder the massive rig, which was probably fully loaded, hadn't rammed into both cars and concertina-ed them together. Ignoring Gemma's wild protestations, Maddie pulled back onto the road behind the rig with the intention of using it as a shelter. When it began picking up speed, Maddie prayed it wouldn't go so fast she wouldn't be able to keep up.

Relief swept over her when she saw no sign of the blue sedan. She could only but hope the jerks inside had given up their little game.

Chapter Four

A desperate need for the bathroom was the only reason Maddie pulled into the roadhouse in Caiguna. Calculations the night before meant she felt certain they had enough fuel to reach the next stop, which was only a further sixty odd kilometres and the place they planned to stay overnight. She would have preferred to continue on without stopping but they'd both been wriggling in their seats for the past half-hour. A scarcity of trees or shrubs of a sufficient density to hide crouching forms meant there had been no place they could stop without being observed by drivers and passengers in passing vehicles. Even if there had been, there was no way she was actually going to stop the car, and then get out. Too many lunatics on the loose. Maddie mused how when you wanted passing motorists to help you, there were none, yet when you wanted a few minutes privacy, there were vehicles in a non-stop stream.

They'd given Balladonia a miss and now Maddie regretted it, but the fear of meeting up with the blue car had her speeding past, although she did search the expanse of cleared white dirt under the sparse trees for any flashes of blue. Even though she hadn't seen any sign of the car, gut instinct told her that if they'd been there they would have spied her.

The retreat from the ladies rest room was a little less hasty than the frantic race from the car, across the pavement to the door. Wiping her hands down the front of faded denim cut-offs after finding the metal container devoid of paper towels, Maddie wandered into the roadhouse to seek out cooling drinks while waiting for Gemma. She headed straight for the glass-fronted drinks' cabinet then stood scanning the contents before opening the door to pull out her selection. The blast of moist, icy air was so welcome she felt tempted to remain standing with the door wide open but the over-large sign printed on iridescent pink paper attached to the front of each door asking to be hasty in your selection to prevent the fridges from overheating, was a rather pointed deterrent.

With two plastic bottles of fruit punch in hand, she turned towards the counter, and paused mid-stride when she noticed a familiar head covered in light gold waves across the top of a row of shelving. A shudder snaked across her shoulders as unbidden scenes of the terrifying journey down the highway, interspersed with the obscene hand gestures, flashed through her mind.

Ducking down, Maddie turned around and crept to the end of the short aisle then peered around the corner, searching for the man's two companions. She spied neither but a quick glance confirmed the redhead was the driver of the blue sedan. He was fingering items on the shelves as though undecided on what to buy. Or was he just waiting for her? Did he know she was there? Far out, their car was sitting out on the concourse like a beaming iridescent bullseye. But she hadn't seen the blue car. Had they just arrived? Then they must know Maddie and Gemma were there. But that wasn't logical. They were ahead of the truck so must have reached here first. Maybe, just maybe the jerks hadn't seen them yet.

When the man sidled towards her, Maddie yanked her head back and scampered back down the aisle with knees bent, her eyes swinging back and forth, watching out for his appearance. Reaching the end of the aisle, she paused then straightened her knees to find out his exact position. He was heading towards the magazine rack across the back wall and since he had his back to her, Maddie scooted across the gap between the aisles and hid behind the next set of shelves.

'Can I help you?' Maddie bit down her squeal of fright at the same time as her body jerked then tensed at the voice coming from behind her. Shaking, she spun around and was mighty relieved to find standing in front of her, the shop assistant who had earlier been serving at the till.

'Err, no, I've changed my mind.' Maddie's voice sounded as though she was being strangled as she thrust the two bottles into the young man's arms and fled the premises, almost colliding with Gemma who was entering through the front door. Maddie grabbed Gemma around her forearm and dragged her towards their car.

'We need to get going – now,' she whispered. In her panic her voice had taken on a squeaky harshness. Reaching the car, she flicked the remote button to unlock the vehicle then yanked open the passenger door and shoved at Gemma, almost pushing her inside. 'Get in. Hurry up,' she urged as she shot around to the driver's seat. Slamming the door, she jammed the key in the ignition and twisted it.

'What's going on? Why the hurry? Where's our drink?' Gemma managed to get out before she was bounced forwards then thrust back into her seat when Maddie planted her foot; kangaroo hopped twice then sped off with the tyres squealing in protest.

'Maddie slow down,' Gemma yelled on her third bounce, both arms outspread, one pressing on the side window and the other on the hot dashboard in an attempt to stop being tossed around.

'Sorry, but we need to get away. Those creeps were there.' Maddie lifted her foot from the accelerator just enough to check the road in both directions for on-coming traffic before swinging onto the highway without stopping.

'What creeps?' Gemma panted out before reaching over to grasp the seat belt she hadn't had a chance to put on. She stretched the strap across her body and clicked the catch into place. 'Now, do you mind explaining what that was all about and you need to put your seatbelt on.'

There was no way Maddie was going to stop the car so she juggled her safety belt from hand to hand while still driving at speed, swerving erratically while latching it in position.

Gemma reached out and grabbed the steering wheel. 'Slow down will you? You're going to kill us.'

'Sorry.' Maddie checked both driving mirrors as well as the rear vision mirror to see if they were being followed. Her breath stuttered before she sucked in long and slow to steady her nerves. 'Those guys in the blue car were at the roadhouse. I didn't see their car but the redhead was inside. I didn't want them to see us.'

'You're crazy, Maddie. They aren't about to hurt us.'

'They've already tried to frighten the living daylights out of me. What they did on the highway was downright dangerous and I want nothing to do with them. It may have been a game to them but to me it is called road rage which is a form of bullying. Besides…'

After a lengthy pause Gemma nudged Maddie. 'Besides what?'

'I didn't want to tell you but one of them made a crude gesture at me.'

'Huh, what kind of gesture? When?'

'Back in Kalgoorlie.' Maddie prayed Gemma wouldn't ask for details. She was no prude but sheesh!

'And?' Gemma's rising voice indicated she wasn't giving in.

'And I didn't like it,' sighed Maddie.

'Do I have to pull your fingernails out to get you to tell me everything?' She'd twisted around in her seat so she was facing Maddie.

Maddie grinned. 'Okay, Miss Stubborn, make a circle with your thumb and forefinger.' She glanced across at Gemma's hands and waited for the penny to drop.

'What's wrong with that?'

Maddie sighed. 'Take the forefinger of the other hand and push it in and out of the circle.' Sneaking another glance, she watched Gemma's actions until the message computed.

Gemma's hands spread apart then fisted as her cheeks reddened. For all the false bravado Gemma put out to the general public, Maddie knew her friend was in fact quite the opposite. Gemma was very insecure and equally naive.

'That's disgusting. Why didn't you tell me this before?'

'The gesture was for my benefit and I didn't know these creeps were going to keep hassling us. At the time I didn't think we'd ever see them again. But now do you understand why I don't want to be in the same place as them at the same time? It's not far to Cocklebiddy. We can stay the night in the motel there and hide the car behind the building so they can't see it when they drive past.'

During the rapid flight to the next highway stop Maddie found it impossible to relax. Her eyes were in a constant motion between mirrors and the long straight road ahead, her tense actions unnerving Gemma who kept muttering for Maddie to relax. She tried – by breathing deep and concentrating on releasing muscle tension limb by limb but no sooner had her upper arm relaxed, then the lower arm was taut again. By the time they spied the large road sign announcing Cocklebiddy only a further five kilometres away, Maddie was more than happy to end this mad drive. She sighed with relief as she slowed and turned off the bitumen into the wide driveway of the roadhouse.

Pulling up in front of the building, Maddie felt uneasy. Something wasn't quite right and she couldn't figure out what was amiss. Four large rigs were parked out the front – which looked normal. There were a couple of cars with vans attached, setting up next to power poles, the only indication that it was the caravan section of the area. There were no green lawns and bitumen roads with concrete pads in the outback. Just the basics: a lone power pole for each van to give electricity, stuck upright from rough crushed limestone. There were no taps, no trees nor even the barest of weeds. Two four-wheel drives were stationary at one end but not a single vehicle stood near the bowsers. Worried, she coasted around behind the main building to park then they alighted from the car. A strong southerly wind whipped her hair into her face. She dragged it away then slid her eyelids down to keep the white dust from penetrating.

Once they reached the front, they glanced into each window as they passed until they reached the main entry. Maddie peered through the window. Then it dawned on her. There were no lights on. She curled her fingers around above her eyes and pressed her face up against the glass to see if anyone was inside. Three men stood in front of the counter near the till, chatting to the woman on the other side. A great peal of laughter rang out, breaking the uncanny silence.

Not recognising any of the men, Maddie had no hesitation in entering the roadhouse. Here, there was safety in numbers if the blue sedan arrived on the scene.

'Hi,' the young woman called out as they stepped inside the door.

'Hello,' Gemma said as they approached the group of people. 'We're looking for a room for the night.'

'Why is it so dark in here?' Maddie asked as she followed Gemma and leant against the end of the counter.

'The generator has broken down which means no electricity, which in turn means no power for the fuel pumps, no power for the water pumps and we can't cook any hot food. But a room we can give you as long as you don't mind the dark.' The young lady's grin looked apologetic as she held out a friendly hand in greeting. 'Call me Susie.'

Grasping the outstretched fingers in a warm handshake, Maddie smiled back then grimaced. 'Maddie and this is Gemma. I presume that also means no shower.'

'Sorry. We can't even pump cold water. We can usually fix the thing but this time it has my husband stumped. The mechanic will be here some time in the morning. There's enough water in the overhead tank to cope with the toilets but I need to ask you to only flush when you have to.'

The sigh emanating from Maddie's lips was deep and loud. She had been really looking forward to standing under hot gushing water. 'Who needs a shower more than once a week anyway?' Her sarcasm was obvious but tempered with a grin.

'Join the club. We'll all smell the same so it won't really matter. Troy's the name.' The oldest of the three men offered his hand. Maddie studied his features as she acknowledged him. He had a stocky build and thinning dark hair but it was obvious he was very fit from the look of the well-defined muscles on his bare tanned arms and legs poking out from a well worn pair of workman's shorts and black, rumpled T-shirt. Scruffy leather work-boots looked as though they were moulded to his feet. A beer belly paunch hung over the sagging waistband of his shorts.

'I'm stuck here until I can get some diesel. People call me Bud.' The youngest man, who looked to be no older than twenty, remained leaning on the scratched red Formica counter, a can of soda in his hand. Tall and wiry, his attire wasn't much different to Troy's only he had no sign of a spare millimetre of flesh. A cheeky grin plastered from ear to ear indicated a jovial type of person.

'Mick.' The single word was quietly spoken.

Maddie turned to the dark haired man whose face held only a hint of a smile. He was very tall and well built. She guessed he was in his late twenties but it was hard to tell.

'That your car hiding around the back?' he asked.

'Yes, why?' Gemma asked. Her body tensed as though ready to attack.

'I'd hide it too after your performance halfway between here and Kal. You two should learn how to drive.'

Bristling, Maddie pulled her already tall height for a woman, up further. 'That would be me you are referring to and it isn't us who need driving lessons – it's those three creeps in the car that had been harassing us for over fifty kilometres. They kept tailgating me at full speed, almost hitting us. Most of the time they were so close I couldn't see their front bumper. I presume it was you driving the big rig. You have no idea how glad I was when you turned up.' She turned her back on the surprised look of the arrogant man, to speak to Susie. 'You said we could have a room. If we had enough fuel, we'd drive on but we are on empty so I guess we're stuck here.'

'Sure. It's the last one but I'm afraid it's a bit crummy. We had a permanent worker living in it for a while and its due for a re-fit so I haven't been letting it out until we can find time to renovate. I just need a few details.' Susie withdrew a blank form from under the counter and slid it towards Gemma who picked up a pen from beside the till and began filling in the required information. Form completed, she slid it back and grasped hold of the proffered key.

'The last unit at the end of the building – number eleven. These guys are joining us at a communal barbecue tonight if you care to join us. We have thawed meat available and I will be making a couple of salads. It's all I can offer you I'm afraid.' Susie spoke while she checked the details on the form then clipped it with an enormous dog clip against a pile of other similar papers.

Gemma glanced at Maddie. 'What do you reckon?'

'Sounds great,' Maddie replied, 'what time?' She looked at Susie, expecting the answer from the woman who appeared to be in charge.

'Half an hour.' The response came from Troy as he headed towards the door.

Bud followed him out, calling over his shoulder, 'Out the front because of the wind.'

When Mick turned to complete the exodus, Maddie waited for an addition to the list of directions but he remained mute, striding towards the cabin of his truck where he climbed up the steps then opened the smaller door of the sleeping compartment and vanished inside. Feeling quite bemused by the sequence of events Maddie turned back towards Susie to garner any more details. 'I assume we pay you for our meals. What about drinks?'

'Ten dollars a head and purchase or bring your own drinks. I'm making up a platter of a variety of meats – all that was already thawed. Without fridges it needs to be used up tonight so there will be plenty. Ten dollars is cost price to us.'

After thanking Susie, Maddie and Gemma went in search of their accommodation. The room was pretty well the same as any motel room in the outback of Australia. It was as though someone several decades ago came up with a standard design for a basic room then mass produced it on a grand scale, dropped them from outer space and each module landed throughout the vastness of the country.

It was obvious which their room was; all the others wore smart new paint. They entered through a peeling wooden door. To the right was a miniscule bathroom containing a shower with a jammed screen door that required one to be a match-thin model to squeeze in and which had so many nooks, crannies and tiny spaces that it was impossible to clean away the mould. Next to a standard white ceramic toilet was a small basin set in a worn Formica bench too narrow to hold anything more than a tube of toothpaste and its companion toothbrush. The obligatory mirror, with patches of black where the silver backing had peeled away with age and moisture, completed the bathroom. Maddie prayed the refurbished units fared better.

Walking further into the room, a small bar fridge containing six foil packets of packaged milk resided under a varnished wooden bench. An equally small cupboard held an electric jug, two cups, two saucers, two glasses and two teaspoons – none of which matched. A ceramic dish had four tea bags, four paper cylinders of instant coffee granules and an equal number of sugar packages. It was too bad if one used sugar in both tea and coffee, thought Maddie as she shoved the door closed with her hip and kept walking.

Next to the bench stood a wardrobe containing a mixture of leftover coat hangers and two extra pillows of dubious age and cleanliness. The spare blanket was brown and had undergone so many washes it was hard with solid balls of pilling. The bed was double with a standard bedspread and built in bedside tables upon which two reading lamps stood. Maddie bet neither light worked, or required one to be a genius to figure out how to switch them on. But without power they were of no use in any case. A wooden desk sat in the corner. Tucked into it was one uncomfortable looking chair that had a definite lean to one side.

Maddie screwed her nose at the odour of stale cigarettes while Gemma, who had tagged behind, groaned at the state of the shower recess. The unit had been cleaned but wasn't what Maddie would describe as clean. The room was in desperate need of a major overhaul. But then Susie had already mentioned this fact. Now Maddie understood the warning – but it was a bed with clean sheets and they had the security of four solid walls and a door with a lock. To her, that was way more important than five star accommodation.

'You drive the car over while I open a few windows to let out the stench,' said Maddie as she strode towards the end with the windows and pulled the curtains back, searching the glassed expanse to ascertain the mechanism for opening. The handle to unwind the chain, which would push out the lower edge of the pane, was locked and looked as though it had been in that state since the day it had been installed. There was a thick layer of corrosion around the lock. A quick but fruitless search of shelves, cupboards and every conceivable hiding place told her they wouldn't be having any fresh air in the unit unless they left the door wide open. After the scare from the kangaroos and the terror of the day's drive – that wasn't about to happen. She grimaced at the sight of the equally ancient air-conditioner. No power meant no cooling air. The night was going to be hot as well as stuffy but they would be safe.

Hearing the crunch of tyres on the dirt outside, Maddie moved across the room and flung the door open. 'The window is locked,' she said as she began assisting Gemma to unload the things they would need for the night. Both girls rummaged in their individual bags for pyjamas, a clean change of clothes and toiletries then carried them inside.

'It's a good job we're used to sleeping in close proximity to each other,' said Maddie as she tossed her pyjamas onto one pillow. 'Bags this side,' she added as she bounced on the mattress to test the springiness of the double bed. The mattress was sound, pillows fluffy and the sheets clean. What more could they want? Luxurious it wasn't but it was adequate for their needs. Not waiting for a response, she returned to the car and piled half a dozen large plastic bottles of water into her arms. She grinned at Gemma's wide eyes. 'We can't have a shower but I have no intention of spending another night without a decent wash so I brought these in. We can replace them from the shop.'

After setting the two-litre bottles upright on the tiny wooden bench, she retreated to the rear of their car and opened the back. Bending over, she shifted items around until she stood up triumphant with a large empty plastic tub held high. 'Bath time. We'll heat up two litres each, add two litres of cold and then keep the other two bottles for a decent wash tomorrow.' It was their emergency supply, a necessity in the outback but she would ensure she bought more before they left. It wouldn't matter if they were not fridge cold. Water was water and when you were thirsty the only thing that mattered was that it was safe to drink. Warm, hot or cold, it still quenched your thirst and kept you alive.

'Exactly how do you intend heating the water if there's no power?' Gemma raised her brow as she stood with her hands on her hips.

'We have a saucepan and our little portable gas stove. Simple.' Maddie grinned at her friend, feeling a little cocky for having thought of the idea.

Standing in the tub, which had been placed on the floor of the tiled shower recess, Maddie felt like a queen. Using her enamel camping mug as a scoop, she tipped warm water over her body then lathered soap over every centimetre of her smoke and soot infused skin, relishing in the feel of the velvety smooth cream before scrubbing with a face washer until she felt clean. She rinsed over and over again, scoop after scoop until the soap bubbles had slithered into the bowl. Having saved half a saucepan of clean warm water, she poured it very slowly from the top, sighing in pleasure while it dribbled down her skin then feeling disappointed when the last drops were shaken out.

Deciding to forgo her bath until after the barbecue, Gemma laughed at Maddie's disdain when she pointed out the fact that they would reek of smoke by the time the evening was over and Maddie's scanty bath would have been in vain.

Chapter Five

Lying on her back with her head turned towards the uncurtained window, Maddie watched the sky turn from dark grey, through salmon to shimmering gold, before deciding her need for fresh air was stronger than her desire for another couple of hours' sleep. Taking care to not waken Gemma who was curled up in a ball with only the cotton sheet covering her body, Maddie slid from the side of the bed then crept towards the bathroom, grabbing her small pile of clean clothes from the top of the desk as she snuck past.

She was more than thankful for the extra bottle of water she had saved as she stripped bare, soaked the washer then ran the dripping cold flannel over her entire body to rid it of the smoke from the barbecue the previous night. She shivered at the icy coldness but knowing how hot it would get during the day, she welcomed the few moments of cool before dressing, cleaning her teeth then sneaking out the door. It wasn't until she had clicked the lock shut that she remembered the key still on the bench inside.

Shrugging her shoulders in resignation, she turned around in a full circle deciding which way to head for an early morning run, although since she didn't want to get all hot and sweaty again maybe she'd opt for a quiet walk. There was not a lot to see except flat white dirt and low sparse shrubs with a few small mallee trees dotted around the landscape. Heading towards the outer perimeter of the compound, she scanned the horizon. Despite the sparseness, the surrounding scene had a unique beauty, especially in the orange glow of the still rising sun. Spying movement in the distance she paused to focus on the speck. A lone emu bent its long graceful neck and pecked at the ground searching for seed.

When she reached the shady lean-to they had sat under the previous night, Maddie settled into a plastic outdoor chair recalling the strange evening. Susie's husband, Bill, the owner of the roadhouse, had joined them, along with most of the population of twenty-five plus a few other patrons who had stopped by for refreshments. Most vehicles had noticed the darkened roadhouse and driven past. As is typical of Australian barbecues, the men had grouped together relating various stories to each other, while the women sat in a smaller group to one side. Most had drunk a fair amount of beer and wine and retired to individual rooms in various states of inebriation. Only Gemma, Mick and Maddie had stuck to non-alcoholic beverages.

Listening in to the men's conversations, Maddie had learned that Bud, real name Bradley Rose, was driving trucks for his father as a holiday job during the summer break from his computer technician studies. She smiled at the way he'd received his nickname. Rose bud had turned into bud. Poor boy.

Troy had been a truckie all his working life, was married and had three teenage children. Mick had been less forthcoming with personal information but Maddie had ascertained he was single and this was only his second trip across the vast continent as a truck driver.

'You're an early riser.' The deep voice from behind broke Maddie's reverie. She turned and smiled at Mick. 'May I join you?' he added, indicating the chair nearest her.

'Sure, I was only daydreaming. Our room stinks of cigarettes and I needed fresh air.' Maddie reached out, grabbed the chair and swung it around on an angle next to her.

'What happened yesterday with the three men in the car?' Mick shifted the chair around a bit further and caught Maddie's eye, the seriousness of his tone a little disconcerting. He lowered his large frame into the moulded plastic with care, as though past experience had taught him how fragile these plastic chairs could become after being left out in the harsh elements and out here the climate couldn't get much harsher.

'Do you know these men?'

'No, we've never met them. They were fuelling up in Kalgoorlie. The redhead made crude gestures to me.' She replicated the action as she spoke, her cheeks heating when Mick hissed in disgust. 'We left before them. About fifty kilometres before you arrived they started tailgating us… and I mean tailgating – right up close. They wouldn't ease up, even when I slowed right down. I was too petrified to stop so kept going at about eighty, hoping they would get sick of the slow speed. You have no idea how pleased I was when you arrived. Sorry about swerving off without warning.'

His frown was serious before his face softened into a trace of a smile. 'Not a great idea when you have so much weight breathing down your neck. It takes a lot to slow one of these monsters. Have you seen them since?'

'They were at Caiguna. That's why we didn't stop to fill up with fuel. As soon as I saw the driver, I grabbed Gemma and sped off. I'm a bit worried they'll stop here and spot the car even though I've hidden it as best I could. I wish we could keep going but...' she shrugged her shoulders, 'no fuel means we're stranded. Gemma thinks they were just having a bit of fun and wanted me to stop and talk to them but I class their behaviour as road-rage. And if guys or anyone for that matter, are so disrespectful then I figure they're not going to be little angels in the flesh. I have no desire to talk to them and there was no way I was stopping.'

'Can't say that I blame you. When we can manage to get away from here, I'll follow ten minutes behind you for as far as we can. Where are you headed?'

'Brisbane. Gemma is starting training in a family business in a few weeks. She needed her car and begged me to drive across with her. I wish I hadn't agreed. Where are you going?'

'Sydney.'

The one word answer followed by silence had Maddie lift her eyes from where she had been studying her sneaker-clad foot making small semicircles in the white dirt. She was surprised to see piercing blue eyes fixed on her face. Mick smiled, startling her. Used to his taciturn nature so far, his smile made him look really hunky and Maddie felt a warm glow shimmer up from deep inside. Feeling embarrassed at her reaction, she dropped her eyes again and felt her cheeks redden.

'How old are you, Maddie?'

'It's not polite to ask a lady her age.' The words were mumbled into her chest but Mick must have heard for he chuckled.

'I know but you seem to be rather young to be driving across the outback of our vast continent.'

'I'm about the same age as Bud and I didn't hear you tell him the same thing.' She wasn't game to add that she was only a couple of months younger and hadn't quite yet turned twenty-one but it was none of his business.

'And I guess I'd be digging this hole I seem to be burying myself in, a lot deeper if I mentioned anything about the fact that he's a guy and you two aren't.'

Maddie bristled as he had intimated she would. She stood so fast the plastic chair she had been sitting in flew backwards and bounced onto the ground. Standing with a glare on her face and her hands on her hips she felt like she wanted to take a swing at him. He hoisted himself out of his chair and towered over her. Well over six feet, he was a big man but didn't carry a spare ounce of fat. Taking a step backwards to break the impasse, he smiled again then paused before he spoke.

'You look really cute when you are mad at me. I can see the fire sparkle in your eyes. I imagine you would be a very passionate partner in bed.'

Her faced heated so much she had no doubts he would notice but Mick turned and hurried away. Maddie stared after him. She wasn't sure if she felt furious or delighted. No man had ever roused her ire like that before or even come close to saying anything nearly so personal or intimate. Sure, she'd dated, but not with Mick and his comment was so blatant, especially to someone he'd only just met. Pulling the chair from the ground, she plonked back into it and sat staring into space thinking about his words.

When the sun's rays began scorching her legs, she decided to return to the motel room and was almost there when she remembered the key still locked on the inside. Leaning forwards, she placed her ear against the peeling paint of the wooden door but heard no sounds of movement inside. Indecision hit. With the sun now well and truly over the horizon and the air temperature rising rapidly, a walk wasn't such a great idea and there was little shelter apart from inside the roadhouse. Maddie wasn't sure if she wanted to confront Mick again so soon. Don't be a coward, Madison Brown, she thought then began sauntering towards the main door.

Determined to show Mick his words had no effect, she lengthened her stride, yanked her shoulders back and raised her chin. A smile was plastered to her face by the time she pushed the door open with the flat of her hand.

Bill, Susie and Mick were seated around a small square table in the corner. A large platter piled high with sandwiches sat in the middle of the table. From her position wavering in the doorway, Mick's face was a mask of indifference.

'Breakfast is on me as my apology. I'm sorry, Maddie.' Mick stood and pulled out the remaining chair then moved over to the drinks cabinet. 'What would you like to drink? You can have anything as long as it's cold.' Pulling a carton of iced coffee from the shelf, he waited for Maddie's response, a wry grin on his face. 'Well, it's no longer really cold but it's not yet warm.

'Water will be fine, thank you.' Maddie settled into the seat and drew a sandwich from the plate, taking care to be studying the filling of left-over cold meat and lettuce as

Mick set the bottle of water in front of her then regained his own seat.

Breakfast was rather quiet with both Maddie and Mick giving monosyllabic answers to any questions, which had Susie and Bill glancing at each other. Maddie couldn't suppress a grin while wondering what the two were thinking. It was more than obvious she and Mick had had words. The tension was only broken with the arrival of Gemma.

All four people glanced across the room when they heard the front door open then grinned at the sight. Maddie couldn't help but groan. Gemma was prone to wearing way-out clothes at times and Maddie knew it was Gemma's way of hiding from her insecurities but today she had chosen the weirdest combination Maddie had ever seen. Gemma's shorts had previously been low slung hipster jeans. In cutting off the long legs, she hadn't bothered to measure lengths. One leg was cut just below the line of her panties and the other was at least twenty centimetres longer. There was a frayed hole in the front of the longer leg. A strip of bare skin showed between the waistband and the bottom of a bright purple and orange vertical-striped sleeveless T-shirt. Her spiky hair had been gelled and stood out on end giving the impression of an echidna in defensive mode. To top it all she wore a pair of tatty sneakers, each with a different coloured lace. On her right foot she wore an iridescent pink sock that reached below her anklebone and the left foot was clad in a bright red sock ending halfway up her calf.

'Does she always dress like this?' The whispered words came from the direction of a stunned looking Bill who stood at the same time and reached over for a fifth seat.

'She's outdone herself today,' replied Maddie under her breath.

'Makes you look tame.' A choked sound came from Mick as though he found it hard to suppress his mirth. He slid the plate containing the remainder of the uneaten sandwiches in front of Gemma's chair then glanced over at Maddie.

'Was that a compliment or an insult?' asked Maddie, her tone wiping the grin from Mick's face.

'Believe me, it was a compliment.' He kept staring at her making Maddie feel uncomfortable.

Gemma's arrival at their table ceased any more comments but neither Bill nor Susie was able to keep from glancing at the outfit. Maddie giggled at the stunned looks on their faces then rose from her seat and headed towards the fridges. 'What would you like to drink, Gem?'

'I'd give my right arm for a very hot coffee but water will do for now.' Gemma waved her right arm in the air as she spoke, an action that drew three mesmerised pairs of eyes towards her fingernails. Each long talon was painted in a different pattern in such bright colours they were like five individual and clashing neon signs.

'Oh, no!' Maddie reeled back then raced across the room and grabbed Gemma's hand startling everyone. 'We have to hide, Gem.'

'What's the problem?' asked Mick.

'That car… those guys… they've just pulled up out the front. You can't let them see us.'

'Behind the counter.' Mick grabbed both girls and shoved them down behind the service desk then strode towards the door. 'I'll talk to them, head them off. Stay down and still.'

'What's going on?' asked Bill as he rose from his chair to follow in Mick's wake.

'Act as normal,' called Mick as the door closed.

Without full comprehension of what was happening both Susie and Bill seemed to understand the urgency of Mick's words. Maddie heard them moving around and couldn't resist peeking around the side of the counter. Susie was making out she was cleaning up the remnants of the breakfast they hadn't even started on while Bill moved into view in front of the shelves as though tidying and stacking, keeping his eyes on the scene unfolding through the window.

***

Mick pretended he was striding towards his truck whilst wondering what had come over him. How had he been so stupid as to vocalize his thoughts? Maddie must think he was a freaking sex maniac coming on to her like that. He never opened his mouth without thinking ahead: too damn dangerous in this game. He was an idiot.

'Hi,' he called then veered towards the three men who were emerging from a rather dusty blue sedan but he recognised it as the one he'd followed. 'Not much point calling in here, their power is down. Can't get any fuel.'

'We don't need fuel. We're looking for a couple of chicks in a Holden station wagon.'

Mick glanced at the man who had spoken. Short and dumpy, his brown hair had been cropped so short he was virtually bald. The man was unfit and looked as though he had slept in his clothes. Probably had. 'They friends of yours?' asked Mick as he moved his scrutiny to the second man who was taller and had almost black hair, which was in desperate need of a haircut. His clothes were of better quality but also rumpled.

'Err… one is my sister. She ran away from home with her friend. Are they here?'

Mick turned his attention to the sandy haired fellow claiming to be a brother to one of the girls. He saw no facial similarities but guessed Gemma could very well be a redhead under the black dyed spikes. He felt certain Maddie's hair was its natural colour.

'Names would help,' Mick said. He saw no need for lengthy statements when just a few words would suffice and after what Maddie had said, he didn't feel these guys deserved more than the basics.

'Err… Maddie. Short for… err… Madeleine.'

The fact that it was the bald-headed man who gave the name convinced Mick they were being less than honest but he was surprised they knew a name. This fact alone made him think of the veracity of Maddie's story. She had said they had never met but a runaway would say anything to prevent being found. He refrained from glancing towards the roadhouse. It would be a dead give away. He needed to confirm both stories before handing the girls over. 'Two young teenagers drove in late yesterday, filled up and then kept going towards Madura. How old is your sister?'

'Seventeen.'

'Kind of young to be driving across the desert don't you think?' He recalled Maddie saying she was close to Bud's age, but that could be a lie although he didn't think so. He was a good judge of character and he felt sure Maddie had been quite open and honest. What else didn't ring true was that Gemma was definitely the younger of the two but must be at least seventeen as claimed since she had a driver's licence. It was possible Gemma could have similar features to one of these punks under all that armour, but not Maddie – no way.

'That's why we're trying to catch up with her… to take her back home.'

Mick figured he had enough information; any more questions and they would become suspicious. 'Sorry fellas, but I would guess they are well on their way now unless they stopped overnight in Madura.' The dark-haired man was eyeing his rig, indicating he recognised it as the one following them so instead of continuing towards it, Mick veered away and began striding towards Bud's truck.

'Thanks, mate.'

At the words from behind him, Mick paused then spun around, relieved to see the three men climbing back into their car. 'You're welcome. Good luck,' he called as he lifted a hand in acknowledgment before continuing on his way. He waited at the side of Bud's truck until he was unable to see the blue sedan driving at breakneck speed down the road, then turned and retraced his steps back into the roadhouse.

'They've gone,' he called once he was inside. He leant over the counter. 'You can come out now.'

'Beats me why we have to keep hiding from them,' Gemma grumbled as she stood and brushed down her clothes.

'Probably because Maddie ran away from home and her brother is after her. He knew your name, Madeleine, which has me mystified since you told me you had never met them. Want to tell me what is really going on?'

'My brother? He's not my brother.' The words came out as a harsh cry of desperation before Maddie bolted for the door. She kept running until she reached the door to their unit where she twisted the knob then dropped onto the doorstep.

Mick stared after her. 'What the…' was all he managed to utter before he was interrupted by a distraught Gemma who began racing towards the door.

'Her brother is dead and her name isn't Madeleine. And just to get things straight – we've never met those guys before. They heard me calling out Maddie back in Kalgoorlie. Why did you have to mention her brother?' Gemma slammed the door then raced after Maddie, crouching down and flinging one arm around her friend.

Completely bewildered, Mick, along with Bill and Susie, stared across the room at each other then back outside at the two girls, the sudden silence unnerving. The arrival of the diesel mechanic to fix the generator had Bill leaving to work with the man and bringing the other two to their senses.

'I guess I need to go and apologise,' said Mick as he made to follow the two men out the door.

'It might be better if I went,' said Susie. 'Maddie might prefer talking to a female. It's obvious her brother's death is still raw. How about looking after things in here in case a customer comes? You know where I am if you need me and you can always call for Bill. I should imagine the poor mechanic will be glad to work without Bill sticking his nose in.'

Chapter Six

Maddie was in the bathroom running a cold wet flannel over her eyes with Gemma hovering behind, when someone banged on the door.

'I'm fine, Gem, really. It was just the shock of hearing them toss Paul around like that.' Maddie sniffed then blew her nose on a piece of toilet paper she tore from the roll near the white porcelain bowl before towelling her face dry.

Hearing a second knock at the door, Gemma backed out of the confined space. 'Who is it?'

'It's Susie; I just wanted to check that Maddie is okay.'

'Let her in,' Maddie said as she squeezed past Gemma and reached out to turn the handle, pulling the door open wide. 'Come in. I'm fine.'

The three of them moved further into the room where Maddie remained standing leant against the desk while

Gemma sank onto the unmade bed. Susie hovered in the archway between the passage and the room, looking unsure of what to say or do.

'Mick feels bad about upsetting you but I suggested he gives you a bit of space.'

Maddie waved a dismissive hand in the air. 'It's okay. He wasn't to know. Paul died three years ago. Drugs. We were very close and I still miss him a great deal. I guess him being my only sibling made it harder. That's why Gemma and I are so close, she lost her sister at the same time.'

Susie winced. 'Tough call. I'm sorry. It can't have been easy for either of you. If you're sure you are okay I must go and start on the rooms though without water I can't do much cleaning.' A loud sigh gushed from Susie's mouth as she turned away, leaving the two girls alone.

'What do you want to do, Maddie, stay here or go back to the roadhouse?' Gemma stretched across the bed and reached for Maddie's hand, giving it a gentle squeeze. This was the one time they completely understood each other – when one or the other was hurting.

'It's too hot and stuffy in here. I'll find our pack of cards and beat you in a game of Rummy.' Determined to shove thoughts of Paul to the back of her mind, Maddie forced her face into a smile then went to hunt down the cards in the car which was still parked behind the main building. At least it hadn't been spotted by those crazy jerks.

'Not a chance.' Gemma laughed as she followed. Maddie was glad to be out of the stale smelling air but knew she was in for a thrashing. Gemma was a master at the game but if it helped push Paul from her mind then that was fine by her. They had an unspoken understanding they had developed over the past three years. If one were on a downer, the other would do their best to bring them out of their slump. She paused when she remembered the key then reached back inside the unit and lifted both the unit key and car keys from the bench.

Once back in the roadhouse, they settled at the table and chairs in the furthest corner of the restaurant section where they spent the next hour in intense concentration. One by one they were joined, first by Bud then Troy and finally Mick. The circle grew and more hands dealt, making the game more interesting, especially for Maddie now she began winning a few hands.

The flickering of lights spelt the end of the competition. 'We have power,' yelled a delighted Troy as he threw his hand into the middle of the pile of discarded cards, making it impossible for the others to continue playing. 'As soon as I'm fuelled up I'm out of here.'

'It's a shower for me first,' Gemma laughed. 'I can't stand myself.' To emphasise her words she made an exaggerated show of sniffing her armpits in typical Gemma fashion.

'Ooh, phew,' laughed Bud as he joined the train heading outside, calling his intention of also wallowing under hot water to scrub off three days worth of putrid sweat.

Mick remained behind to assist Maddie in collecting up the strewn cards. 'I apologise for my insensitive words. I had no intention of upsetting you. Susie told me about your brother. I'm sorry.' He handed her his small pile of cards, which he'd tapped into a meticulously neat pile.

'Thank you, but you don't need to apologise. You weren't to know. Mention of Paul doesn't usually upset me any more. I guess it was more the situation of someone pretending to be Paul, although they couldn't have known either.'

Mick leant back in his chair. 'Which brings me to what I want to discuss with you. I believe you are right to be concerned about those three guys. It's obvious their intentions are not in your best interests. I don't trust them. I can follow you as far as Port Augusta to make sure they aren't laying in wait but I need to ring my boss to let him know of the situation.'

'You don't have to do that. We'll be fine. We'll be camping out most nights.' And that scared the Bejesus out of her.

Mick must have picked up on her tension for he frowned. 'Now I'm really concerned and I would never forgive myself if something untoward happened to either of you. Where are you headed today?' He leant forwards, his arms sliding across the table to almost, but not quite touching her.

'I'm not sure. Since we're having a late start I'll have to study the distances on the map.' Maddie fed the cards into the box but several escaped and splattered across the table.

Mick scooped them up, then again tapped them on the surface to get them aligned before handing them back to Maddie. This time skin touched skin, sending a wave of warmth up her arm. Why he had this affect on her she couldn't understand, but it felt kind of good.

'How about meeting me at my truck in half an hour? Does that give you enough time to shower and pack?'

'I guess so, thank you.'

As Maddie shoved in the tabs on the box, Mick rose and pushed his chair under the table. From what she'd seen so far he appeared to be a neat and tidy kind of guy. He reached out with one hand and curled his long fingers under her chin, lifting her eyes up to face him. 'You're very welcome, my good deed for the day. See you in thirty minutes.'

It took Maddie a few minutes to recover her equilibrium from Mick's touch that seemed to have lingered longer than necessary. Once back in the unit she wasted little time in packing the few items they had removed from their car while Gemma showered. Then it was Maddie's turn to luxuriate under the hot water while Gemma went to buy a new supply of water and settle their account with Susie. She waited until she heard Gemma return before turning off the water. After a final check of their room they stowed the last of their belongings into the back of their car and drove around the front to where Mick waited by the cabin of his truck speaking to someone on his mobile phone.

Noticing them arrive, he completed his conversation then hung up. 'Are you ready?' he asked.

'Yes. I didn't think mobiles worked out here,' said Maddie as she pointed to the bulge the phone made in his shirt pocket. Neither she nor Gemma had bothered turning theirs on because of the lack of coverage.

'They don't. This is a satellite phone. Let me get my road book out.' He began climbing the steps up to the cabin.

'Can we see inside? I've never seen inside one of these,' asked Gemma.

***

Mick paused for a moment. 'Sure. Just let me check I've got nothing lying around that would embarrass me.' He chuckled at the innuendo and noticed the heightened colour in Maddie's cheeks at the same time as Gemma released a sheepish giggle. Climbing into the cabin he eased between the two seats and reached into the sleeping compartment where he lifted his holster and pistol from the hook against the wall and hid the firearm under the mattress of his made bed. He thumped the mattress to check the gun couldn't be felt through the bedding. He already knew his clothes were well packed but nevertheless, he scanned the interior to check there was no more incriminating evidence. It wouldn't be wise to let the girls know what he was up to. Reversing back into the cabin, he remembered the notebook he'd been jotting his information in while waiting. Closing it up, he shoved it into an overhead cupboard above the dashboard then settled into the passenger seat. 'Come on up,' he called.

His skin tightened when Maddie's head emerged first. It gave him an excuse to touch her again. He knew it was ridiculous to be attracted to the young woman but something about her quiet manner made him want to protect her. He reached out to take her hand and hoisted her up onto the driver's seat. Gemma followed close behind. The difference between the two girls was so remarkable. They were complete opposites and he wondered why they were such close friends.

'Welcome to my temporary home. Feel free to take a look in the back.' Both girls screwed their bodies around and knelt on the seat to peer into the interior.

'It's much roomier than I imagined,' said a muffled Maddie.

'Cool, I wouldn't mind sleeping in one of these.' Gemma wasn't content to just look, she had to climb right in and stretch out on the bed. Where Maddie was reserved in nature, Gemma appeared to be impulsive and seemed to act before she thought of the consequences.

'While you make yourself comfortable in there, maybe Maddie and I can study this map,' said Mick with a laugh.

'I gather you don't smoke. The place doesn't stink like our room did.' Gemma sat up and stuck her head out of the opening. The sight of Gemma's way-out clothes and electric-shock style hair still startled Mick and he grinned at her.

'No, I never had the desire to kill myself from the inside out.' Without further comment, he pulled his road book from the side pocket of the door and flicked through the pages until he found the right one. Leaning towards Maddie he drank in the perfume of the shampoo she had used to wash her still wet hair. She was so natural. No make-up, no way-out hairdo and modest yet trendy clothes. To calm hormones that had decided to race through his system, he concentrated on the map, mentally calculating distances as his finger paused on each stop.

'What say we drive on to the Nullarbor Roadhouse? It's about four hundred and seventy kilometres. We'll stop at Bordertown since it's the border between the two states and I'd love to show you the South coast from there. We can go down in your car. The coast is not far from the highway around there and the scenery is quite spectacular. I'll keep behind you but within sight. Stop at any roadhouse if you need a break and I'll pull in. How does that sound?' He glanced up at Maddie and smiled at her stunned face.

'Sounds good but why are you doing this?'

'I guess it's my male protective instinct but I didn't like the attitude of those men and I wouldn't be able to sleep if I didn't know you two were safe. Besides, we're heading in the same direction and neither of us can drive over the speed limit in any case, so I've got nothing to lose.' He actually had a lot to lose but couldn't say a thing.

'I don't believe they meant us any harm,' piped in Gemma as she poked her head out again.

'Speaking as a man, I think you are wrong. They spun me a story filled with lies. If they meant no harm they wouldn't have even stopped to ask about you. I hope they keep driving while searching for you but if they ask around and you haven't been seen at any of the roadhouses, they may lie in wait. The thought scares me. Three grown men against two young females are not very good odds.' He eyed Maddie who began to bristle at his perceived sexist comment. 'And don't get uppity, Maddie. I didn't mean that to sound sexist. I'm sure you are quite capable of looking after yourself but my experience tells me they could overpower the pair of you quite easily if they really wanted to.'

'Okay, you've convinced me. Shove over, I'm coming through.' Gemma grinned as she wriggled her way between the two, settling onto the console.

'I think it's time we left,' Maddie murmured as she began to slide from her seat. She twisted around then climbed down the steep steps.

'What about lunch? Will you need to stop off somewhere to buy lunch?' asked Mick.

'No, we have enough snacks in the car,' replied Gemma as she followed her friend down the side of the truck.

'So do I. Slow down as you go through the Madura Pass. The scenery is quite spectacular. Wait until I fill up with diesel before you drive off. It takes longer to fill these massive tanks.' In reality he had more that enough fuel but he had to play the part. No fuel was his reason for staying the night. He had to make it look real.

Mick slid into the driver's seat and started the engine then eased his vehicle to the truck bowser, while the girls filled their car on the other side of the concourse.

Chapter Seven

With Gemma driving, Maddie enjoyed the luxury of pushing her seat right back so she could take in and appreciate the passing scenery, which wasn't so easy since they were driving directly into the sun. What she had always thought to be a desert containing nothing but sand, the Nullarbor Plain had its own unique beauty. Low sparse scrubland with few trees of any height was forever changing and there was a continuous stream of different wildlife. Her heart lurched each time they approached some form of road-kill - usually kangaroos or birds. After watching a pair of magnificent soaring wedge-tailed eagles for quite some time, she felt particularly saddened when she spied a dead bird of the species on the side of the road, its partner hopping around the recently departed creature. She thought she recalled some snippet of information that these birds mated for life and she felt for the remaining bird, knowing it must be devastated – just as she had when Paul died. Far out, why did Paul keep creeping into her mind? Determined to rid her brain of his image, she turned her concentration back to the birds. Close up, the black and brown feathers of the two birds appeared to glisten bronze and she realised how huge the birds were, especially the long, thick, curved talons.

Seeing the large green and white road sign for Madura Pass, Maddie reminded Gemma to slow. At half their normal speed, they drifted through a sudden higher embankment that looked like a roofless archway. The appearance of high ground on each side of the car after so many hundreds of kilometres of virtually flat land was a welcome surprise but what was even more amazing was the sight of a lower plain stretching out forever below their lofty height. Vegetation was suddenly much denser with an abundance of trees, which indicated an underground water supply fairly close to the surface.

'Wow!' Gemma exclaimed as she slowed even more.

'Pull over, Gem, I have to get a photograph of this.' Maddie unbuckled her seat belt then knelt on her seat as she searched around on the rear seat for her digital camera.

They were still standing on top of the embankment above their car when Mick pulled up behind them, a knowing grin plastered across his face. He slid over into the passenger seat then wound down the window. 'Impressive isn't it?' he called.

'It's fantastic.' Swinging around to face him as she spoke, Maddie aimed her camera and snapped a photograph of the grinning Mick.

***

Startled, Mick yanked his head back inside and swore under his breath. He hadn't reckoned on the girls having a camera, although, why shouldn't they. It was logical they would but he now either had to get a hold of the camera and delete his photo or pray they didn't show it to anyone or worse still, upload it to some social media. Then he could be in all sorts of trouble. 'Damn,' he muttered under his breath as he slipped back into the driver's seat and waited for the girls to clamber back down to their car. His mind was in turmoil of indecision while the girls drove off. He'd revealed too much about himself already and the problems with this trip were mounting by the hour. Keeping track of the girls meant he was losing sight of his objective but for the life of him, he couldn't expose the girls to danger from the three thugs in the dark blue sedan. Some inner gut instinct had told him they were nothing but trouble when Maddie first explained about the games the men had been playing. And his gut was rarely wrong.

While keeping the Holden in sight, Mick spent time on the two-way radio and the truckie grapevine in an endeavour to garner information about the dark blue sedan. He passed on the memorised number plate along with a brief description of the three men then added an outline on why he thought they were possible trouble. Calculating times and distances in his head, he became alarmed that the car hadn't been seen beyond Eucla. They should have reached the town by now. He prayed the girls didn't pull into the tiny town for a pit stop, or there could be more trouble than he wanted.

A brief stop at Mundrabilla for use of the facilities and the purchase of hot coffee had Mick feel his nerves tighten. Knowing that Eucla was only another half hour away and it would be unlikely the girls would stop again so soon, he sent a wish skywards that they wouldn't. As he eased through the hamlet of Mundrabilla and passed the clean long building of the roadhouse, Mick scanned the vicinity and grounds for any sight of the blue sedan, but as far as he could see it wasn't there. The fenced outdoor beer garden contained a group of four workers wearing bright orange safety jackets. From his height it was easy to see over the fence. He tried to peer into the small reception area then the fast food bar but couldn't see anything other than vague shapes. The girls emerged with cardboard mugs of hot coffee and since both were smiling he assumed no unwelcome person had been laying in wait.

A further few kilometres later, he pulled up behind the already stationary car belonging to the girls. Once on the ground he glanced around to search for their whereabouts.

'Over here!' The shouted words accompanied by a giggle came from the irrepressible Gemma. Each girl stood either side of the prominent road-sign marking the border between South and Western Australia.

Striding across the red dirt, which had been compacted to almost concrete hardness by thousands of feet over the years, posing for the same snapshot, Mick figured he had an opportunity to delete his photo from Maddie's camera. 'If you give me your camera, I'll take a photo of the pair of you on this momentous occasion.' He forced a laugh to make sure he sounded casual.

With an unrestrained skip, Maddie returned to their car where she lifted her camera from the front seat, turning it on as she ambled back to the signpost. Handing it to Mick, she pointed to the button he needed to press. What he didn't bargain on was the sensation of an electric shock when their fingers met briefly.

Stepping backwards, Mick made out he was playing with the telephoto lens as he scrolled backwards to the last photograph. Grimacing at the very clear image of his mug, he pressed the delete button. Taking his time to focus and frame the girls gave the camera time to re-boot to the correct setting. He shot several photos of the girls in various poses then shut the camera down. Keeping it held in his hand he moved closer to the girls.

'About forty kilometres further along, this road runs fairly close to the coast. There's a well-worn track. Wait for me at the turnoff and I'll take you down to the cliffs. We'll have to go in your car because I can't take the rig down there.' He paused for a moment, wondering whether he should mention the lack of sighting of the three men. As far as the girls knew, the men were a couple of hours ahead of them. Better to let things lie for the time being. No sense in causing undue grief unless it was unavoidable.

At the turnoff Mick pulled his rig well off the road, climbed down to the ground then double-checked all the doors and windows were locked before joining the girls who had pulled onto the hardened red dirt track that only existed because of the number of tourists who travelled across it each day. He found it difficult to fold his large body into the confining space of the back seat after Maddie had cleared a space for him.

'Drive all the way along this track but be careful you don't keep going over the edge. The cliffs are about ninety metres high and end up in the Great Southern Ocean. I don't relish the idea of becoming shark bait.' Mick grinned at the shocked reflection of Gemma's face in the rear vision mirror before she dropped her eyes to concentrate on the road ahead. Her speed matched her fear.

'You can go a bit faster, Gemma. There's a sign warning you about the cliff.' He chuckled at her harrumph of displeasure at being sucked in by his teasing.

To make sure she didn't go over the edge, Gemma pulled up about fifty metres before she even reached the sign.

'Looks like we're walking,' Mick's sarcasm was tempered with a laugh as he lifted the black plastic catch on the door.

'My camera?' asked Maddie.

'I've still got it. Allow me to take the photos so you are both in them,' Mick replied as he held the camera up.

After a short stroll, Mick stood back a few metres, watching the awe on the faces of the two girls as they scanned the magnificent scenery. Ahead and below them were miles and miles of rolling blue water, the white caps tumbling over and over, looking like white meringue coils. The waves pounded as they hit the solid cliffs with traces of rising spume eddying high in the air. To the right and left, they could see the creamy whiteness of the sheer cliff walls topped off by a flat mesa of red dirt that had been baked salmon by the intensity of the sun. The wind was strong, hitting them in their faces. It whipped Maddie's hair around in the air but had no effect on the rigid gelled spikes adorning Gemma's head. Even though they were standing several metres from the edge, it was scary. Making it obvious she wasn't keen on heights, Gemma clung to Maddie's arm.

Mick wandered along the edge of the high cliff then turned and snapped a photo of the girls who, unbeknown to them, were standing on an overhanging ledge. He felt a sudden perverse fear that the cliff would give way and the girls would tumble to their deaths but knew the area was reasonably safe. Regular checks were made of the stability of the cliffs at all the popular tourist lookout points.

Returning to the girls he knew he had a way to get them to leave poste-haste.

'Do you want to see the photos I took?' He scanned back to the last photo. After just the briefest of glances, both girls turned and fled back to the car in panic.

'You could have told us,' exclaimed Maddie as he neared them, grinning.

'Let me look at that again?' Gemma grabbed the camera from Mick's hand and pressed the button. Her eyes widened at the sight of the two of them standing on the overhang. Both girls studied the photo, heads together. 'I can't believe you let us stand on that,' whispered Gemma in disbelief.

'You were perfectly safe. The earth is a lot thicker than it looks in the photo. Besides, didn't you read the sign? It does tell you to take extreme care as some areas jut over the ocean. He took the camera back so the girls wouldn't be tempted to study the other photos or take another one of him, then he bent to concertina himself into the car. 'Time to go if we want to reach Nullarbor before dark.'

Back at the turnoff, Mick waved to the girls as they continued along the highway. Reaching his truck, he noticed a mass of footprints at the side of the cabin. Following, he studied them closely then swore aloud when he figured there were three different sets, all made by men, by the size of each. At the back of the second trailer, it became apparent they had attempted to open the rear door to establish what he was carting. Were these the men he was looking for? Or were they the girl's admirers? Could they possibly be the one and same? He followed the trail all around the truck then stared ahead for a moment, his hand brushing through his hair in agitation. He didn't need to follow the prints back to where they had emerged from a vehicle – he knew in which direction they had driven. So where had they been hiding?

Worried, Mick wasted no time in starting up the powerful motor and pulling back onto the highway. He accelerated until he was well over the limit in a bid to catch up to the girls. It took time to ease through the mass of gears but once in top gear he was able to push the rig along until he had the Holden station wagon in his sights. This time he didn't leave as much distance between the two vehicles. Only then did he begin to enjoy the regular glimpses of the ocean from the road that trailed near the coastline for many kilometres.

His concern mounted once he began talking on the two-way to other truckies. All reports indicated the three men were not far ahead of Maddie. He assumed they would be stopping at Nullabor Roadhouse to make enquiries. His only hope was that the men didn't realise he had been with the girls. He prayed the men had thought that he had walked down to the coast or that he was asleep in the rear compartment when they weren't able to rouse him, but real life never went the way one wished. His gut told him things were not going to be that simple.

Hearing a sudden blast from his rear he peered into the side mirrors then smiled when he recognised the triple rig belonging to young Bud. Contacting him on the two-way, he asked where Bud was staying overnight.

'Nullarbor, why?' Bud responded.

'I could need your assistance, mate. Those three punks who were harassing Gemma and Maddie are hanging around again.'

'Righto, I understand. I heard you on the two-way. I'll keep on your tail.'

Switching off his microphone, Mick set it back in its holder and smiled. All of a sudden things were looking up. The needle had eased its own way out of the proverbial haystack and was in full view. His only problem now was keeping three men away from two attractive young women. A vision of Gemma's outfit for the day flitted into his mind: well, maybe one gorgeous young woman and one really weird teenager, who he wouldn't be caught dead squiring around town on his arm. But Maddie – he would love to have her on his arm, or better still, in his arms. She was one very special young lady but for the life of him he couldn't figure out why he had taken to her so quickly.

Reaching the large road-sign warning of Nullarbor Roadhouse in five kilometres, Mick closed the gap until he was sitting on Gemma's tail where he stayed until Gemma pulled into the grounds of the roadhouse. From his height, he scanned all the area he could see for any signs of the blue sedan. It wasn't difficult for they had really reached the *treeless plain* of the Nullarbor. The surrounding area was flat and covered in small shrubs of saltbush and brown Spinifex; all that would grow on the two hundred thousand square kilometres of limestone rock which was up to a hundred metres thick in places.

He felt more than relieved when he couldn't spot the car. He pulled into an overnight truck parking-bay at the front. A couple of caravans had already set up for the night behind him. Of all the roadhouses along the route, this one seemed to be the most desolate looking with white limestone dust eddying around in the gusty wind. A sign indicated that the camping ground was behind the backpackers unit. Mick groaned. The girls would be sitting ducks camped so far away. Somehow he had to convince them to take a motel unit. He jumped to the ground and strode to the reception area but even though he was fast, the girls were already inside booking a campsite when he reached them.

'Hi girls, are you booking a unit?'

'No, we're camping. Our funds don't go to staying in motel rooms every night.' Maddie reached over to sign the registration form already filled out.

'Maddie is just a poor student,' laughed Gemma.

'You don't have to make it sound as though I'm a pauper. We don't all have mega rich parents like you.' She looked embarrassed by Gemma imparting personal details. 'I just like to make sure I spend my limited funds wisely. We're sharing costs and I only agreed to come if we did it on the cheap. I'm used to camping so it doesn't bother me.'

'Well it bothers me and when you've finished up here I want to show you why.' Mick waited, an idea forming.

All visited the rest rooms before Mick led them out to his truck. Handing both girls up into the cabin, he climbed in beside them then turned on his two-way radio.

'There were three sets of footprints around my rig after you dropped me off. I've been making enquiries via all the truckies in the area. Your three admirers are hanging around. Listen to this.' He made the call to any truckies listening. 'This is Big Mick. Anyone sighted my prey?'

'Johnno here. They were parked in a rest bay about two clicks east of Nullarbor Roadhouse five minutes ago. Seems they were keeping an eye on the road. My guess is they are waiting for the two chickadees.'

'Thanks, mate, I'm parked at the roadhouse for the night. So are the girls.' Mick signed off then glanced at the ashen faces of the girls. 'I guess they'll be back here snooping around when you don't drive past them. If you did pass them, then I assume they would follow you.'

Maddie gasped. 'What are we going to do?'

'I have an idea. Set up camp with your car next to your tent and go to bed as normal. Bud and I will keep watch from this truck. No car can drive in here without us spotting it. They'll probably recognise my truck as the one that spoilt their little road-rage game but they won't be able to see in at night. Bud is also staying here overnight and has agreed to help me if these punks turn up. I'm planning on setting up a bit of a surprise for them but I promise we won't let them get to you. What do you say?'

'I feel embarrassed that you have to keep looking after us like this.' Maddie wasn't able to look Mick in the eye.

'It's cool,' said Gemma. 'I still don't think they are out to harm us.'

Mick frowned at Gemma's words as he cupped his fingers under Maddie's chin and lifted her face up. 'Don't feel embarrassed. It's not your fault these thugs are behaving like wild animals. I'd like to give them something to think about although I'm not so keen on sleeping in such close proximity to Bud. He's not my type. I'd prefer someone prettier, softer, more feminine.' His wicked smile told both girls to whom he was referring, resulting in Maddie blushing bright red and Gemma giggling.

'I think he likes you, Madison Brown,' she quipped.

Surprised at the name Mick swung his head to look at Maddie. 'Madison. An unusual name. It suits you.' His fingers lingered longer than they should have but he found it hard to release his hold. But at least he now had positive confirmation that their story was the truth.

Before he allowed them to leave, Mick discussed his plans with the girls. When they left to make preparations and set up their camp, he sought out Bud to see if he would agree to the plans. Being young and ready for any type of adventure, Bud was more than willing to go along with Mick's ideas although he did baulk for a while at the thought of sleeping alongside the huge form of Mick.

'I'd prefer sleep next to Gemma,' Bud quipped.

'Really? In that get-up.'

'She's all right. Gemma is sassy and the clothes are just a wall she's hiding behind. I kinda like her.'

'To each his own. Give me Maddie any day. But what makes you think she's hiding behind clothes?'

'I have a mate who has a rough home life. He dresses in black – gothic like, you know, with lots of piercings. The get-up is only to give the impression he's tough but it's all show. Deep down, he's hurting and afraid. Gemma gives me the same impression.'

Mick was surprised at the way Bud saw things. It showed maturity beyond the young man's years and thinking about it, Bud was probably right.

Chapter Eight

The atmosphere over a shared cooked meal in the roadhouse restaurant was amiable with most of the chat between Bud and Gemma. They seemed to have formed an easy camaraderie. Afterwards they all went there own way to attend to showers and final preparations, which included a game of cards until late in the evening. Mick found Maddie to be quick witted, smart but a little reserved. Every now and again a grin split her face and her eyes sparkled, which did something to his insides. Before retiring to bed they ambled around the outskirts of the compound until the shutdown of the majority of the lights. Limited lighting remained for the running of the twenty-four hour service station. On their stroll, Mick and Bud kept sweeping their eyes around, seeking sight of the three men or their car but none appeared.

In the darkness, they dropped the girls off at their tent, waiting until they were settled before leaving for Mick's truck. 'Sleep tight, girls,' murmured Mick as they turned away.

'As if we'll be able to sleep,' came from Gemma.

'We're not even sure if they know where you are, so try to relax,' said Mick.

'You hear that, body. Mick says to relax.'

Mick laughed at Maddie's pointed sarcasm as he and Bud strode away. The girls certainly had a great sense of humour.

It took less than thirty minutes of slouching back in their seats while chatting about nothing in particular before a darkened sedan drifted to a stop on the far side of the roadhouse grounds. Nudging Bud, Mick straightened then pointed. 'That has to be them. Why else would they have no headlights?'

'Hell, are we going to be able to reach the girls in time?'

'I don't think they're sure yet, that the girls are even here.'

'Then why are they skulking around?'

'Scouting party – looking for the station wagon. Watch.' They both leant over the dashboard.

Sure enough, one man emerged from the car, leaving the door wide open. He crept along the side boundary of the roadhouse compound, his movements so obviously covert he looked ridiculous.

'Couldn't be more obvious he's up to no good,' chuckled Bud in an undertone.

'They don't know anyone is watching.' Mick leant further forwards for a better view, his heart pounding when a sole dark figure jumped up and began frantic arm waves beckoning the other two over.

'Now they know, let's go.' Bud made to open the door.

Mick put a restraining hand on his arm. 'Not so fast, we don't want to scare them off.'

'Isn't that what we're here for?' Even in the gloom of the darkened cabin, Mick could see the concern on Bud's face. There was more than enough light from the high gibbous moon and the lights along the front of the roadhouse. Too much damn light.

'Patience, we need to catch them in the act.'

'In the act? Go to hell! I can't let anything happen to the girls while you're pussyfooting around.' Bud dragged his arm from Mick's hold and snicked open the catch on the door.

Knowing he had no choice but to prevent Bud from tearing after the three by himself and scaring them off, Mick yanked his pistol from the holster under his arm and flicked it in front of Bud's eyes. It only took a second for things to register.

'Christ, where did that come from?' Bud turned. 'Is that thing legal?'

'That information is on a need to know basis and right now, you don't need to know and it doesn't really matter. Let's just say that in this job, one always needs some kind of protection and I do know how to use it.' He pointed the butt towards the window. 'Look.' The other two men had only just emerged from the car. They joined the first then grouped together halfway along the side rim, looking as though they were having a discussion.

'We'll give them a head start then both get out my side of the truck.' Mick paused while watching the men. 'Ready? Let's go.'

His muscles tensing, Mick snicked the catch open as silently as he could, knowing the sharp click couldn't be heard so far away even though it sounded like a bullet being fired in the confines of the truck. Replacing the gun, he stepped down the rungs then slid to the ground, holding the door wide as Bud followed suit. Bud had his fingers clenched tight around a long tyre lever. It was a wieldy piece of metal when you had to change a punctured tyre but its length and weight made it a good weapon.

Stealthy steps made slight scraping sounds as they edged between the trucks, waiting at the end of each trailer long enough to flick a glance into the gap to ensure their approach went unseen. Mick noticed one shadow move to one side of the backpacker's units while another took a few steps in the opposite direction. Damn, where was the third man? He held his arm up in the air to stop Bud then lifted one finger indicating the way the two men had gone. With the third finger he shrugged his shoulders.

'There!' Bud whispered as he pointed.

The other man had crouched down and looked to be peering under the block of units. Damn it, why couldn't they have kept together? Scrambling for ideas on what to do next, Mick paused. A loud crunch split the air. Mick peered around the corner. Two men were standing together while the third had neared the gap between the units and the lonely tent, which glistened in the moonlight, the nylon strands indicating the newness of the fabric. It looked like a neon lit sentinel but it sure wasn't standing guard. More like, *Here I am, come and get me!* He'd never seen a more obvious target.

With the two beginning to creep forwards, there was no time left to waste by standing around. Mick leant towards Bud and whispered in his ear, 'You go that way,' he pointed to the left, 'but keep well back so you're not seen.' He waved his open hand towards the solo figure. Bud nodded and immediately crept away, knees bent to keep low.

With practised stealth, Mick bent at the waist to hunch over and moved in an arc so that he would come up behind the pair who was now out of sight behind the far end of the units. He quickened his pace, cursing under his breath at what sounded like a heavy footstep to his right. Yanking out his pistol, he swung around, gun aimed chest high. There was no immediate movement so he paused while swinging his steady gaze from side-to-side until he was satisfied no-one had back-tracked.

He crept forward but had only managed a few paces before he heard a muffled squeal. Even though he wasn't certain it was female, he sped across the last gap and raced down the side of the building since both men had vanished. Damn it, where was everyone? All of a sudden things were going pear-shaped. A strong surge of adrenaline sent alarm bells along every nerve fibre in his body.

Another squeal, this time definitely female and a lot louder, had him surge forwards then dart around the end of the building. The tent had flattened underneath the weight of two men. The third knelt on the ground at what should have been the entrance but who could tell when the entire mass of nylon was writhing like a giant python. A hand wielding what looked like a heavy branch lifted in readiness. Mick ran full pelt and rammed the barrel of his gun into the back of the crouched man's head.

'Looking for something, my friend? Well you found it,' he growled as the man stilled. 'Bud!' he yelled then added, 'all of you stand still or I shoot.'

Panting at his side accompanied by the sliding of feet told him that Bud had arrived.

'Shit, where did they come from?' was muttered before a scuffle ensued.

One lurched towards Bud. Someone swung a weapon, the thwack followed by a groan indicating it had connected with something hard. A loud whack then a moan was clearly heard and was followed by a man crumpling to the ground. Mick could make out the lanky form of Bud leaning over then kneeling on the fallen man's back with the lever pressed against the man's shoulders.

The fracas, even though it had lasted for all of ten seconds, had given the other two men a chance to figure out what was going on and that it was three against two.

'Run!' yelled one and both took off in different directions. Mick aimed his gun in the air, flicked off the safety catch and pulled the trigger, bringing everyone to a sudden standstill at the echoing sharp crack that cut the air like a whip, which is what he'd hoped to achieve. It even stilled the two girls who had been squirming under the fallen tent.

'The next bullet goes through the first man that moves,' Mick growled as he swung the gun between the two who had attempted to run.

Neither man moved, which delighted Mick for he had no desire to fire again. He was already in trouble if anyone mentioned his use of a firearm.

'Back off very slow, my friends,' Mick spat out, paused then pressed forward when the men failed to obey. They just stood there, gaping before they both began creeping backwards, their eyes in unblinking stares.

'Maddie, Gemma, are you all right?' Mick called.

'Oh, just dandy,' came from Maddie.

Micked smiled as he attached the handcuffs he'd fashioned out of plastic cable ties, to the two standing men. He was more than thankful Bud had the good sense to keep the other man on the ground. 'Come out girls,' Mick said as he indicated for Bud to give them a hand, while he secured the wrists of the third man.

Gemma emerged first with tears streaming down her face. Mick held back his smile at the sight of Bud slipping his arm around the distraught girl. Even in the kerfuffle, the hair spikes hadn't moved. When Maddie crawled from the flattened nylon she stood tall, eyeing the three trussed up men then catching Mick's steady stare. She jerked when she spied his gun but then slung an arm around the other side of Gemma. Maddie looked to be holding up but her tense body indicated she was only just holding it together through sheer willpower.

'Let's go where there's some light,' Mick suggested. 'Bud, how about staying behind these three to give them a hurry up? Use that lever if needed.'

A sound of pounding feet neared. 'What the hell's going on here?' The shape of a large man emerged from the gloom.

Mick took a few steps towards the man, recognising the manager he'd spoken to earlier. 'These filth attempted to attack these two girls. Everything's under control now but let's move to the building.' He indicated towards the rear of the main building.

The three assailants were shoved through the small camping ground containing only the flattened tent then ushered into the enclosed back section of the roadhouse where each was trussed up against steel posts. Best invention in a long time – these cable ties, Mick thought as he wound, shoved ends through holes then tugged to tighten each enough that any struggling to free themselves would result in a tight pinching. Whenever a man attempted to speak Mick aimed the gun at his head. Bud stared bug-eyed at the waving firearm. Once he was satisfied each of the men was secured, Mick pulled out three chairs and asked Bud and the girls to sit.

'Now gentlemen, you can begin talking. The police are on their way. Let's see, Ceduna is three hundred kilometres and I rang them over two hours ago which means they'll be here within the hour.

'But how…?' squeaked Maddie.

'We meant no harm,' Baldy interrupted, 'just wanted to have a bit of fun with the pieces of skirt.'

Mick sent the man a withering glare and had to force his fist to his side to prevent it from landing a blow on the smug face.

'In the middle of the night! Waiting until after they had gone to bed! I can imagine what type of fun you were envisaging. Now let's see what charges are going to be laid against you.' He thought hard, imagining what sounded like genuine crimes.

'There was fifty kilometres of road rage as a start, to which I can verify since I witnessed it. Stalking – which can be proved by the number of times you asked if the girls had been at each roadhouse along the way. You were even foolish enough to spin me your porky pies. The fact that Maddie doesn't have a brother and Madeleine isn't her name didn't help your cause.'

'Dumb arse,' was muttered by someone but Mick didn't see whose lips had moved.

'Then you left your footprints at my truck and I should imagine your fingerprints where you attempted to break in. Did I mention that the police are bringing their forensics kit with them? My friend here,' he pointed to Bud, 'can testify how you crept towards the girl's tent in the middle of the night – armed with knives.'

At the shocked gasps from Bud and the manager, Mick straightened, slid his gun into the front waistband of his jeans, pulled on a pair of white latex gloves which he withdrew from an inside pocket of his jacket then searched pockets, withdrawing three different types of knives, a handful of condoms, rubber washing-up gloves of the common variety. They were so common Mick bet that they could be purchased at every supermarket and hardware store in the country - even out here. Three individual lengths of nylon twine, two balled up handkerchiefs and three rolls of grey, adhesive insulation tape completed the haul.

Bud gawped at the pile of items. 'How could you have known?' he asked, 'and is that thing legal?' He indicated the gun with a flick of his hand.

'Seems to me that raping was on the agenda with all this stuff,' muttered the manager. 'Guys like you disgust me.' At his words, the manager stood and aimed a hefty kick at Baldy. His aim was deliberate and accurate. The fact that Mick had trussed the men on the floor with legs spread and tied to different posts meant that the kick didn't miss its intended target. The man yowled in agony then slumped forwards but was unable to protect his crotch since his hands were handcuffed to the post.

'That's enough!' Springing forwards Mick dragged the manager back. He hated the idea of what would happen if the men were physically harmed. 'The police will handle things in the appropriate manner.' He leant over to the manager and whispered in his ear. 'You don't want to be up on charges. Take it easy. I feel the same way, mate.' And if anyone mentions his firing a gun, he'd be the one on charges.

'All right. I need to get back on duty in any case.' He stalked away but turned as he opened the back door.

'Yell if you need any assistance. I've got a rifle.' He sent a pointed look towards Mick 'Licensed.' The door shut with a resounding bang; the sound echoing off the walls causing Gemma to whimper and Maddie jerk in her seat.

Mick crouched on his haunches in front of Maddie. 'Are you two all right?'

'No,' sniffed Gemma. A new bout of tears began puddling from her eyes. 'They squished the breath out of us when they jumped on the tent.' She raised her face. 'I thought you said they wouldn't hurt us.' The "in your face" teenager had gone, leaving behind a vulnerable youngster who'd had her confidence battered by three brutes. It was a harsh lesson for her but maybe now she realised how dangerous the men's behaviour was. Mick leant forwards to give the girl a hug but she pulled away and turned to Maddie, who wrapped her arms around the distraught Gemma. So Maddie was not only her best friend but also the security blanket. He recalled the scant information he'd been given about when the two met. It appeared there was more to this friendship than one could see from the surface.

'Maddie, what about you?'

'I'm fine,' she mumbled without raising her head. 'Who are you? Those gloves…' she pointed towards his hands.

'A necessity when you have to drag dripping animal remains from the roo bars or under the wheels. It beats getting blood and gore all over your hands in the middle of nowhere.'

He hoped she bought his explanation. It sounded logical. He eyed her to see if there was any doubt in her face. What stood out was how pale Maddie was which meant she was far from fine. Studying her more closely he noticed a tremor skip across her shoulders. She was hanging together by the merest of fine threads; probably because she was the older and more mature of the two. He suspected Maddie was the one always picking up Gemma's pieces and patching her up.

'Yeah, and I'm the King of England. Neither of you are what I'd call fine. I'm sorry we weren't there to prevent the oafs jumping on you but the less than subtle approach wasn't something I'd anticipated. They separated, giving the two of us three different ways to follow.' He was about to add more but wailing sirens followed by a loud skid as at least two cars slid to a halt meant the police had arrived.

It took only a few minutes before the manager led four uniformed officers through a rear door of the building. Mick outlined all he knew to the bulky but tall officer who wore the more senior stripes while the three captives were bundled into the rear of a paddy wagon. One officer remained behind to take statements then set off in the culprits' car for Ceduna.

Allowing Gemma to walk on ahead, Mick tugged Maddie aside as they made their way towards the tent. His heart felt heavy at what he was about to tell her. How he wished things could be different. 'Maddie, I probably won't be here when you wake in the morning. You'll be safe from those three now. They'll be held in custody until they go before the courts for the crime they committed this side of the border. Then they'll be extradited to W.A. to face the charges on the other side. They'll be in custody either here or in Perth until you reach Brisbane. The officers are going to make enquiries to see if they are responsible for any other crimes. I need to get back on track and see if I can make up time. You two take care.'

Maddie took her time mulling over his words. For a while Mick thought she wouldn't say anything.

'Why do I feel so sad?' she finally said so quietly that he wondered if he was meant to hear.

Mick paused. Did she feel the same way? He shook his head. It would never work. She was so young, so inexperienced, so gorgeous, so damned alluring and intriguing. Hell, there were times when he hated his work. But he had too many secrets – especially now. He sighed as he stepped forwards with outstretched arms. 'Give me a hug.' He enveloped her in a tight embrace. The scent of her shampoo wafted into his nostrils and he knew without a doubt, he would never be able to rid himself of the memory of this woman. Damn but she felt so good, so right. As he planted a lingering kiss on top of her head he felt her tremble in response.

'You've made quite an impression on me, Madison Brown. Gemma was correct in her assumption. I like you a great deal but right now I can't even think about taking things further, much as I would like to.'

After a final squeeze he forced his arms to release her. Standing back, he took one last look then turned and strode away as fast as he could without seeming to run. He felt the pressure of Maddie's eyes boring into his back, had noticed the sparkle of reflected light from moisture on her lashes. The way his innards were twisted into such a tight clench, he knew he had fallen in love for the first time in his life. The rapidity with which she had stolen his heart whammed into him. How could a man fall in love so quickly? Up until this moment he had been too cynical to even believe in love but now, hell this was too hard. It took a monumental effort to keep walking, to prevent his head from turning around, from striding back to her, but he managed by trying to convince himself that it was lust

– pure and simple lust that wouldn't last beyond a single bedding to get her out of his system.

Despite a silent mantra of 'lust, it's only lust,' instead of counting backwards to lull his body into relaxation then sleep, Mick lay awake on the mattress in his cabin with images of Maddie naked in his bed, careening around his brain, which allowed no relaxation and preventing sleep.

When Bud started up his rig at sun-up, Mick crawled into the driver's seat and followed him down the highway, headed for Sydney.

Chapter Nine

At the not too gentle shove, Maddie dragged her eyelids open. 'Go away. What's the time?'

'Seven. Come on, we need to get going to make up lost time.'

Gemma's bright words were met with a very loud groan followed by silence when Maddie buried her head under the pillow. Less than three hour's sleep! Nowhere near enough and it was her turn to drive. Re-erecting the tent in the dark had been a farcical exercise and had eaten into most of what was left of the night. She continued lying on her mattress, dozing and thinking of Mick. It wasn't until after she had heard him leave that unbidden tears flowed. She'd felt bereft, kind of when Paul had died but different. She had no idea why she'd cried. It had left her feeling foolish. Maybe the reminder of Paul had done something to her subconscious.

Gemma packed up around her and then had the nerve to jog to the ablutions block for a shower. Where does she get all her energy? Hearing Gemma return, Maddie played mouse, pretending she was still asleep until Gemma crawled into the tent, grabbed a firm hold of two corners of the thin foam rubber mattress then yanked it upwards, turfing Maddie onto the hard ground.

'All right, I'm coming,' Maddie mumbled as she began freeing her body from the tangled sleeping bag. She became really alert when she spotted Gemma's hairdo. It was obvious she had washed her hair because it was still wet but it was just as obvious Gemma had used as much gel as the previous day but instead of the porcupine look, she had opted for a Mohawk. Her hair had been swept back from the sides and stood up on end right down the middle from her forehead to her nape. Oh, wow, this was about as way-out a hairdo that she'd ever seen.

Sitting up, Maddie swept her eyes lower, taking in the torn, bright green T-shirt and dark blue shorts. Gemma's attire was a little more subdued than the previous day in that it didn't have so many patterns but not a lot. Today it was vivid colours. At least she was wearing matching white socks under the same tatty sneakers. Knowing it was a subconscious indication of how confident Gemma felt, Maddie knew better than to comment about how her friend was dressed. The more outlandish the attire, the more afraid Gemma was of the world around her. Today Gemma felt more secure than she had yesterday, but with the hair – not much more. So she had been really afraid of the men despite her comments and now that the creeps were in police custody, Gemma appeared a tad more secure.

'Give me five minutes for a quick shower while you scrummage up something to eat. How about a hot coffee from the roadhouse?' Without waiting for an answer, Maddie reversed from the tent on all fours, dragging her sleeping bag and mattress with her. After rolling both up into a tight roll, she stowed them in the back of the car then collected her towel, bag of toiletries and a clean set of clothes. Passing by the front of the car, she noted several folded pieces of paper tucked under the windscreen wiper. Easing them out, she opened the pages, scanning quickly until she saw Mick's name scrawled at the bottom. A grin split her face as she refolded the pages and slid them into the waist band of her pyjamas to be read later.

Even though she said she would hurry, Maddie lingered under the warm spray until her token giving the allotted time, ran out. A five minute shower token each came with their camping fee. It didn't sound a lot but usually two minutes to get wet, soap up, scrub away the grime then rinse off was all Maddie needed. She could never figure out what shower lingerers did when they stood there for ages. Her brother included. Sure, hair washing took another couple of minutes but Paul, along with a few of her friends took forever in the bathroom. The need to limit water use out in these remote areas was obvious with water being such a scarce commodity. While dressing her thoughts centred on Mick and his parting words, wondering what he meant. Before returning to the car, she very carefully scoured the pages Mick had written. He had outlined in minute detail the best route for them to take. His final sentence said, *One day, I hope we will meet again. You made quite an impression on me. Keep safe, Mick.* Knowing it was useless to dwell on him since neither had sought or given contact details, Maddie made up her mind to forget about the only man she had taken an instant liking to as she hurried from the ablutions block. When she returned to the campsite,

Gemma was in the throes of forcing the carelessly rolled tent into what appeared to be a bag way too small for the task.

Forcing Mick from her mind, Maddie gave Gemma a hand in refolding the nylon flaps before easing it into a bag that had taken on the sudden appearance of being more than adequate in size for the now neatly folded tent. She settled into the driver's seat for what she knew was going to be a long hot journey. They were at least a day behind their planned schedule but it didn't really matter because they had a couple of days up their sleeve: days she had intended spending on a brief exploration of Brisbane. If nothing else went wrong she'd still have at least one day before catching her already booked flight home.

Nullarbor to Ceduna was three hundred kilometres along the Eyre Highway with only three tiny settlements to break the boredom. One of those was the Yalata Aboriginal community, which they had already decided they weren't going to detour the few kilometres to visit. They'd only just passed the boarded up Yalata Roadhouse when the scenery changed. A few sand dune sized hills covered in slightly taller trees were the precursor to a more undulating landscape and road. Undulations meant relief from the boredom of the dead straight road and flat vista.

The expected heat hit with a vengeance, the sun pouring into the passenger's side. It didn't take long for Gemma to lower the window a fraction to feed the end of a towel into the gap to gain some relief. Even the air-conditioning wasn't enough. Maddie was admiring the angular branches of knobbly trees that had been burnt during a bushfire in the not too distant past. They looked like the bony fingers of the grim reaper. Apart from the grisly skeletons, the trees were taller, bushes bushier and undergrowth far more dense.

All of a sudden the sun dimmed as though someone had turned down the dimmer switch. Maddie turned to see what Gemma had done to create the effect when they were bombarded by a swarm of insects, the brown bodies splatting against the windscreen and leaving splodges of yellow entrails and dribbles of pink blood radiating outwards like sloppy paint splashes.

'Oh, gross,' Gemma squealed as layer upon layer of pulverized bodies burst open on impact then unceremoniously slid down the glass, some of them still quivering in the last throes of death. Watching a bent leg quiver again and again as the bilious yellow innards oozed out was nauseating yet at the same time mesmerising with both of them staring at individual death rites until the insect finally stilled.

'What are they?' Gemma asked as she dragged her eyes from the base of the windscreen where the bodies were mounding in a steadily growing pile.

'Locusts.' With vision almost nil, Maddie had no choice but to decelerate then steer off the side of the bitumen, ensuring they were far enough on the verge they wouldn't be hit by oncoming or following traffic, although Maddie guessed any vehicle travelling would have to do the same. 'We're going to have to clean the windscreen before we go any further. I can't see.'

For a moment they sat still, just staring out, stunned at the density of the enormous swarm. With the car stationary, individual insects weren't hitting so hard then bursting open. Those flying into the sides of the car were able to settle, rest, then finding the pinging hot metal as no source of food, spreading their delicate wings to rejoin the impenetrable mass. The tracery of fine vessels amongst the sparkling transparency of the intricate wings was a vast contrast to the ugliness of the beady yellow eyes, twitching hooked feelers and thick yellow-brown bodies.

With the flying swarm appearing to be never-ending, Gemma grew restless.

'We can't sit here all day.' She lifted the latch of the door then shoved it open, immediately stepping outside.

'No, Gemma, don't get out,' Maddie yelled. But it was too late. Scores of the critters managed to find their way inside the car in the few brief seconds the door was open. They flew around the car, thudding against windows, doors and ceiling in panic then finally settling. With her arms over her head to protect her face from attack, Maddie waited for the frenzy to die down then watched the insects slowly tuck their wings in while beady eyes flicked, antennae swung around and bent legs clung to surfaces. The rustle of sticky feet settling and the clicking murmurs of insects communicating gave Maddie the creeps but she knew better than to panic and upset the calming animals.

A loud screech from outside had Maddie twist around. Gemma was prancing around waving frantic arms as she was being bombarded as though a cyclone was whipping small stones in hurricane force winds. Her hands flew upwards, covering her face as thousands of tiny feet landed on the bare skin of her arms and legs, setting up wave after wave of tremors rippling along her skin. Maddie was awed by the way Gemma's skin shivered. Bodies pounded into her as the maelstrom of insects, unable to evade her body in the frenzy, slammed into her. Another panic-stricken scream of utter terror echoed through the eerie atmosphere darkened by the dense cloud of grasshoppers.

Scream after scream rattled Maddie's ears. Knowing her friend was terrified she figured she had to do something - but what? Wracking her brain for ideas she reached over to the back seat and grabbed the first thing she could find to cover her head. The towel she had used that morning had been spread out over the back seat to dry. Dropping it over her hair, she fashioned a hood, leaving just enough room for her eyes to peer out before sucking in a deep breath. With Gemma still screaming and prancing around, her feet pummelling the ground in a frantic tattoo of terror, Maddie shoved her door open, leapt out then slammed the door shut. As fast as she was, she knew an awful lot more insects had managed to enter the car.

Convincing her brain that they were just grasshoppers and weren't going to kill her, Maddie shot around the other side of the car, grabbed a hold of Gemma and frantically brushed down her arms and body, sweeping clinging insects from clothes, limbs and hair trying to get rid of as many as she could. Then she realised Gemma was wearing a green shirt: food — as far as the insects were concerned. As fast as she swept, other insects clung. Noting the naked fear in Gemma's eyes and realising she was on the verge of hysteria, Maddie gave up denuding Gemma's body of locusts. It was a futile exercise. Instead she steered Gemma towards the passenger door, whipped it open and shoved her inside. Then she dived in after her, flinging the towel covered in clinging locusts from her head as she dived, not caring where it landed as long as it was outside.

Gemma continued whimpering like a terrified two-year old as she sat huddled in the seat with Maddie sitting on her lap. 'Get them off me!' Gemma choked out as her hands beat and rubbed against her body.

'Calm down, Gem.' Feeling like a contortionist, Maddie eased over the console then twisted around to face her friend. 'They won't kill you, sweetie. Relax, take deep breaths.'

'They feel so… creepy. That horrible clicking noise…' Gemma choked out between sharp whines.

Despite her attempt to pacify her friend, Maddie knew Gemma was so petrified she was beyond being calmed with any ease. 'I have an idea.' Crawling onto her knees on the seat and facing the rear, Maddie leant over into the back seat then searched around for the can of insect repellent she had insisted on bringing, telling Gemma it was a necessity. But grasshoppers were the last things she thought she'd be using it on. Mosquitoes and flies and maybe the odd spider had been on her mind at the time. Finally finding the can she asked Gemma to close her eyes then waved her arm around as she pressed on the button to release the aerosol spray, ensuring she covered every part of Gemma's body in a fine mist. Then she aimed the can in her own direction, wriggling around until the can emptied.

They both began coughing in the choking chemical laden atmosphere but Maddie didn't care two hoots about the prospect of dying from poisoning. It was far better than being bombarded with millions of crawling legs. One by one, sedated insects either dropped off, or were picked off. Verbose utterances of sheer disgust filled the cloying, stinking atmosphere as the pair wriggled and squirmed each time they found another twitching body and shook it to the floor.

It seemed to take forever to cease the continuous contortionist acts until Maddie was certain there was not a single remaining insect clinging to their bodies, or invading their space on the seats. Neither had their feet on the ground where the floor space was covered in a tan, writhing mass of insects. There was a continual *plip, plip, plip* of sound as some gassed locusts still slowly moved.

Sitting perched on the seats with arms wrapped around their knees and feet tucked tight to their bodies, they sat staring at the continuing waves of insects still swarming outside.

'There must be trillions of them,' Gemma muttered in awe, her body still shuddering in disgust every now and again.

'Yes, and they are all looking for food to devour so they can mate then lay trillions more eggs. Wherever they land, they will pick the vegetation bare then move on to the next source of food. I've seen them before but never this thick.' Maddie turned to face Gemma, noting how her rigid Mohawk was about the only thing not affected by the past few minutes of mayhem. Under her hair, Gemma's face was porcelain white.

'It makes the Hitchcock film about the birds seem meek and mild. I've never been so petrified in all my life,' said Gemma.

'I don't know, you were pretty scared of the kangaroos.' Maddie managed a grin as Gemma stared at her.

'The kangaroos were nothing compared to these ghastly aliens. How are we going to get rid of them?' As Gemma turned her eyes towards the floor, her entire body shuddered in disgust.

'They probably aren't dead, just stunned. I emptied the entire can. We'll have to wait until the swarm moves on. I imagine there are masses of them clogging the radiator vents. We have to clean them away otherwise the car will overheat.' Reaching up. Maddie flicked another locust that had emerged from behind the sun visor, onto the floor then cautiously turned the visor down with the tip of one finger, recoiling backwards when three more locusts dropped.

'You sound as though you've done this before.'

'Once, but it was only a small swarm. We were on a camping trip before…' Maddie hesitated as she recalled the trip. Paul had still been alive.

'It's okay, Maddie, you don't have to tell me. I understand.' Gemma reached over and gave her friend a hug. Even though they were complete opposites in almost every aspect, the connection through the understanding of the loss of a sibling tied them together in a way any outsider couldn't possibly understand.

While they waited, they munched on muesli bars, washing the dry cereal down with tepid water. 'You want to tell me exactly why you went out there?' Maddie indicated with a wave of her hand.

Another tremor snaked down Gemma's body. 'I thought they'd be scared of me and fly away.'

'They're grasshoppers: very hungry grasshoppers.' Maddie tugged the hem of Gemma's shirt. 'Right now green is their favourite colour and you getting out there was like an oasis in the desert for them.'

'They wanted to eat me?' Gemma shuddered then rubbed her hands vigorously up and down her arms.

'They were probably attracted to the colour but when they landed they discovered your shirt wasn't tasty enough.'

'I didn't think about that.'

'A bad habit of yours – never thinking about the consequences before you act.' As soon as she said it, Maddie realised she should have kept her mouth shut, but far out, Gemma was always leaping into things without thinking and it was Maddie who was always getting Gemma out of the resulting pickles.

'Bitch,' hissed from Gemma's mouth.

Maddie reeled back. The accusation hurt but to retaliate would only escalate an already uncomfortable atmosphere and they were only about a third of the way through their journey. 'I'm sorry, I shouldn't have said that.' Even if it was true, she added in her mind.

Gemma turned her head away and stared out of the window. The silence was unbearable until the locust swarm disappeared as suddenly as it arrived. One minute they were surrounded by a heaving, swirling mass of tan then the air was clear, the dark cloud sweeping southwards towards the coast on the never-ending search for food.

Maddie began cleaning out the bodies by using a small hand-brush they had for sweeping out the tent. She had just folded sheets of newspaper to scoop out the piles when Gemma joined her. They swept and scooped until the car was clean of bodies, many of them still writhing. They then turned their attention to the outside of the car, sweeping away body remnants from the windscreen and bonnet then brushing away those caught in the vents in front of the radiator, even lifting the bonnet to denude the engine of dead insects. The final gesture of cleansing was scrubbing the windscreen clean, using an entire two litres of precious water to rid the glass of all traces of small spots of insect droppings. No way did Maddie want to be looking at grasshopper gizzards for the next few hours. Even when they were settled back into their seats, her eyes were always searching for an elusive creepy body.

Maddie eased back onto the road. For the first few metres the sound and feel of crunching bodies on the bitumen had the girls screwing up their faces in revulsion. Then they were free – the road clean – the foliage untouched. It was as though they had just passed through a brief time warp on another planet and then been returned.

Maddie turned on a CD of pop music to break the silence. She sighed in relief when Gemma began bopping and rocking to the catchy rhythm.

As they approached Nundroo there was evidence of the beginning of farmland, the recently harvested paddocks a golden tan. Lucky people had got the crop off before the locusts arrived. A strong wind caught the top layers of dirt, turning them into swirling masses of mini dust storms.

Penong was the first actual settlement of any size since Norseman. It looked to be a sleepy hollow but with the wind still blowing up a dust storm it didn't give a welcoming feeling. It was probably a haven for the outlying farmers and their families, Maddie thought as she drifted through the town. She noted the police station and wondered if the three creeps were held in a cell there or if they'd been taken to Ceduna. She thought it better not to mention it, especially since Gemma had hardly spoken a word since the locusts. Then again, Maddie wasn't feeling in the space to chat either. The past twenty-four hours had been rather – she couldn't think of an apt word to describe how she felt about the past day but it was something she never wanted to repeat.

Ceduna felt like an oasis in the desert with the bright cerulean blue of the ocean on the right. The town was clean and gave Maddie a feeling of reassurance that they were once again amongst a large number of people. Well, relatively large compared to the past couple of days. After a drive around taking in the sites of the first real town since before crossing the Nullabor Plain, they ate a late picnic lunch of fresh salad rolls and cartons of fruit juice, sitting on the sand of Murat Bay. Before continuing on their way they dipped their feet in the ocean. Maddie lapped up the pleasure of feeling the cool waves against her ankles. Such a pleasant relief.

Maddie would have liked to stay overnight but they were already running more than a day over schedule so they headed for Kyancutta with Gemma taking over the wheel after filling the fuel tank. It was a two-hour drive in the sizzling heat of the hottest part of the day but at least there were now more regular small towns to pass through to break the monotony of the journey. A short stop at Kyancutta to top up the fuel and take a toilet break at the general store cum roadhouse was all they dared once reaching the small town. The biggest feature was the huge wheat silos making the couple of houses gracing the tiny settlement's streets, look miniscule and desolate. Maddie was glad they were heading for Port Augusta where they decided to spend the night.

Chapter Ten

It had been a stupid idea, Maddie thought as she studied the broken vanes of rusted skeletal windmill remains. Looking at what was left of the town of Iron Knob she felt a sense of despair and loss. It was uncanny how the feeling was similar to how she felt the day they had buried Paul.

She recalled the shocked daze she'd felt after being told of his death. For a week and a half she'd lived in a weird Twilight Zone, feeling numb and empty and yet there had been a tonne of concrete sitting in her stomach at the same time. It wasn't until watching Paul's casket being lowered into that deep dark hole that the meaning of his death had hit so hard. It was as though someone had slammed her in the heart with a massive sledge-hammer, the sudden pain buckling her at the knees. She'd slumped to the ground with tears she hadn't realised were there, streaming from her eyes. She'd had no control. Something inside her broke apart, leaving an intense sensation of emptiness. In the weeks after, that feeling had never left, leaving her walking around like some brainless zombie. It must have concerned her parents for it was after two months of barely existing that she'd ended up in the counselling group. They had never spoken of the why's or how's but now she was glad they'd insisted for the sessions had saved her sanity and brought her back to life. She wondered if Gemma had felt the same. She should know but didn't. She'd never asked and never would.

Maddie glanced at Gemma who was studying the vista in front of them. Maddie followed her line of sight. The place looked like a ghost town yet hardy folk lingered. How they survived was a mystery. Behind a rusty fence held up by a variety of make-do posts, a mob of scraggly sheep searched for something more succulent than saltbush on the flat ground. They looked as depressed as Maddie felt.

They drove past the motel. Smashed windows and a peeling *Closed* sign greeted intending patrons. It was the tall antenna that had lured them to take the short detour to explore the first iron ore mining town in Australia. Up close, the mast was as sad looking and dingy as the rest of the town.

The hill that had given the town its name looked like a giant loaf of bread that monster rats had gnawed at over the years leaving behind tiered sludge heaps. The entire knob had been eaten away leaving crumbling crusts.

As they retraced their route to the highway, Maddie was sorry they'd come yet glad to see the beginnings of the Australian iron ore industry which was now one of the biggest sources of mining income in the country. It was depressing to think that many current iron ore towns could end up the same way once the hills had been dug out and carted away.

Back on the main road, the scenery was just as depressing and not nearly as exciting as the Nullarbor. Here there were flat, saltbush plains with a base of salmon coloured clay. Maddie spotted the odd spindly tree with a few denser rows in the distance following level creek beds.

The power poles stuck out. They were concrete tapers with iron railway line supports up each side. Trident tops supported a trio of electric cables. King Neptune wouldn't be out of place except for the obvious lack of water.

An occasional windmill and dam were welcome relief from the tedium of flat land mirrored by a flat horizon. The spinning vanes of working mills gave a sense of hope in a desolate part of the country. In Maddie's experience, the outback had a unique beauty but not this particular spot.

'Look at that!' said Gemma.

Maddie roused from her introspection and turned her head to follow the line Gemma's hand was pointing. A mob of nine rams were stalking the fence line seeking a way out of their barren paddock to the richer pickings along the road side. They probably deserved the better feed as a result of managing to escape but after filling their bellies in bliss they'd probably end up as road kill. Sometimes life just wasn't fair.

Gemma slowed to a crawl as they passed Little Nutbush. The campsite was lush and looked like an oasis in the desert. 'Should we stay there?' asked Gemma. 'It looks pretty good.'

Maddie thought. It did look gorgeous, especially after the last few nights. 'No, let's go on to Port Augusta. It's only about thirty kilometres and I'd rather be somewhere with lots of people. I'm looking forward to some civilisation.' And no way was she letting on exactly how spooked she'd been.

Gemma laughed. 'Sounds good.'

Maddie felt a sense of expectation as they neared Port Augusta. Traffic both ways was dense compared to the Eyre Highway. It was hard to believe she would appreciate having to slow because of traffic but numbers meant safety. Where were all these drivers when she had needed them?

A brief stop at the visitors' centre yielded directions to three caravan parks. There were also a couple of out of town camping spots but Maddie was adamant. No way. Nothing remote. Not tonight. Still spooked by the past couple of days she wanted people – lots of people. After driving around and inspecting the position of each park it was a mutual decision to stay at the Shoreline Caravan Park. Sitting on the edge of the water near the apex of Spencer Gulf, it looked lush, green and inviting.

Even as they set up the tent, Maddie couldn't stop yawning. 'I'm pooped,' she gushed on the expelled breath of yet another yawn as she whacked in the final tent peg with a hammer. After eyeing the tool, she tossed it into the corner of the tent instead of putting it back in the car. It was a handy weapon.

'Yeah, so am I. We shouldn't have driven so far today. How many k's did we do? And I virtually had no sleep last night.' Gemma unrolled her sleeping bag then shoved it through the flap before following it inside, crawling on all fours.

'Almost eight hundred kilometres, which made up some lost time.'

'Too much. I'm knackered.'

'Let's not bother with a meal tonight. We've still got some fruit and a few energy bars. I'm all for a shower and bed.'

'I don't think I can even make it to the shower.' Gemma's voice sounded muffled.

Maddie fisted the flap aside. Gemma was stretched out on her sleeping bag with eyes closed. Maddie laughed. 'We could shower in the morning.'

One eye cracked open. 'Suits me. Goodnight.' Gemma rolled over and tucked one hand under her cheek.

It took ten long minutes for Maddie to secure their belongings in the car, unroll her own sleeping bag, fight Gemma's pillow under her soundly sleeping head, spread her sleeping bag over the top then curl up in her own bag. The need for sleep far outweighed the need for food.

Chapter Eleven

'Slow down!' Maddie growled as Gemma ignored the road signs and maintained her speed.

'Why?'

'Didn't you see the signs? Road works ahead.' Maddie twisted her head to look at Gemma who hadn't slowed one iota and didn't look as though she was going to. Maddie wished she was still driving but after four hours on the Barrier highway she had started to lose concentration. It was as hot as hell outside with a strong cross-wind whipping down from the north making it difficult to keep the car steady. The constant struggle to keep the wheels straight had sapped her energy. It hadn't taken long for the early morning clouds to burn off once the sun had risen high enough to suck away all the moisture. The bare fresh-harvested paddocks seemed to stretch forever with only an occasional dot turning into a sheep or cow as they neared it. And to top it all off, they had lost the time they'd made up yesterday by sleeping in. And now Gemma was driving like a maniac.

'Sure but there are no workers so why slow?'

Maddie straightened. 'How did you ever pass your driver's licence? You're supposed to obey all road signs. They are there for a reason. Slow down to eighty.'

Gemma flicked two fingers in Maddie's direction and clamped down the accelerator even more. Anger surged. That was the second time Gemma had been downright rude. Maddie had ignored being called a bitch because at the time Gemma had been scared witless but this… this was uncalled for. Should she say anything? After mulling things through her mind she decided, better not or it might inflame the situation and Gemma might accelerate even more.

Thoroughly miffed, Maddie turned her head and stared out of the window. They'd meandered through the higher hills of the South Flinders Range for a couple of hours, which had been pretty but now, just past Olary, there was less vegetation than most of the Nullarbor. Who'd live out here? And the town, if you could call it a town, was so uninviting with just a run-down pub and a circular toilet block for tourists. At least there were basic amenities. The only reason they'd stopped was to swap drivers and make use of the facilities.

Determined to keep her mouth shut, Maddie closed her eyes and thought about the little settlements they'd gone through during the day. Mannahill had boasted a police station and a quaint railway siding which looked rather cute. There were a few houses and, joy of joys, a roadhouse where they'd stopped for a burger and coffee. The burger wasn't what Maddie would call fabulous but it was fresh made, filled a hole and had mostly healthy ingredients.

She smiled at the memory of Yunta. Now that had been a surprise. The few small houses led to a brilliantly set up area for caravanners and truckies. A pub and two roadhouses indicated the town was well patronised by travellers from all directions. What made the place even more attractive was the pretty creek just out of town that still had deep ponds of water teeming with bird-life – obviously run-off from the range running along the north. But she still wouldn't want to live there. Way too isolated.

Whump!

The car jerked and bucked. Maddie's head whacked against the side window. 'Whoa, what happened?' she yelled as she straightened and glanced around while rubbing at the sore spot. 'Oh, God, slow down, Gemma.'

The road had been dug up and looked like the cratered lunar landscape. A detour sign loomed. Maddie made a grab for the steering wheel and swung it upwards to turn the wheels onto the track going around the small bridge that was under repair. Workmen dressed in iridescent jackets gawped, their shovels and tools held in mid-air.

Then a single worker loomed. They were going to hit him. Gemma screamed and gripped the steering wheel as she jammed on the brakes. They skidded past the man as he leapt out of their path. How they missed him must have been a miracle for there was barely a space between them. The car came to a shuddering halt and a dust cloud swept up around them.

'Idiot,' was yelled from somewhere beyond the still hovering dust.

Maddie gritted her teeth then hurled out, 'That's why you obey road signs. You've probably wrecked the tyres. And that poor guy!' Her mind stuttered. She was so shocked and so irate she couldn't get any more words out.

'Oops, sorry,' said Gemma in a little voice.

'Sorry! That's all you've got to say?' Stunned, Maddie rubbed at the sting on the side of her brow. 'You'd better keep going or these men are going to want a piece of you.' She flicked her other hand to indicate the gravel track which was at least rolled gravel and better than the cut up section. 'And CRAWL.'

'All right, there's no need to get your knickers in a knot,' Gemma mumbled as she began edging the car forwards.

Maddie bit her tongue to prevent it from forming more words. She wanted to say plenty but none of it would have been pleasant. Her heart was trying to fight its way out of her rib cage and her hands had taken on a definite tremor. They passed the bridge which looked as though it had collapsed and was being rebuilt then veered back onto the road which consisted of large chunks of dug up blue metal embedded in bitumen. It was impossible to tell if the jolting was due to the condition of the road or whether they had in fact done a tyre in and were running on the rims. Maddie tried to figure out if the car was listing in any one direction. She didn't think so but with all the juddering who could tell?

They bumped up the ridge delineating the dug up section and the smooth tarmac. Gemma sped up but Maddie noticed that she appeared to be a little unnerved. Her knuckles were white and had a death grip on the steering wheel and the speed was restrained. Well good. Serves her right. Maybe next time she will take heed of the road works sign.

Even though her nerves were strung tight, Maddie settled back in her seat and resumed her perusal of the passing vista. She needed to concentrate on something – anything other than the near tragedy. A train line ran alongside the road and by the neatness of the vegetation along the sides it looked as though the track was still in use. It was better maintained than the road. There'd been few cars, maybe one every five kilometres and even less trucks, although it was a major truck route. No-where near as many as the Nullarbor highway. She shuddered at the remembered thought of the lack of trucks when they were being harassed then smiled as she remembered Mick. He was a mystery: all hunky muscle with brooding good looks but kind and caring. But at the same time there was something dark about him. That gun. She didn't do guns although her dad had a service pistol for work.

Pop!

The loud explosion rocked the car, tossing Maddie forward. Her seat belt tightened and sucked the breath from her. She struggled upright as the car veered with a squeal of tyres. Gemma let loose with an ear-drum piercing scream as she tried to twist the wheel against the swerve.

'Steer into the skid,' Maddie yelled as she grabbed the steering wheel and wrenched it in the opposite direction.

The car jerked the other way at speed then rocked from side-to-side tossing them around like they were in a tiny boat on an angry ocean in a force five hurricane.

'Brake slowly,' Maddie said, forcing her voice to calm.

But panic-stricken Gemma jammed her foot down forcing the car to spin one hundred and eighty degrees then it rocked to the left on two wheels then counter-balanced on the other two wheels before juddering to a standstill facing the wrong way, but at least they were on the verge and still upright.

Maddie felt sure her heart had ceased beating for what felt like forever, then it sped up at a thundering pace to make up for the missed beats. She couldn't move but sat with her head bowed and her hands gripped in her lap willing her body to calm.

'What happened?' squeaked Gemma, the words hardly audible but with a definite tremor.

'We blew a tyre.' Maddie had no doubts. She turned her head sideways, 'You damaged it back at the road works because you couldn't be bothered slowing when the sign said to slow.' She knew she was sounding terse but that was how she felt. 'You could have killed us because you were reckless and didn't care.'

Jamming her teeth together, Maddie unclipped her seat belt to ease the pressure on what she knew were bruises. It stung across her chest, especially her breast bone. She winced at the sharp pain as she shoved the door open.

'I didn't know…' whimpered Gemma.

Maddie slid from the car and teetered as she stood. Her legs felt like jellified rubber. She grabbed the car door and sucked in a few deep breaths until she felt she was safe from toppling over then bent to glare at Gemma whose face had taken on the appearance of a ghost. 'Well now you do know. Maybe next time you'll do what the sign says. Idiot!'

'You're mad at me aren't you?'

Even though Gemma sounded and looked contrite, Maddie was too stirred up to cut her any slack. 'Angry isn't a strong enough word. I'm beyond angry. Try hopping mad or furious.' She wheeled around and stalked down the road in an attempt to use up the bucket loads of adrenaline that were surging through her veins. If she stayed she'd throttle Gemma.

A car door slammed then there were the slap of hurried footsteps coming closer. God, give me strength, Maddie threw heavenwards.

'Where are you going?' asked Gemma as she drew alongside.

'Just leave me alone while I cool off,' hissed Maddie through clenched teeth.

'But what are we going to do?' Gemma's voice sounded like a petty wail.

Maddie stopped and spun around. 'WE are not going to do anything.' She jabbed Gemma in her chest. 'YOU are going to change the tyre.' She spun back and kept stomping.

'But I don't know how.'

Maddie jerked to a standstill. 'Excuse me?' She turned. 'You go driving across the continent in your own car and you don't know how to change a tyre? What have you got in that head of yours? Cottonwool? It sure isn't brains?' With that Maddie pounded back to the car, yanked the boot open then began tossing tents, sleeping bags and whatever she could lay her hands on, out onto the ground.

'What are you doing?' Gemma dared to ask.

Maddie paused then took a step back as she whistled a long sucked in breath through clenched teeth. 'You're right. What the hell am I doing?' There was a hiss from Gemma at Maddie's blasphemy for she rarely let loose like that, but she was much too mad to care. She wanted to yell every blasphemous word she'd never used and would have if she thought it would have made one iota of difference.

'I'm not doing anything. YOU are. The spare wheel is under the board in the back and if there is a God up there,' she wavered her fingers skywards knowing full well that Gemma came from a devout Catholic family, 'then there will also be the repair kit such as jack and tyre wrench so we can get the damn thing off! YOU are going to shift all our gear and get the tyre and tools out. Yell when you are ready then I will teach you how to change a tyre and believe me… you are going to do it.' Noting the shocked look on Gemma's face Maddie turned and began jogging back towards the bridge. Hopefully she could find somewhere to dump her simmering temper over the next few minutes. If she stayed she might just wring Gemma's scrawny neck, then she'd drop her to the ground and stomp some sense into her head. Hopefully it would take Gemma at least an hour to shift all their gear. Then maybe, just maybe, the real meek and mild Madison Brown might return to teach Gemma how to change a tyre without killing her in the process.

Chapter Twelve

With her hands planted on her hips, Maddie studied the array of tools scattered on the ground. She kicked the spare tyre to check that it was hard then stood and jumped on the wall of the inflated rubber. It barely budged. At least something was going right for a change but it wouldn't have surprised her if it wasn't fully inflated and then they'd be stuck. Next she toed through the tools, ignoring the black dust that billowed like tiny mushrooms then shoved the jack aside. It was puny and hardly adequate for the job but it came with the car so she figured it would hold it up long enough.

'That's the jack,' she said to Gemma. 'You need to put that little flat bit with the lip', she indicated with her toe, 'under the jacking point beneath the edge of the car.' She hid her grin as Gemma picked up the jack and studied it as though it was an alien from some way-off universe. Gemma didn't have a clue.

'How do I find the jacking point?'

'Lie on your back and slide under the car. It should be right below the main supporting frame of the car.'

It was farcical watching the princess dropping to her back in the dirt. Getting down and dirty wasn't in her vocabulary, especially since for once she was wearing co-ordinated clothes – all white. Maddie grinned at the thought of what those cut-offs and frilled cotton top were going to look like after this little exercise. Sometimes Karma showed its face in mysterious ways. It was also pathetic the way Gemma whimpered and moaned about sharp stones, dirt and dust. Sighing at the Prima-Donna's performance, Maddie squatted on her haunches, felt around with her fingers and found the spot.

'Here. Set it up under here.'

Despite explicit step-by-step instructions, the jack slipped and fell in every direction except the right way. Maddie sighed again then took over, having the jack up in ten seconds flat. Making sure Gemma was standing back in case the car slipped from the support, Maddie then pumped the lever until the front wheel was free from the ground. Then she pumped some more since the tyre was so shredded there was little rubber left on the rim and the new tyre was going to need enough clearance.

Just as she reached for the multi-purpose brace/come lever a huge semi-trailer pulled up in front of them. That was all they needed; another maniacal he-man to take advantage of them.

'Get behind the car, Gemma.' Maddie kept a tight grip on the metal lever as she shoved Gemma behind her.

'Why? He'll probably fix the tyre for us.'

'Yes, just like those other jerks only wanted to talk to us,' Maddie parroted, taking off Gemma's words. 'I'm not taking any chances.'

Gemma scuttled to the rear end of the car. For once she was heeding advice so maybe she'd learnt a lesson.

'Afternoon, ladies, need a hand?' The truckie was stocky and dressed in what appeared to be the current fashion for truck drivers. A tatty khaki shirt with torn off sleeves and a pair of shorts showing permanent faded creases from sitting in the same position too long, showed off toned limbs. These guys might sit endless hours behind the wheel but climbing steps and loading and unloading obviously required physical strength. A protruding paunch told a different story; too much greasy fast food from road-houses and perhaps a few too many beers at night.

'We're fine,' Maddie said at the same time Gemma yelled out, 'Yes.'

The man grinned while Maddie winced.

'I can handle it,' added Maddie after elbowing Gemma to shut up.

'And I could change that wheel in a quarter of the time. A car tyre is a piece of cake after changing one of those buggers.' He waggled a hand in the direction of his truck. 'Why don't you hand over that wheel brace and let me do it.' He took a few steps towards them with one hand stretched out.

'No way,' said Maddie. 'I mean, thank you for the offer but really I can manage.'

The man paused as Maddie shoved Gemma further back. Then he withdrew a mobile phone from his shirt pocket, pressed tapped and slid before holding it to one ear. Thank goodness he turned away and headed back towards his truck.

Maddie released the breath she hadn't realised she was holding. Good, he was going away but she was staying right where she was until he drove off. She knew it was stupid but her trust levels with men in general had slid to an all time low. And they were miles from anywhere - although she could go back to the workers on the bridge; she could run that far. Maybe not. After Gemma's brilliant display of driving, the guys there would probably want to string the both of them up or maybe dig a hole with those shovels they'd been waving around and bury them up to their necks for the ants to feast on.

'He's coming back,' whispered Gemma from behind her.

Maddie glanced up then her entire body tensed as the man approached.

'Someone wants to talk to you.' He pointed right at Maddie.

Huh, who would want to speak to her? Maddie shook her head and took a few steps backwards, ready to run and shoving Gemma as she went. This was getting beyond a joke. Her innards managed to tie themselves up into a tight knot within seconds.

'Look, lady, I'll set my phone on the bonnet and move away. The worst that can happen is that I'll lose my phone. You need to talk to this guy.' He lifted the phone in her direction. 'I promise I mean you no harm. I've got a daughter about your age and I sure wouldn't want anyone to hurt her.' He slid the phone across the top of the bonnet then turned and strode away.

Mystified and wondering if she was taking leave of her senses, Maddie shot to the front of the car, grabbed the phone and raced back to Gemma. She wasn't taking any chances.

'Hello.'

'It didn't take you long to get into more strife, did it? Give Thommo the brace.'

She recognised the voice immediately. 'Mick! How did you… how did he…'

Mick laughed. 'I figured you would be smart enough to follow the route I mapped out. It's a truckie route. I sent a message along the grapevine to keep an eye out for you for the next week. Seems I was right. You do get yourselves into some pickles, don't you? Now give Thommo the brace. I promise he won't harm you. Stand well away while he works if it makes you feel safer.'

'Okay, but you can't blame me for being a bit wary.' She held the brace up into the air then tossed it towards the busted wheel. Thommo grinned then set to work.

'What happened, Maddie?'

Far out, how did she explain this little predicament? Keep to the basics. No need to tell about almost cleaning up a workman. 'Gemma hit a rough patch in the road at full speed. The road had been dug up. The tyre must have gotten damaged. It burst about a kilometre later.'

'Are you okay?'

'A few bruises.' Maddie wriggled to test out the muscles then winced. Probably more than a few.

'Bruises? Why?'

'The car veered and Gemma didn't know to steer into the skid then she jammed on the brakes instead of applying gentle pressure, which resulted in some hairy manoeuvres before we spun out. It was a bit scary.'

'Dear, God. You sound as though you know what to do when something like that happens.'

'I should. The day I got my licence, Dad booked me into a defensive driving course. After that I did an advanced course.'

'Wise man but wasn't that a bit over the top?'

'Not really when you consider his job.'

'And what might that be?'

'He investigates car accidents.'

There was a sound of a long sucked in breath then a pause. 'He's a cop?' The way Mick said it sent a shiver snaking across Maddie's shoulders.

'You sound as though that disturbs you.'

'Not at all. It's an honourable profession.'

'Yeah, well, Dad has a physics degree so he gets to do all the measuring and calculating to figure out what causes accidents.' She snorted. What would Dad think of this little episode?

'And what conclusion would he draw with your bingle?' asked Mick.

Maddie felt spooked when Mick virtually said exactly what she was thinking. Was he a mind reader? 'Sheer stupidity on Gemma's part. She ignored the road works sign but somehow I don't think she'll do it again any time soon.'

'Can I have my phone back?'

Maddie jolted and spun around at the sound of the voice so close behind her. 'You've finished already?' she stuttered then added to Mick, 'I've got to go. And thank you.'

'For what?' asked Mick.

'For the grapevine. Bye.'

Mick laughed. 'You're welcome and keep safe.'

Maddie held out the phone. 'I'm not sure which button to press to turn this off.'

Thommo took back the phone, pressed something and slid it back into his shirt pocket.

'I really appreciate your help,' said Maddie, 'and I'm sorry about not trusting you.'

Thommo gave a casual two finger salute and smiled. 'Not a problem. Big Mick explained what happened and it's probably wise to be cautious when a complete stranger approaches. I just pray that my own daughter takes the same precautions. Now, you need to get that tyre replaced in the next town.' He rubbed his hand over his balding head. 'Well probably not in Cockburn but Broken Hill is only about fifty clicks. It's a big place so will have what you need. I wouldn't go any further without a spare. Good luck.'

With another casual wave he strode to his truck. A strong whiff of diesel hit them as the truck passed. Maddie turned towards the car to see Gemma sitting in the driver's seat ready to go but she hadn't bothered to pack up any of the still scattered gear. Amazed at Gemma's arrogance, Maddie moved to the front of the car and hoicked her thumb sideways to indicate that Gemma needed to get out.

'What?' mouthed Gemma as she shrugged her shoulders.

Maddie strode to the driver's door and yanked it open. 'You plan on sleeping out in the open without your sleeping bag for the rest of the journey?'

Gemma screwed her mouth in displeasure and glared at Maddie. 'I unloaded it so it's only fair that you put it back again.'

Unbelievable! Maddie grabbed the car keys.

'Hey! What are you doing?' squawked Gemma looking as though she'd been served the worst injustice ever.

'We can stay here all night and all tomorrow if you like but unless you get out and share the work load then the keys stay with me.' Maddie tugged the front of her T-shirt outwards and dropped the keys into her bra and stalked to the pile of tools, wincing at the discomfort of metal poking into an already tender breast bone. She was getting a bit fed up with Gemma's selfish antics.

'Jeeze, Maddie, you can be such a bossy boots.' Gemma tossed her head to emphasise her pique as she strutted past and picked up her own sleeping bag then proceeded to stuff things into the rear compartment one item at a time. There was no orderliness about her packing. It was pick and toss with a glare and humph accompanying each item until all that was left was the damaged wheel. Gemma ignored it and headed back to the driver's seat.

'So are you going to leave the wheel on the side of the road?' Maddie asked as she ran to reach the door first. She planted her body against the metal, crowding Gemma's personal space. They were so close Maddie could feel each of Gemma's petulant breaths brushing against the skin of her face. 'We can't continue without a spare so if you want to put our lives in danger then as soon as we get to Broken Hill I'm heading for the airport to catch a flight home.'

A brief look of fear washed over Gemma's features before she dropped her eyes. 'You're still mad at me aren't you?'

Maddie so badly wanted to say yes. She drew in a breath and glanced skywards seeking the right words. Getting on a plane sounded so, so good. She took a step to the side to give them both space then eyed Gemma.

'Look, Gem, yes I was peeved that this happened because you chose to ignore road signs warning us of road works ahead. It was reckless and we were dead lucky we didn't roll over.' She winced at her choice of words. Dead wasn't all that appropriate considering what had just happened. 'I was plain scared and shaken when we spun out. But it happened and we were lucky to escape with just a busted tyre. I'm doing you a favour by coming with you when I could be working to earn some money but I get the feeling you don't appreciate that and are taking my presence for granted.' She spun around a full circle; sure she wasn't saying the right things.

'Gem, we've still got several days driving to get through. Why don't we put this behind us, slap on a positive face and work together?' She stepped forwards with her arms outstretched asking for a hug.

'I'm sorry, Maddie.' Gemma threw herself forwards and almost knocked Maddie over with her exuberance.

Maddie laughed as she stumbled then righted herself. 'Okay, let's get this wheel in the car and get ourselves to Broken Hill for the night.'

Chapter Thirteen

The next bridge passed over the railway line and wasn't, thank goodness, under repair. It pointed them into Cockburn, which, Maddie read on the sign that was too large to be missed, had the distinction of being on the border of New South Wales. Maddie laughed at Gemma's insistence of shooting each of their images under the humungous sign. It was hard to believe they'd driven the width of two entire states. So many hundreds of kilometres with the sparsest of inhabitation caused by such a lack of natural water resources. There were no vast river systems like the mighty Mississippi in America and no mountain chains to do what they did in regards to forcing clouds to rise and drop their precious moisture or prevent the winds from sweeping across the plains uninhibited, stripping the land of viable topsoil. A hot spell in Perth on one day meant that a few days later it would hit Adelaide then Melbourne. Similarly with a cold stormy front in the winter. It was so predictable and unrelenting.

The road took them up into the Thankaringa Hills and although it wasn't far to Broken Hill, Maddie couldn't help willing all four remaining tyres to stay intact. She flinched at every bump and dip in the road that was a little rougher than she'd like. She tried to concentrate on the scenery which was gorgeous compared to some they'd been through. Just being on a road with a few bends was a pleasant relief but also the hillier country after so many hundreds of flat kilometres was magical.

When the sun shining directly into the passenger window became too hot to tolerate a moment longer, she wound down the window a fraction and jammed in the edge of a towel. The relief was instant. All she needed was for Gemma to turn down the infernal racket of heavy metal that was so loud the speakers seemed to physically shudder at each booming bass note. Another reason Maddie should drive more for they'd agreed that whoever was driving chose the music. Now it seemed like such a stupid idea, as dumb as her agreeing to accompany Gemma. Why couldn't Gemma have shipped her car either by train or on one of those never-ending road trains?

Maddie twisted her head to study Gemma. Why had they ended up as friends? They were opposites in almost everything. Standing out was the frilly blouse. It was so out of character, especially with streaks of dirt that Gemma had tried to brush away without success. All she'd managed was to spread the marks and ingrain the dark particles into the fine weave of the cotton fabric. Maybe she had run out of clean clothes and was scraping the barrel as to what to wear, even though they had decided to pack enough changes for two weeks so they didn't have to bother with doing any laundry along the way. But, then again, Gemma had two full suitcases of her belongings since she was training in Brisbane for a full year.

Maddie noticed how Gemma's collar bone protruded. She was skinny, too thin, but then she was always active, probably on the border of hyper-active. Hmm, that gave her food for thought. Was Gemma A.D.H.D? It could explain her impulsiveness. Her hair today was only lightly gelled – enough to give it the sticky-outy messy look, which, for Gemma, was tame. A smooth, sleek style wasn't in Gemma's make-up. The blackness was so black that it could only come from a bottle and it was a recent change. Maddie grinned at the memory of the many colours her friend had dyed her hair. Nothing was off limits. If Gemma's mood for the week demanded canary yellow hair then that's what happened. And that particular colour had been a real shocker. Yellow did not suit Gemma's complexion. It sapped her to the extent she had looked anaemic with a green tinge.

Maddie shuddered at the memory of green and the millions of locusts. Funny, Gemma hadn't worn a scrap of green since and it is one of her favourite colours. Ha, that's the reason for the white frills. She's too spooked to wear green. Maddie wondered just how many tops bearing the colour were packed in Gemma's bag. She guessed the white was a recent purchase for the up-coming job. It looked brand-spanking new.

The shirt hung over the top of a pair of white denim capris bearing the same dark smudges. The only items of the normal Gemma attire were the sneakers, this time worn with white socks and wonder of wonders, they were matching.

'What are you staring at?'

Maddie jerked upright at Gemma's words. 'I wasn't staring, I was just thinking.'

'About what?'

'Several things.' No way did she want to reveal her thoughts.

'And?'

Amazing how a single word could be such a demand. 'How come we are friends?'

The car jolted to one side as Gemma tightened her grip on the wheel. 'You don't want to be friends any more?' There was a distinct edge to Gemma's voice.

'I never said that. Don't read things that aren't there. All I was thinking was how come we are friends when we are so different?'

'Different in what way?' asked Gemma as she shot a quick glance to Maddie before centring her eyes back onto the road. A worried frown creased her otherwise flawless brow. She had beautiful skin with a natural olive tinge.

Maddie laughed. 'In almost every way. I'm always careful and reserved where you are uninhibited and impetuous. You like this awful loud heavy music where I prefer something a little more sedate and catchy. Our hair,' she swept her hand up and tousled Gemma's black strands.

'What's wrong with my hair?'

'There you go again, twisting my words. There's nothing wrong with your hair, it looks great today but you love way-out styles and colours where-as I couldn't be bothered changing colours and I prefer my hair to be a bit neater.'

'You mean boring,' said Gemma without taking her eyes from the road.

That stung a bit. But maybe she was right. 'Okay, maybe my style is boring but that's the way I am and you are just the way you are. You think nothing of wearing really weird combinations of clothes while I like to be neat and have my colours at least match.'

'Like I said – boring.'

Did Gemma really think that? Did other people see her as boring? Far out, she hoped not. Maybe she needed to ask some discreet questions amongst her peers when she managed to get home. Oh, boy, home was sounding pretty darn good.

'So I'm boring but the point is, we are so very different in just about every way imaginable so why are we friends?'

'Maybe because we like each other and are you forgetting about Leah and Paul?'

Leah and Paul. How could she ever forget? Paul still managed to creep into her thoughts several times a day. How many times did some action by a complete stranger or something some-one said, remind her of Paul? How many times did she go to speak to her brother only to remember he was no longer there? It didn't hurt as much any more but boy, she still missed him something awful. It was like he'd taken a huge chunk of her heart with him and he was only her brother, not some love interest. It still amazed her how much she cared. When he was alive he was just her pesky older brother who always thought he knew everything better than her. He had forever teased her and delighted in playing dumb pranks just to get her riled. They had fought over the most stupid things. She'd hated it at the time but now she'd give anything to have a fight with him. Just to have him back she'd put up with his teasing – she'd even relish in it.

'Do you still miss Leah?' she asked Gemma when the silence got to her. For the last few minutes it was like they were having a competition – who could stay mute the longest and it was a heavy unbearable silence weighing down the atmosphere.

'That's a dumb question. Of course I do. She was my sister.'

'Was she like you?'

'In what way?'

'You know, the way you dress, the books you read, your nature.'

'Not really, no.' Gemma peeked at Maddie. 'She was more like you.'

Maddie reeled. She never knew that. How many times had they bared their souls in group therapy and talked about their grief and their respective siblings? And not once had Gemma compared her sister to Maddie. Then it hit. Leah had been the same age as Maddie. Was that why Gemma had become so attached? And it had been more of a one way street with Gemma always seeking out Maddie, mostly in times of crisis. Maddie fought to visualise any time she had gone to Gemma to seek advice on her own problems and she couldn't see a single time. Did Gemma see Maddie as a pseudo sister? Maddie wasn't sure how she felt about that. Should she be honoured or was it creepy? It felt creepy now that she knew. She needed to think about this.

Chapter Fourteen

Two things stood out to Maddie as they drove into Broken Hill. The streets were wide – very wide, left over from the days when long bullocky drays could be turned around in the main street and what a street it was. It was bedecked with hundreds of small houses built out of corrugated iron. The more modern ones were of Colorbond where the colours were powder coated onto the raw metal before it was sold. Of the older houses, many wore the dulled silver of weather-worn galvanised iron whilst others had been hand-painted in Federation green or red.

The town was the birthplace of one of the world's largest mining companies. BHP Billiton started out as Broken Hill Propriety Limited. Maddie recalled learning about it in history classes early in her secondary schooling. At the time she hadn't really cared about what the character of the town was like; it was just the name of a place developed on the back of some ore discovery. But now she wished she'd researched more into what these towns had developed into. She snorted at the thought that she'd find history so interesting now. She had detested the subject in secondary school.

'This place is huge,' said Gemma as she slowed a bit. 'Ooh, look, a caravan park up there.' She pointed to a sign indicating a road to the right. Broken Hill Tourist Park sat on the rise of a small hill.

Well that will be a change, thought Maddie, having to find a flat spot on which to pitch the tent. 'Let's drive around first. There might be another one closer to the centre of town.'

'Are we staying the night here?' asked Gemma.

'I think we should since we have to get a new tyre and it could take time if the garage is busy. Look out for a tyre place.'

They continued down the main street noting various buildings. The police station on the left stood out with its badge of blue and white squares. On the opposite side in the next block was the Theatre Royal Hotel, a two storey building graced by the traditional open and wide veranda on both levels. It looked to be old but well-maintained. Even more attractive was the Royal Exchange Hotel perched on the opposite corner with all the charm of an Art Deco building. Maddie had always been particularly fond of the Art Deco as well as the Art Nouveau designs maybe because they were all curves and not so angular.

There were several eating establishments and signs pointing in various directions to art galleries and museums. Heading out of town on the right was evidence of a still thriving mine. Maddie wasn't sure but she thought it originally started when large deposits of silver and lead were found. So many early mining towns were now deserted ghost towns but this place was alive and doing well. It felt heartening to see, especially after the utter despair of Iron Knob.

A sign led them up a viewing hill which lived up to its name. The panoramic scene from the top was spectacular. They found the Lake View Caravan Park and searched around for the lake. It should have been called Lake Glimpse for the actual lake was so far away it looked like a tiny silver discus but the sight of the body of water glinting in the sun told why the town was so successful. They had a good supply of fresh water: enough to run a mine as well as cater to the largish population.

After discovering that the first tourist park was the closest to the town hub they booked in then set up camp on a shady spot that was flatter than Maddie had at first imagined. The dense canopy of leaves from an ancient eucalypt cast a cooling shadow over their little camp although it didn't seem to be as hot as the past few days – thank goodness. As it was unlikely either would ever pass through this town again, they agreed to go exploring after first stop dropping off the wheel.

'Just as well we decided to stay the night,' Gemma grumbled as they made their way back to the car after having to spend a good fifteen minutes convincing the owner/manager and only worker in view that their need was as important as anyone else. The truth had been expanded a bit, well more than a bit, as to the urgency of their particular trip.

'I can't believe we can't pick it up until tomorrow,' Gemma added as she folded into the driver's seat.

Maddie got in the other side. 'We're in the outback. Roads are not so well maintained so more tyres get wrecked which means constant business for the fewer places that do repairs.' Gemma turned onto the main street. 'So I guess they have a constant stream of cars and trucks booked in, especially from the mining companies. We have to wait our turn. It could be a lot worse.' Maddie reached out and tapped Gemma on the arm. 'Let's go into that gallery. Jack Absolam is quite a well-known artist.' Maddie pointed to the sign.

'Art!' Gemma scoffed. 'Who wants to look at boring old art?'

'Well I do. Drop me off. We have plenty of time so we can do our own thing for a couple of hours.' Maddie pointed to a sign down the road. 'See that milk bar sign. Why don't we meet up in there in,' she glanced at her watch, 'say, two hours? Then we can go back to shower and find somewhere nice for a decent meal.'

It was a relief to be able to wander on her own and linger where she wanted. Maddie fell in love with one particular Absolam landscape and wished she could afford to buy it but the price was beyond her means and then she'd have to cart it without getting damaged and she figured getting it on to the plane would create a whole heap of problems. Instead she sneaked a photo after disregarding the prominent sign forbidding such things. Then she felt the weight of guilt pressing onto her so she slunk away, sure she was being watched as she skulked out the door and down the pavement. Relief swamped her when no voice yelled out for her to stop or no hand grabbed her from behind, demanding she hand over her camera.

The Afghan mosque, left over from when Afghan cameleers came with their ships of the desert to provide transport in the time before trucks, was interesting. The history held Maddie's interest for ages. The cameleers left a fascinating legacy. Once the camels were superseded by road transport the animals were simply left to forage for themselves all over the continent. Australia now had a huge population of feral camels roaming the outback. There were so many that there were regular culling programmes to keep the numbers down for they destroyed the fragile environment, leaving nothing for the native animals to survive on. The irony was that Australia now had a profitable trade in exporting healthy, strong animals back to the countries from whence they originated. Apparently Aussie camels were regarded as far superior to the local ones. Ridiculous, thought Maddie as she left the building and strolled down the main street, popping in and out of various buildings that piqued her interest.

It took a while before she realised the streets were all named after metals, minerals and mining managers. After that little discovery she took particular notice of every road sign she came to. When she reached the milk bar she was delighted to find it was also a museum. Glancing at her watch she saw that she still had fifteen minutes so she went in, thankful to not have Gemma tagging along. No way would Gemma have joined her, or if she had, she would have bitched and complained the entire time.

After a pleasant twenty minutes perusing various displays and interesting items while reading short snippets of history, Maddie reached for the silver knob that had been dirt-smeared by many hands, on the door leading to the milk bar. She paused mid-stride when she heard the rumble of voices followed by laughter. Unmistakable was the distinctive high-pitched squeal that could only come from one person – Gemma. There was never any lady-like held back restraint from our Gemma. She always let loose when she laughed, which was good in one way for it meant she wasn't inhibited when she found something to be amusing.

Maddie twisted the knob and pulled the door open then brushed her greasy hand down the back of her pants. She glanced up and sighed. Hadn't Gemma learnt her lesson? Obviously not for she sat at a table with the moisture beaded silver canister of a milk-shake in front of her. Two lime green straws peeked over the top. They just had to be green. Three men surrounded her. One sat each side of the small square table with their chairs turned facing Gemma while the third stood behind one man, his hand resting on the back of the chair. They were all dressed in smart casual attire of shorts, collared T-shirts and reasonably clean quality sneakers. The discussion looked animated. All four were grinning as if they were enjoying the aftermath of some joke or humorous anecdote. What really concerned Maddie was the age of the men. They all looked to be in their mid-twenties or maybe a bit older. It was difficult to tell sometimes. But Gemma was only seventeen – too young for these guys.

For some reason Maddie's body tensed as she stepped into the café but she shrugged her annoyance away. She wasn't Gemma's keeper, her parent or even a relative. She had no right to interfere or pass judgement on who Gemma spoke to. But far out, after what happened just three days previous, where did Gemma get off? Didn't she have any brains? Hadn't she been scared enough by their recent brush with hormone crazed idiots? What would it take for her to learn a lesson?

Feeling frustrated, Maddie forced a smile and crossed the café floor. 'Hi, I can see you enjoyed the past two hours.' She pulled out the chair opposite Gemma and plonked into the seat, ignoring the squeak of one leg scraping across the tiles: a squeal that set her teeth on edge.

Four grinning mouths opened in surprise and four heads turned her way in a single synchronised motion. Oh, boy, Maddie felt as though she had come in with some fatal disease that was going to kill them all in an instant. Talk about unwelcome vibes. Her face began to ache as she kept her smile moulded into a still-life pose but inside her innards jolted in delight as a flush rushed up Gemma's face. It was such a rare occurrence. So Gemma felt guilty about something. Just how much of the past two hours had Gemma spent flirting with the three guys, who up close, had ten years on her. Darn it, but the girl never learnt. This was exactly the position Leah had got herself into, which resulted in so much agony and grief.

'Err, I just met these three in here,' stuttered Gemma her face suffusing from a pink blush to bright crimson. That body betrayal told Maddie heaps. Gemma was lying through her teeth. The startled glances between the three guys confirmed her suspicions. The last thing she needed was to come across as some frigid spinster aunt so she grabbed a menu from its spiral holder in the centre of the table and studied the print.

'I think I'll have a good old-fashioned spider,' she said as she rose and sauntered to the counter as though she didn't have a care in the world. A rumble of harsh whispers followed her then she felt the pressure of eyes boring into the back of her head as she placed her order of a red creaming-soda spider and handed over a note. She felt like some freak star attraction in a side-show as she took her time in plopping the change back into her purse. She forced her breathing to calm and schooled her features into what she hoped looked nonchalant. And why should she care? If

Gemma wanted to persist in pushing the boundaries and be careless about her safety then Why. Should. Madison. Brown. CARE?

Because, her inner voice answered, you do care.

'Hi, I'm Maddie,' she said as she returned to the table.

'Oh, err, this is Josh.' Gemma indicated to her right. 'And this is Matthew.' She looked up at the man still standing and who looked a bit put out. 'And Liam,' Gemma added with a glance that went beyond friendly. She looked smitten.

Just met, huh? The familiarity of Gemma's smile at each as she introduced them told an entirely different story. How dense did they think Maddie was?

'Are you guys local?' asked Maddie, determined to be friendly.

'They all work at the mine,' jumped in Gemma before any of them had a chance to respond.

'I'm sure they all have tongues in their heads and can speak for themselves,' said Maddie as she eyed each man in turn. She kept on tossing out question after question and directing them to each guy in turn, not giving Gemma a chance to butt in. The surrounding air soon lost its icicles as Maddie forced the conversation towards the men's interests, her skills from the few years as a member of the university debating club becoming useful. But, boy, her innards were on tenterhooks, screaming at her that this was not good. But then, maybe because of what happened, she was over-sensitive? She hoped it was so.

By the time Maddie stood and indicated that they needed to go, she felt a little more comfortable about the guys. None had shown any inappropriate behaviour or comments, not like the creep back in Kalgoorlie. They all seemed to be every day normal guys getting to know the new chicks in town. But at the same time Maddie couldn't let her guard completely down and trust them entirely.

'It was nice chatting to you,' said Maddie as she shoved her chair in and slid her small money purse into her pocket.

'Nice meeting you, too,' said Liam with a grin.

Gemma looked as though she didn't want to leave but she gave a harrumph with a careless shrug of her shoulders then followed suit. She stood then slung the long leather strap of her tiny bag over her shoulder. 'See you later,' she called as she followed Maddie outside.

'See you,' chorused back three male voices.

No you won't, thought Maddie, glad they could pick up the wheel at eight in the morning and then be on their way.

The drive back to camp was filled with a silence that weighed a tonne.

'Well, are you going to say anything?' Gemma grumbled as they turned into the park.

Here it comes thought Maddie but instead she said, 'About what?'

'You know.' Gemma pulled up next to their tent.

'I have no idea what you want me to say,' Maddie lied as she peeked at Gemma from the corner of her eye and grinned inwardly. Gemma's face was turning bright red.

'You know – the guys.'

'The guys?' Maddie turned and faced Gemma. 'You met some guys; you talked to some guys, so what. They gave the appearance of being all right but I would have thought they would be a bit too old for you. They work in town, have decent jobs but we're leaving in the morning. Do I trust them? They'd have to earn my trust over more than a half hour chat: especially after our experience over the past few days. Now are we going to freshen up and find us a decent meal? I saw a little Indian restaurant in the main street. If I remember right, you like Indian.'

'Indian sounds good, so you're not mad at me?'

Yes, I'm mad at you – again, but more because you lied to me, she thought then said aloud, 'No, I'm hungry.'

Chapter Fifteen

'This tastes kind of funny,' said Gemma as she waved her fork around and screwed her face in distaste.

Glancing at Gemma's almost empty plate, Maddie was stunned. An embarrassing rattle echoed through the tiny restaurant as she dropped her own fork. She shuddered at the noise and peeked around to see if anyone else had noticed before eyeing Gemma. 'You've almost eaten the entire meal and now you decide it tastes funny? Funny how?'

'I was hungry and funny… I don't know, just funny.'

Maddie gave the plate a longer scrutiny. What little was left looked just what the menu described. 'Let me taste.' Maddie retrieved her fork and leant over the table. She scooped up a forkful of the chicken curry Gemma had ordered and held it to her nose. She sniffed. It smelt like curry, but curry spices could hide a lot of sins. With the tip of her tongue she took a tentative lick. The sauce tasted just like it should so she shoved the food into her mouth, chewed, swilled then grabbed a paper napkin and tried to be discreet in emptying the contents of her mouth before turning back to Gemma.

'I can't believe you ate that. The sauce is okay but to me the chicken tastes kind of metallic likes it's off.' She grabbed her glass of chilled water and sipped in a mouthful, swishing it around her mouth to get rid of the tinny taste before swallowing.

A shudder ran across Gemma's shoulders while her face took on a horrified look then she shoved her plate into the centre of the table, knocking over the tiny vase of artificial flowers in her haste. 'All of a sudden I feel ill.'

As Maddie reached out to steady the flowers she laughed. 'You were fine before I said it was a bit off.' She pushed her own dish of beef vindaloo forwards, her appetite having dissipated all of a sudden. 'I don't think I want to eat any more. You've put me off. Let's go. Maybe that cute milk bar is open for something to sweeten the tastebuds.'

Gemma reached for her little tote bag. 'I reckon we shouldn't have to pay for dodgy food.'

Maddie stood and pushed in her chair. 'You ate most of it and didn't complain. We'll offer to pay but let them know why we're leaving and see what happens.'

It took a good ten minutes to convince the head waitress, who very well could have been the owner by the way she reacted, of their suspicions. She went all huffy and looked affronted as though nothing like that would ever happen in her restaurant. It was only when, much to Maddie's horror, Gemma began trawling nearby diners offering them a piece of the uneaten chicken and asking them for an opinion that they were offered a discount by the furious woman as she chased after Gemma. Maddie heard mumbled apologies to the patrons and hissed pleas hurled in Gemma's direction. Maddie felt for the woman who, despite her olive complexion, wore an embarrassing redness in her cheeks. Who could blame her? In a small town like this she didn't need customers to know that someone was complaining about dodgy food. News travels fast. It would be economic suicide.

After paying the halved bill, Maddie felt mortified and was desperate to leave. She stepped outside with so much adrenaline surging through her veins she felt as though she was about to explode. It was dumb to be feeling guilty, especially since she'd done nothing wrong but she wasn't used to making a public exhibition of herself and an awful lot of eyes had followed them outside. She'd felt them boring into her back as though someone had used her back as a dart board with her spine being the bullseye. Gemma had been a lot gamer than Maddie would ever dare; another huge difference between their personalities but in this instance Maddie felt proud of Gemma for she was well within her rights. The chicken was well past it's safe to eat date.

Maddie hurtled along the footpath and crossed the street, anxious to get well away. Unrestrained giggling followed then a rapid slap, slap of sandalled feet caught her up. She was nudged in the back then her elbow grabbed, bringing her to a standstill.

'Did you see her face?' Gemma panted.

Maddie snorted, sucked in her breath then couldn't suppress the grin that shot across her face. 'Poor woman had no choice but to give in. I can't believe you did that.'

Gemma stalled then her face altered in a split second from joyful glee to deep worry. 'You're mad at me again.'

Wow, Maddie didn't see that coming. Was Gemma really so dependant on Maddie's approval? How could she handle this with subtlety and not let Gemma down? 'No way! In fact, I was proud of you. The chicken was definitely off and should never have been used. What I meant was that I would never have been so bold. I would have just paid the full amount.'

Gemma came to a sudden standstill, her face taking on an awed look. 'You were proud of me? Oh, wow.'

Maddie laughed. 'Don't look so shocked. Yes, I was proud of you. I think I may have learnt something from you tonight.'

'You did? But what could you possibly learn from me?'

Maddie laughed, 'That I should stand up for myself more often if I'm sure I am right.' She slung her arm around Gemma's waist and turned her around. 'Come on let's pig out on something sinful.'

As they strode down the street with a definite winning swagger, one thing centred in Maddie's brain. Gemma's need for Maddie's acceptance indicated a lower self-esteem than Maddie had ever realised. It added more fuel to her earlier thoughts and it began to worry her. How was Gemma going to cope when she was on the opposite side of the continent and couldn't come running for advice or security when something went wrong. She'd always thought Gemma was much stronger.

There was an unbelievable racket of loud voices as they passed the cute art deco pub. It was supposed to be a quiet piano bar but a glimpse inside indicated a private function. It sounded as though the hundred or so voices were trying to all be heard over the others.

Linked arm-in-arm, they crossed the intersection, running the last few steps when a car sped around the corner without slowing and almost collected them. Maddie wasn't sure who got the biggest fright, them or the driver who looked startled when he spied them.

'Idiot,' mumbled Gemma as she flicked a finger towards the driver.

Maddie tugged at her arm. 'Leave it; he probably didn't see you in any case.'

'Let's go in there,' said Gemma.

Maddie paused and twisted around to see where Gemma was pointing. Catchy rock tunes were coming from the Theatre Royal Hotel across the wide main street.

'You're not eighteen. You might not be allowed in,' said Maddie.

'It's a pub. Anyone can go in as long as they are with a responsible adult and neither of us drinks alcohol.' Gemma gave Maddie a tug as she stepped onto the road. 'Come on, the music sounds really good. Sounds like a live band.'

Maddie laughed as she resisted and held back. 'And who is the responsible adult?'

Gemma tugged harder and laughed back. 'You, of course and they might not even check our I.D's.'

Knowing how young Gemma looked, Maddie shook her head. 'Oh, they'll check.' She gave in. Why not? They hadn't had any fun since they'd left Perth. Maddie wasn't a big fan of the pub scene but on occasion she joined her uni mates for a night out, especially if there was a good band playing. She loved the dancing and relaxed atmosphere and it wasn't so bad now that smoking was banned in enclosed spaces. Well, it was in the west. She wasn't so sure about the rest of the country. One way to find out, she thought as she ran the final few steps and mounted the opposite footpath.

Light interspersed with jerking shadows spilled from the windows and two open doors. The music was loud and accompanied a steady thrum of voices. They were met at the door by two burly security guards who let Gemma pass without a murmur.

'I.D.,' the shorter of the two said as he fronted Maddie, barring her way. What he lacked in height he made up for in width. Maddie bet to herself that the guy was a gym junkie and had muscle on muscle underneath the too tight shirt and expensive looking black leather jacket.

Maddie shook her head in disbelief. No way did she look younger than Gemma even though, for once, Gemma was wearing respectable jeans teamed with a classy top and smart denim jacket. She opened out the flap of her purse to show her driver's licence, which proved she was over the legal age.

'You don't look old enough,' the man mumbled from a crooked mouth as he ran a finger along her personal details printed on the tiny plastic card. A scar from the top of his lip to the centre of his cheek gave a slight tug to one side of his mouth. Apart from that he was good looking in a rugged kind of way. Maddie wasn't sure if his comment was a compliment or not. The way he said it sure didn't sound in the least bit complimentary. But she figured that when she was fifty she'd probably enjoy people telling her she didn't look her age.

'And she did?' Maddie asked as she flapped her hand in Gemma's direction. Guilt stabbed at referring to Gemma as *she* but Maddie wasn't about to mention Gemma by name. She couldn't figure out why, after all they now knew Maddie's full name and her birth date, and her address.

'She looked much older,' the man said as he hitched his thumb towards the door. She figured it was his permission for her to go in. She sniggered at the idea of Gemma looking much older.

'If you only knew,' she mumbled under her breath. She flipped the flap of her purse over and pressed the stud before sliding her purse into the large pocket of her black jacket and hurried inside as she slid the hidden zipper closed: a zipper that made it difficult for her pocket to be picked.

Gemma was no-where to be seen. Damn you, Gem, where are you? Maddie scouted around the outer edges of the long room with her eyes darting in all directions until they settled on her prey. Then tiny clues tumbled into place. 'You sneaky little witch, she thought and made a bee-line for her rapidly falling out of favour, friend.

Chapter Sixteen

'You planned this, didn't you?' Maddie hissed into Gemma's ear. Miffed, she shoved her way between Josh and Liam, not caring when they both stumbled backwards a few steps and ignoring their grunts of displeasure. She faced Matthew who was half sitting on a bar stool, one leg on the rung and the other supporting his weight on the ground. He was dressed in black: black jeans and black shirt with the top two buttons undone and exposing the glint of a heavy gold chain around his neck. Of the three, Maddie had liked Matthew the best. He wasn't drop dead gorgeous but a strong square chin gave him an air of strength. The dark clothes darkened his eyes, or maybe it was just the lighting that made him look forbidding. Even his short brown hair had taken on a darker hue. Earlier, he had been quietly spoken and less boastful than the other two but wasn't there some old saying about beware of the quiet ones?

He tipped his head in acknowledgement. The beginnings of a grin crawled from the corners of his mouth but didn't quite make it to a full smile. 'Maddie,' he said then hooked one foot around an empty stool and dragged it into place. 'Take a seat.' Well at least he had manners.

'I don't know what you're talking about,' Gemma whispered back. 'I'll get the drinks. Ginger Ale?'

'Please and yes you do,' Maddie said in an undertone knowing she had been well and truly sucked in. She wriggled and perched on the wood slats, wincing when bruised flesh protested. When she'd inspected her torso during her shower, she'd been adorned with blue seat-belt stripes. Plus there was a sore lump on the side of her head courtesy of the window. Right now, she had a couple of choices. She could make a scene and drag Gemma outside. She snorted under her breath. Walking back to their camp and leaving Gemma with her new-found friends sounded like a wonderful idea but she was only seventeen. She was under the legal age and Maddie was technically responsible for her well-being. Or she could suck it up and put on her nice friendly persona even though she was inwardly fuming and not only at Gemma. Part of the blame lay with her. Why hadn't she taken more notice earlier when Gemma had said, *see you later*. And why had she agreed to come in against her better judgement when Gemma had oh, so innocently pointed the place out. Innocent, my foot!

'What would you like to drink?' At the sound of a deep drawl, Maddie twisted slightly and studied Liam. Shabby chic with different layers was trendy but somehow Liam hadn't pulled off the chic side of things. His tan T-shirt bore an inappropriate slogan above a crude picture. He probably thought it was funny or smart but since it was derogatory towards women, Maddie thought the shirt reflected his attitude, otherwise why would he wear it? He'd need watching. Draping over it was a brown striped shirt with all the buttons undone and the sleeves rolled half-way up brawny forearms. The tails hung over low slung pants. She couldn't understand how anyone could wear pants with the crotch halfway down the inner thighs. It must feel mighty uncomfortable when walking. Yeah, it was the latest fashion for guys but didn't any of them look at their rear view in a mirror before they left home. From behind they looked as though they'd had an accident in their pants, or wearing a droopy, soppy wet nappy. Liam's dark grey pants clashed with his top half.

'No thanks, Gemma's getting it,' Maddie replied. She darted a glance in Gemma's direction and attuned her ears towards her to make sure she heard what the order was. She wasn't in the space to be lumbered with more surprises tonight. Never before had Gemma added alcohol to her cola but after the past few days of revelations Maddie's instincts had gone on full alert.

A weird silence surrounded them for the next few minutes. It was as though no-one knew what to say. It sent a whole heap of strange vibes vibrating towards Maddie to the extent she felt as though something wasn't quite right. She was about to move away when Gemma returned and handed her a huge glass of chinking ice and ginger ale. Well, Maddie hoped it was only ginger-ale.

'I'm going to dance.' Gemma's high vibrant voice penetrated the gloomy atmosphere and sent the spooks away. She settled her own glass on the bar behind Maddie.

'I'll join you,' said Josh and he followed Gemma into the squashy writhing crowd.

Despite knowing she was over-reacting, Maddie sniffed at her drink before taking a tiny sip. It was ridiculous because Gemma was more cautious than Maddie about allowing alcohol to dull the senses. It was Gemma's edict, Gemma's suggestion that they never imbibe for it was drunkenness that had got Gemma's sister into so much trouble which ultimately resulted in her death.

Determined to let go of her angst at her over-sensitive suspicions, Maddie sighed, wriggled to get more comfortable then made a conscious effort to relax each muscle in her body one-by-one. She took another sip then slid her glass onto the bar in a position where she could keep and eye on it. Paul's death had taught her that little habit. Just to be sure, she reached around and grasped Gemma's drink to place next to hers then grimaced when she realised she was sniffing and tasting the cola as well. Far out but she was strung so tight and was being too damn suspicious when there was absolutely no reason to be so.

Shake it off, Madison Brown. Let it go and have some fun. For the next ten minutes she watched Gemma flinging her body about in time to the tempo of the vibrant band that really was top-notch. Josh danced opposite Gemma but they were not touching with Liam making up a threesome. So caught up in her own mind games she hadn't noticed Liam moving away.

'Are you going to join them?'

Maddie jolted at the quiet deep words. She glanced sideways to find Matthew eyeing her.

'I will soon. I'm just letting my dinner digest a bit. I feel a bit too full,' she lied. It was the only excuse she could come up with on the spur of the moment. No way was she going to leave the drinks unattended. Paul had done that and ended up dead less than twenty-four hours later. The so-called friend who'd laced his drink hadn't known that Paul had taken a cocktail of prescribed drugs to counteract a severe asthma attack earlier in the day. The interaction between the drugs had been dramatic and fatal. A cold shiver beset her at the memory. She slid her eyes shut and fought to rid her mind of the memory.

Think of something beautiful, she told her brain and pictured a rainbow arched over a verdant grassy hill with hundreds of different coloured blooms waving in a gentle breeze. Shimmering crystal water tumbled over a rocky riverbed and flashes of silver glinted from the backs of darting fish. Paul's image peered at her from the under the water.

'Are you okay?' A hand touched her arm causing her eyelids to bolt apart. Matthew was leaning towards her looking concerned.

'Of course, why?'

He reached up with one finger and brushed it against her cheek. 'You're crying.'

Oh, my gosh, how did that happen? Maddie sniffed then forced a sappy grin as she swiped at her cheeks. 'Sorry, just a bad memory.' She scrabbled for something to say to change the subject for the last thing she wanted was to have to explain about Paul. 'Just how long were you guys with Gemma this afternoon?'

A hoot of laughter escaped Matthew's lips. 'What did she tell you?'

'I never asked but it sure wasn't what she said at the milk bar.'

'And how do you know that?' There were still the traces of a wry grin around his mouth.

'Because none of you were in there when I went into the museum section a few minutes earlier and you were all too cosy and comfortable with each other to have just met.

'So what is it to you?' There was an edge to his voice which sent her alarm bells clanging again.

She sobered. 'Nothing really. I'm not her keeper but Gemma is only seventeen and I promised her folks that I'd keep her safe.

Matthew reeled upright. 'Seventeen! Shit!' It was as though he'd been taken over by a racing millipede the way his body shivered. 'She intimated she was twenty.'

'Gemma said that?'

'Well, not exactly.'

Maddie paused. 'What do you mean – not exactly?' She gave him the eyeball treatment.

'Gemma was a bit vague but mentioned two ages and we figured she was the oldest.'

Wow, that was the second time in the same night that Gemma was classed as the elder of the two. 'Why would you think Gemma was older than me?' This was going to be interesting.

'I don't know, the way she said it, the way she dressed. You seem a lot more… umm… reserved and inexperienced. Matthew waved his hand up and down her body as he spoke. For a split second she felt as though he was visualising her naked. And just what experience did he think Gemma had. She might present as a confident world-wise young woman who thought she knew everything but she was a virgin in more ways than one. As far as Maddie knew, and she'd been Gemma's confidante for three years, no alcohol or illicit drugs had passed Gemma's lips and she'd certainly never slept with a man. Oh, she talked as though she had all the experience in the world but her tell-all private talks after dating a couple of school mates had indicated Gemma was as green as, when it came to intimacy. She freaked out after one particular boy had got to the heavy petting stage. Disgusting, yucky and gross were three of the words Gemma had used during her way too explicit descriptions of the night.

Disconcerted, Maddie didn't know what to feel or say. She gave a wry grin. 'And how old am I supposed to be?'

Matthew had the good grace to look a little embarrassed. 'Eighteen, but you're not are you?'

'No.'

'Then…'

'None of your business,' Maddie snapped and pushed a path through the crowd, seeking out a pair of long legs clad in new dark jeans and a black tank top studded with sparkles, under a denim jacket. It took what felt like forever to find her target. Positioning her body between Gemma and Josh she began swinging her hips from side-to-side, grimacing at the pain then she leant towards Gemma until there were mere centimetres between them. They were so close Maddie could feel the body heat radiating from Gemma.

'You don't like me being mad at you yet you keep doing dumb things to stir me up,' she said close to Gemma's ear.

There was an instant slowing of movement from Gemma but her body still bucked to the rhythm. 'What are you talking about?'

'One, you didn't meet in the milk bar. You met much earlier and you lied to me.'

Gemma bit the corner of her mouth and glanced around until her eyes settled on Matthew still at the bar. Josh had joined him.

'Two, you planned on meeting the guys here tonight but very conveniently didn't tell me. That's being underhanded.'

'I didn't!' stuttered Gemma as she twisted away as though trying to escape.

Reaching out, Maddie grabbed her arm and reeled her back. 'Don't add another lie. We've always been straight with each other so why the sneaky act now? And three, you told the guys that you were twenty and I was eighteen. Why would you do that? It's plain dumb.'

Gemma stalled and cast her eyes downwards. A deep crimson rushed up her neck. 'It's what they thought and I…'

'Didn't correct them. Damn it, Gemma, these guys are way too old for either of us and especially you.'

'But we'll never see them again after tonight and they seemed like okay types of guys. I only wanted a bit of fun. It can't do any harm.' Defiance replaced the redness.

Maddie stilled and grasped Gemma's arm and hauled her to the edge of the dance floor. 'Leah only wanted a bit of fun and looked what happened to her.'

Poor Gemma looked stricken in an instant. The blood drained from her face and her eyes popped wide. 'That's not fair. I'm not drunk. I'm not that stupid. Jeeze, Maddie, you're worse than Mum.' She stamped a foot and jerked her stiff arms down her sides. 'All right we didn't meet in the bar but it was only half an hour before we got there. They were headed there in any case so I tagged along since I was meeting you there. And yeah, they said that they'd be here tonight but I never said we were coming because I knew you wouldn't want to. I just said maybe. And I didn't tell them I was twenty.'

'But you didn't tell them the truth either.'

'If they knew my real age they wouldn't have had anything to do with me.'

'Well they know now.'

Gemma paled even more. 'You told them?'

'Accidently. We were just talking and it came out. But, gosh, Gemma, being seventeen is nothing to be ashamed of and you have to remember that Leah never reached eighteen. I, as well as your folks, want you to get there safely and have a wonderful full life. Your Mum might be hard on you but do you honestly think she wants to lose another daughter. And I'm supposed to be keeping you safe on this journey but gee whiz, Gemma, you're making it hard for me to keep my promise to them.' Frustrated, Maddie spun away. 'I'm going back to have a drink.'

She only managed one step before she was grabbed on the arm.

'I'm sorry, Maddie. I'll come with you. All this dancing has made me a bit nauseous.'

Concerned, Maddie eyed Gemma, seeking signs of some sort of malaise. 'Are you okay?'

'Yes, just a bit queasy. I'll be all right after a rest.'

They headed towards the bar. 'Could be the chicken. Why don't you drink my Ginger Ale? Ginger is known to settled stomachs. Better for you than cola.'

'But you don't like cola.'

'That's fine, I'll get something else.'

As they crossed the room and approached their possie near the bar, Maddie could see that the three guys were having what looked like a heated discussion. Matthew looked as though he was losing an argument. He lifted a hand and shushed them when he noticed Maddie looking at him. Once they reached their seats, it appeared that whatever the disagreement was, it was over. Liam seemed chirpy and Josh sidled along the bar to order more drinks. Maddie handed her Ginger Ale to Gemma. 'Here, drink this slowly; I'm going to the loo.'

Chapter Seventeen

Unbelievable! It was so unbelievable. A simple trip to the loo took, Maddie glanced at her watch. Oh, my gosh, forty minutes. She screwed her nose at the still lingering stench of cubicle one. The ghastly smell seemed to have attached itself to everything: her clothing, her hair and even her skin. She shuddered. Talk about gross to the nth degree. Some charmer had hurled the contents of their stomach everywhere except in the pan and fingers of poop coloured slime had oozed into the next cubicle. So gross. Cubicle four had displayed a note saying it was out of order, leaving only two working toilets, well three if you were game enough to puddle through the grunge in number one and no way was Maddie that desperate, nor had anyone else been game. The queue of nose holding and cringing desperate ladies had been so long it was a wonder there had been any women at all still dancing or in either of the bars. And typical, to top it all off, *everyone* had taken forever. At one stage Maddie had considered storming the men's room but uncrossing her legs to go anywhere, let alone down the passage, would have been beyond embarrassing.

She sighed. There never seemed to be enough loos for the ladies, anywhere, especially on a busy night and this night sure was busy. It seemed as though the entire district's population was in the pub tonight despite the other pub they'd passed having been full with a private function. Just how many people lived in this town? Another sigh, longer and heavier, slipped from her lips as she strode down the passage, each footstep echoing and sounding spooky. All these people and all of a sudden not one other single body was in her vicinity. Weird.

Giving her hands a final swipe down the outside of her thighs to ensure they were dry, she shoved at the swing door with her shoulder and stepped into the main bar. The noise level rose as though someone had turned up the volume switch all of a sudden. Clinking glasses, a thwack of snooker balls hitting and ricocheting, along with hundreds of voices all vying to be heard over the others, assaulted Maddie's ear-drums. She wove her way through the throng, getting jostled and bumped as she fought a path across the room. This saloon bar seemed to be full of mainly guys, many of whom looked as though the pub was first stop off point after their shift for there was a predominance of bright orange safety vests over navy or khaki work clothes. Scuffed leather safety boots far outnumbered more casual footwear.

'Oops sorry,' Maddie muttered as an elbow swung around and connected with her shoulder. A strong tang of bitter hops sloshed from the glass. Maddie stepped back to avoid getting splashed only to get nudged from behind for her troubles. Far out, this is bedlam. Surely there is a limit to how many people could be crowded into the place, especially with so few loos.

'Sorry,' she said again then spun sideways past two guys poking each other in the chest as they spewed unsavoury epithets that burned her ears. Oh, boy, there was going to be serious trouble pretty soon. At last, the archway to the lounge bar loomed.

She heaved her shoulders in relief as she stepped into the next room and honed in on the bar to her left where Gemma and the guys had parked themselves. Spotting none of them she stilled and swept the room with her eyes. For some reason it seemed much quieter, then she realised there was no music. Bringing her eyes to a standstill on the corner where the band had been stationed, she saw two band members perched on the edge of the raised dais. One had his elbows on his knees and was chatting to the other who was taking regular sips from a plastic bottle of water. Break time and she wasn't sorry for the slightly lower level of noise.

So no music explained the lack of people on the three metre square of parquetry dance floor. So where was Gemma? And the three guys for that matter? Another sweep of the room netted no familiar faces. Worried, Maddie trawled around the room seeking another doorway leading to another room or bar. Was there an attached dining room? Or maybe another set of restrooms? She searched then returned to the overcrowded saloon bar. There were so many people in there that it was possible Gemma was amongst them.

It was a battle to search. Standing at the archway and using eyes was impossible. Gemma wasn't all that tall so if she was in there she could be hidden behind wide shoulders and brawny arms. Maddie raised her shoulders on a long sigh and waded into the melee keeping as close to the walls as she could so she could make a full circuit of the room. It took a couple of minutes of dodging and weaving before Maddie was certain Gemma wasn't there. She went back to the rest rooms. The queue was much shorter and didn't contain Gemma. Holding her breath to avoid sucking in yucky fumes Maddie waited as far back as she could until both cubicles emptied before turning around and backtracking.

Pausing at the bar, she asked if there was another set of rest rooms and was directed to the restaurant section, reached by going outside and entering through a separate door she'd not noticed before. The place was like a maze. Maddie felt the pressure of many eyes boring into her as she studied the patrons while walking through the large eating area to the rest rooms at the rear. Why hadn't she asked about these earlier? There was no queue and no sickly stench. There was also no Gemma.

Concern gnawed at the pit of her stomach as Maddie returned to the outside then cased the gardens, pathway, roadway and as much of the grounds as she could reach. She figured two padlocked gates barring her way would work just as well with Gemma. Not only was there no sign of Gemma but the three guys seemed to have vanished as well. The niggles of worry were turning into gnashing bites.

By the time she reached the lounge bar again the band was back at work and the dance floor filled with writhing bodies. The noise was unreal. Maddie sidled up to the bar and waited for either of the two barmen to notice her. They were flat out taking orders, filling glasses with various potions and working the till. How they could actually hear the orders was a miracle.

'Excuse me,' Maddie said as one man neared.

'Wait your turn,' he growled and took another order.

Maddie waited then when worry overtook her patience she raised her hand and her voice. 'This is important. Do you know what happened to the three guys and young girl who were sitting up the end there?'

Despite being in the middle of filling a glass with beer, the man glanced in the direction Maddie pointed, frowned then eyeballed Maddie. 'Yeah, you were with them.'

'That's right but I got held up in the ladies and now I can't find them. I've searched the place.'

'The chick was drunk so they took her home,' the barman said and turned away, ready to serve someone else.

Stunned, Maddie pounced upwards and reached out, grabbing the man by the elbow of his shirt. She ended up with hips on the bar and her feet dangling in mid-air but no way was she letting go.

'No way was Gemma drunk!' Maddie yelled so loud that the nearby chatter ceased in a split second.

'Listen lady, I'm telling you she was out of it, staggering around. Liam said she was drunk and he was taking her home.'

'No!' Maddie yelled. 'I'm telling you that Gemma didn't have any alcohol. She's only seventeen for heaven's sake. She never drinks alcohol and I know for a fact she didn't have any before I went to the loo and there's no way she could have consumed enough to get drunk in the time I was away.'

'Look, miss, all I know is that your friend was virtually comatose and Liam and Josh Evans were holding her upright as they left.'

'You know these guys?'

'Sure, everyone knows Liam. He grew up here.'

'What about the guy called Matthew?'

'He left earlier. They had some sort of a tiff.'

'Where did they go?' Worry had turned into fear and was now knocking on the door of sheer dread.

'They were taking your friend home.'

'Whose home?'

'Your friend's home I guess. How am I supposed to know?'

'Well, since Gemma lives in Perth that's going to be one mighty long journey.'

'Shit. Look I've got to serve. I don't know where they went.' The man tugged his arm free and shot to the other end of the bar.

Maddie had no idea what to do. Her heart was palpitating wildly in her chest and her stomach was churning. She spun around trying to get her brain to function and come up with some logical thought. No way was Gemma drunk. But if she had been staggering and had to be helped from the room it meant… Oh, God, no! Not again. It couldn't happen to Gemma. No!

Realising she didn't have her jacket with her Maddie skittered to the corner of the bar and searched around. There. Her jacket was on the floor under the edge of the bar. She bent to retrieve it and spied…oh, God, one sandal. Now she knew something bad… really, really bad had happened and her gut was telling her exactly what it was.

She grabbed the sandal, her jacket and searched for more clues. Gemma's tiny bag that held only the car keys and a few dollars in notes was hooked over the backrest of the stool. She reached for it and stilled. Gemma's still full glass of cola, now flat, was sitting in the middle of the bar. Maddie's glass was empty and lying on its side but there was no pool of ginger-ale and no evidence of any having been spilt. The drink Maddie was supposed to have drunk. Gut instinct had her grabbing the empty glass and shoving it in the pocket of her jacket before she turned and ran.

Chapter Eighteen

Once outside, Maddie twisted left and pelted down the footpath, her sandals slapping and scraping in synchronisation with her laboured breaths and pounding heart. Panic seized her, shrivelled up her innards. A claw wrapped itself around her windpipe and tightened making it difficult to find sufficient air. Checking to see that nothing was coming either way as she ran, she veered right and raced in a diagonal path across the wide road, the blue and white chequered logo of the police station in her sights. Thank goodness she'd taken note of it when driving into town and remembered where it was. And it was probably only because her Dad was an officer that she took such notice. She knew it wouldn't have stood out if her dad had been anything else.

'Please be open,' she stuttered under her breath.

Lights were burning inside, which hopefully meant an officer was on duty. It wasn't always so after hours in some police stations. There might be someone inside on call in case of emergencies but it didn't mean they would open the door. But heck, that was in the west. Who knew what happened in other states? She skidded as she neared the glass door but the soles of her sandals failed to grip on the smooth concrete. Instead her feet seemed to have a mind of their own and kept sliding when the rest of her body had halted. In a pure unconscious reaction she shot her hands in front of her chest.

Whump! She slammed into the glass and rebounded then lost her footing, yelping as her legs gave way. As she landed on her backside, all remaining air whooshed from her lungs. It took a few seconds, too many precious seconds to disentangle legs that felt liquid. She managed to get on all fours, gathered up Gemma's shoe and bag then tried to find the strength to stand.

Whoosh. The door in front of her eyes hissed and opened.

'Are you all right?' a deep voice said as ugly black boots appeared, followed by the cuffs of khaki twill trousers. Then a hand reached down, long thick fingers outspread. The moment Maddie gripped the proffered hand she was hauled upright.

'Sorry, I slipped… I'm fine… but my friend… I'm certain she was drugged and kidnapped.' Maddie paused. She was rambling and what had just slipped out sounded so ridiculous, even to her.

'You want to run that by me again?' The officer, a rookie by the absence of stripes on his shirt and his still boyish features, took a step backwards. There was a look of disbelief on his face. 'Who are you?' he added.

'Sorry, Maddie. We were at the pub across the road…'

'Who are we?'

'My friend, Gemma and me. Anyhow I got caught up in a long line at the ladies and when I got back to my seat Gemma was gone.'

'You mean she wasn't on her seat. She could be anywhere in that pub.'

Maddie sighed. This was going to be harder than she'd at first thought. Then again it did sound a bit far-fetched. But Gemma had disappeared and Maddie believed the barman. Her stomach muscle sent her a severe reminder by wrenching tight and her eyes went scratchy. She blinked. No way was she going to start blubbering. 'I've searched the entire pub, inside and out. We were with three guys. The barman said one left… um, Matt left. The other two were seen assisting Gemma from the hotel. They said they were taking Gemma home.'

'Have you been home to see if this Gemma is there?'

Frustration began gnawing at her innards. 'We live in Perth.'

The man scratched his head then eyeballed Maddie. 'So she was drunk.'

'No way! Gemma doesn't drink alcohol.'

'That you know of. Just because you didn't see her drinking alcohol doesn't mean she didn't.'

Maddie didn't like the way this conversation was going and they were wasting so much valuable time. She drew herself up tall and planted her hands on her hips. 'Gemma. Does. Not. Drink. Alcohol. Apart from the fact she is only seventeen, she's never touched a drop and nor have I.'

The man snorted. 'Then you must be the only two teenagers in Australia that doesn't.'

Anger spurted. Man, this guy was such a prat. Maddie hefted one finger in the air. 'One, I'm only three weeks away from turning twenty-one.' She cocked one eye at him then added a second finger, enjoying the stunned look on his face. 'Two, I don't like your attitude.' His chin jutted out and chest heaved in a puff. Another finger went up. 'Three, I don't tell lies and we are wasting time here. When you realise something really nasty is happening to a seventeen old girl, I'm laying half the blame on you.' A fourth finger joined the others. 'Four, I can give you the phone number of my father to confirm my credentials and when you do ring him he's not going to be a happy camper.' Maddie glared at the man. 'My Dad is a cop and he'd never treat a member of the public who comes to him for help with such contempt.'

The man's jaw gaped then he reddened. 'Err, sorry. Look, what was your name again?'

She gave it again then spelt it out but was bowled over to see the man waste even more precious seconds by fiddling with the button on the breast pocket of his shirt. Then he had the audacity to withdraw a small note book and begin flicking through the pages. He paused and read then gave Maddie the once over giving her an uncomfortable feeling.

'You say your name is Madison Brown?'

Maddie harrumphed in disbelief. 'Yes. Isn't that what I just said?'

'And your friend is Gemma.'

This man was unbelievable! 'Gemma Thomas, yes.'

'Come in and sit over there.' He indicated a rather tatty vinyl bench set against a brick wall painted misty green then vanished through a door into the bowels of the station, closing the door behind him with a definite click.

The ensuing silence lengthened beyond comfortable as interminable seconds ticked by. Then at last, the door opened and a different officer, a constable this time, came out and approached.

'Miss Brown, Sergeant McKay said we were to believe everything you say. I'm Constable Peters.'

She had no idea who Sergeant McKay was but she muttered, 'Alleluia,' under her breath as she stood. Someone was finally going to believe her.

'Could you explain why you think Gemma Thomas has been drugged and kidnapped? We might be a mining town where men let off steam with sometimes some rough behaviour, but drugging and kidnapping isn't something that happens around here.' As he spoke, the constable clicked the end of his pen several times then poised it over a yellow note pad. He scribbled down notes as Maddie detailed all she knew. As she spoke she proffered the single sandal and pulled the glass from her bundled jacket. She was surprised to see it in one piece since it had been the last thing on her mind when she'd crashed into the door. Then she un-slung Gemma's bag from her shoulder and held that out as well.

'Gemma wouldn't leave her bag behind, nor would she go anywhere with only one shoe.'

Constable Peters studied the three items before using the tips of his fingers to place each on the reception counter. He jotted down a few more notes then caught Maddie's eye. 'Do you often take illicit drugs?'

Affronted, Maddie gaped at the man. So shocked at the implication, words eluded her for a few seconds then she screwed her eyes in determination.

'I understand where you are coming from but neither Gemma nor myself take any form of illicit drugs. Lord, but I have to be bedridden before I'll even take an aspirin.' Sucking in a breath, she slid her eyelids shut and paused. She hated having to recall the past but she figured that unless she detailed what had happened to Gemma's sister, Leah, and her brother, this man just wouldn't understand. She blew her held breath out between clenched teeth in a long, slow hiss.

She sucked in another breath and hefted her shoulders back and up as she eyed the constable. 'Three years ago, Gemma's sister, Leah, got drunk at a party. She was gang raped and left a bloody mess. Leah found it hard to cope and even more so when she discovered she was pregnant to one of the perpetrators. She was so distraught and depressed that she committed suicide. DNA from the foetus led to an arrest of one of the men. To soften his prison term he gave up the names of the other three men involved. The whole tragic mess caused a great deal of heartache for Gemma and her parents.

'Around the same time my brother died from a drug overdose. Someone slipped something into his drink at his graduation party. Normally the drug wouldn't have killed someone but my brother was a severe asthmatic. That day he'd had a bad attack and had dosed up on prescription medication to alleviate his symptoms enough so he could attend the party. The illicit drug reacted with the asthma medication and sent him into a coma within minutes. He never recovered and was pronounced dead the next day. Gemma and I met at grief counselling. We vowed to never imbibe in alcohol or illicit drugs and have kept to that promise. Tonight, Gemma ordered a cola and I had ginger ale. Gemma was feeling a bit queasy after eating some suss chicken at the Indian Restaurant in the next block so she drank my ginger ale.'

Maddie pointed to the glass on the counter, which by now had so many different fingerprints it was probably useless but maybe they could get samples of the drug from the inside. 'That was my glass but I'd only taken a sip from it before I went on the dance floor for about twenty minutes then the loo. It was on the bar for about an hour. There is absolutely no way Gemma was drunk and she definitely didn't knowingly take any drugs.'

Taking a much needed breath because she was rambling trying to get it all out in as short a time as possible, she noticed the constable had ceased taking notes and was watching her.

'I'm sorry about your brother,' he said.

'Thank you but right now I'm more concerned about Gemma. Can't we do something… anything other than standing here wasting time?'

'Okay, right, look do you have names for the men?'

She thought she'd already said the names but maybe she hadn't. Far out, her brain felt like mashed up fruit salad. Every muscle and nerve in her body was so tense with worry she couldn't remember half the things she'd said. 'Matt was one but the barman said he'd left earlier after the guys had some heated words. Liam… I don't know his surname but the barman said everyone knew Liam because he grew up here and the other one was Josh… um… Evans, that's it, Josh Evans.'

'Josh Evans and Liam Faulkner? Are you sure?' The constable had a stunned look on his face.

'I never heard the Faulkner bit but the rest I'm certain about. You know these guys?'

'Unfortunately, yes, let's go.'

Maddie's arm was grabbed and she was dragged behind the counter, stumbling as she grabbed her jacket and

Gemma's shoe and bag then she managed to get her feet working.

'Mack,' the constable yelled so close to Maddie's ear that she jumped and a surge of adrenaline spurted through her veins. 'You drive… the Faulkner place,' Constable Peters continued as he tugged harder on Maddie's arm.

For a moment Maddie thought he'd asked her to drive but then the rookie she'd been talking to earlier rushed past, grabbed some keys from a hook near a door in the rear of the building and bolted outside. By the time she reached the squad car the engine was rumbling. It sounded like a high performance engine but she supposed they would need powerful cars if they had to travel any distance in an emergency out in these parts. Constable Peters whipped the rear passenger door open and bundled Maddie inside before slamming the door and sliding into the front seat.

'Seat belt,' came a terse order from the front.

Maddie straightened, searched for her belt and slipped it over her shoulder before clicking the metal lock into its catch. For the life of her she couldn't think why she was even in the car but before she could ask the car took off, rocking Maddie off balance as it peeled out of the yard onto the road.

Chapter Nineteen

Consumed with worry, Maddie hadn't noticed that they'd even been moving until the car shuddered to a standstill in the centre of a short driveway: the shaking bringing her out of her reverie. If she was ever asked to describe the route they'd taken, she wouldn't have a clue.

'Stay in the car!' barked the constable before he turned and shoved his door open. Mack eased from the driver's seat and slammed the door before rounding the front of the vehicle and joining Constable Peters as they mounted the front steps.

Then why am I here, Maddie thought as she peered into the gloom. It took only a second or two for her eyes to adjust. The house attached to the drive appeared to be more upmarket then those in the main street. It was larger with a wide veranda running all the way along the front. Like almost every other house in town it was built of corrugated iron but these walls emitted a lighter glow. Cream, she thought, or maybe coffee coloured.

Bluish light flickered from the furthest front room. The T.V. was running but she couldn't detect any other lights burning. The room closest was bathed in darkness.

Movement caught the corner of her eye. Maddie twisted her head and peered straight ahead. A car with open doors on each side sat perched so far at the rear of the property that it appeared to almost meld into the fence. A shadow emerged from the right hand side. Someone had been bending over and leaning into the car. Oh, my gosh! Gemma. Was that Liam or Josh leaning over Gemma? Oh, God, no! Were they in the process of raping her?

Taking a quick glance in the direction of the front door she noticed the two officers were side-by-side with their backs to her and holding open the fly screen door. Should she or shouldn't she? How dangerous could it be with two policemen less than ten metres away?

The thought of Gemma in danger decided her. It was a no-brainer. She eased the door open, peeked at the veranda then crept rapidly on tip-toe around the rear of the car. She ducked below the window-line then waddled to the front. Another sneak peek then she shot down the drive making a bee-line for the open door of the car that was opposite to the person who had bent at the waist again and was leaning into the car.

'Stupid cow,' she heard mumbled as she skidded to a stop.

'What the…? How the hell?' the man muttered.

Oh, oh. Maddie recognised the voice. Liam. She grabbed the open door. 'Gemma,' she whispered as she ducked her head inside. 'Oh, yeuw… gross!' She jerked backwards at the odious stench. Some-one had puked all over the rear seat – the otherwise empty rear seat. Maddie glanced into the front. It was devoid of human bodies.

'Where's Gemma?' she hissed as she met Liam's eyes over the roof of the car.

He winced for a split second then masked his features but despite his attempt to not look guilty, he failed miserably.

'How the hell should I know?'

Maddie scoffed as she held his gaze. He knew all right and there was no way she was going to be the first to break eye contact. 'Could be because you were seen carting Gemma out of the pub.'

His eyes flared and a muscle twitched along his taut jaw line.

'I thought I told you to stay in the car.'

Maddie reeled around at the new voice. Caught – but darn it she couldn't just sit there like some dumb idiot and do nothing when there was a chance Gemma was being raped – or worse.

A mumbled string of four letter words came from Liam's direction. Seems he figured out how Maddie had gotten there. She couldn't hold back a grin that dared to creep out from the corners of her mouth.

'Do you know the whereabouts of Gemma Thomas?' The constable had positioned himself in front of Liam so that it wouldn't be easy for him to make a run for it and he sure looked like he wanted to run and then keep on running.

'Son, answer the man!'

Maddie jumped at the new voice that bellowed from just behind her. She hadn't even been aware of anyone else approaching. Her heart skipped a few beats then raced to catch up as a few more gallons of adrenaline squirted through her blood vessels.

'And don't beat around the bush,' came a third voice but one Maddie recognised as belonging to the rookie.

'I don't want to waste time checking the CCTV from the hotel but I will if I have to,' said the constable as he sidled around a bit to keep Liam boxed in against the side of the car. Now where is the girl?'

Liam swore under his breath then glanced around, his eyes stopping as he peered over Maddie's shoulder. Maddie twisted her head around. What could only be Liam's father stood behind her, glaring fiercely at his son.

'Jesus, son, what have you done?'

'Nothing, Dad. It was Josh.'

'And wherever Joshua Evans goes, you manage to follow. How many times do I have to tell you that, that boy is nothing but trouble? Where the hell is the girl? She's only seventeen for God's sake.' Mr Faulkner rounded the car and shirt-fronted his son. 'Please tell me you haven't harmed a seventeen year old kid?'

'It wasn't me. Josh slipped a Mickey into the drinks. He thought it was this one's.' He pointed towards Maddie. She felt positively ill as a vision of Paul's dead body centred in her brain.

'We didn't know she was only seventeen.'

'That's no excuse, for Christ's sake. What were you thinking?' Liam received several jabs to his ribs and Maddie suspected that if there hadn't been so many witnesses he would have been on the receiving end of a lot more than a few jabs. Boxed ears or a right hook to his jaw was more than likely if you took into consideration the fierceness of his father's words and face.

The constable thrust his shoulder between father and son. 'Liam, just tell us where the girl is. She was in your car wasn't she?'

'Gemma threw up in the back seat of his car,' Maddie butted in. She never thought she would thank someone for giving them crook food but now she was overjoyed that Gemma had scoffed down so much of the rotten chicken.

There was a startled silence followed by three heads peering into the car. 'Jesus, son,' Mr Faulkner stepped backwards shaking his head as though he was completely bewildered. He blew out his breath then sucked in another very long one. It looked as though he was fighting to rein in his temper. He turned back to eye-ball his son. 'Where is she?'

'I dropped her at the park.'

'Which park?' came from Constable Peters.

'The caravan park,' came out as a sneer.

'Don't get smart, son,' said the constable. 'You're in a whole heap of trouble. Now tell me she is unharmed.'

'She threw up. She was conscious when I dropped her off.'

'And did you touch her?' asked the dad.

'What do you mean?' Liam's attitude was that of a drowning man not wanting to face the truth that he was snookered.

'Christ, son, don't act so damn stupid. There is only one reason you would drug a young woman. Now tell me you didn't rape a seventeen year old kid!' Mr Faulkner reeled away as he swiped his fingers through his hair. 'Jesus, I can't believe my own son would be so damn stupid.'

'We didn't touch her,' Liam yelled then wheeled around. 'God, this is such a freaking mess,' he muttered under his breath. He rubbed a hand down his face and seemed to be fighting for control. 'It was all Josh's idea,' he yelled even louder.

'But you were a party to it. You didn't stop him but went along for the ride.' The constable grabbed one of Liam's wrists. 'I'm sorry, but you're under arrest.' Before Liam could say or do anything he was handcuffed and read his rights.

'Dad?' Liam begged his father. The edges of his eyelashes glinted with what looked like moisture as he stared at his father.

'Take him away and lock him up before I kill him.' Mr Faulkner turned away. 'I'm going to find the girl. Come.' He turned to Maddie. 'Come with me. Young Gemma is going to need you or else she is going to think that I was a party to this idiocy and scream blue murder if I approach her.' He grasped Maddie by her elbow and tugged.

Maddie wasn't sure what to do. Yes, she wanted to find Gemma as quick as possible but going with a complete stranger didn't seem to be the smartest idea. Especially when his son had behaved with so little regard for Gemma's welfare and Maddie believed behaviour like that was usually learned as a youngster from their parents. So she planted her feet and tugged back. She eyed the constable.

'Go with Mayor Faulkner. We'll meet you at the caravan park as soon as we've locked this idiot up.'

The mayor? Good grief! No wonder he's not arguing about his son being shoved in a prison cell. Maddie shrugged her shoulders and followed Mr Faulkner. Not that she had a whole lot of choice because she was virtually dragged along by the elbow. Mt Faulkner was not a happy chappy.

In less than two minutes she was belted into the front seat of a flash SUV and they were speeding towards the caravan park after Maddie told the man at which park they were staying.

Chapter Twenty

'Where's your spot?'

Maddie twisted her head towards the mayor. They were the only words that had been uttered during the entire drive, not that the distance had been great: a kilometre at the most. She still couldn't believe he was the head honcho of the community. No wonder the barman had said everybody knew Liam.

'We're in the tent section near the amenities. Go that way.' Maddie indicated with her hand as she scanned the area with her eyes. They hadn't thought to ask exactly where Liam had dropped Gemma off but if she was conscious then surely she would have told them which one was their tent. There were plenty of lights beaming from tall steel power-poles making it relatively easy to see and so far she'd seen nothing out of the ordinary. There were no huddled forms that looked like comatose humans. But it was more in the deeper shadows that Maddie searched.

'Over there. That station wagon is ours.'

'You didn't drive into town?'

'No it wasn't that far and after sitting in a car hour after hour, we needed the exercise.' Maddie straightened and leant forwards as Mr Faulkner turned the last corner and came to a standstill. The headlights outlined their tiny tent. It looked exactly as they'd left it. A shiver skittered across her shoulders. But that was how it was supposed to look even if someone was inside. They always locked all their odds and ends in the car overnight, with only the basic necessities inside the tent. It meant fewer things to pack each morning and fewer things to catch the eye of less than scrupulous people. Even their thongs for a trip to the conveniences during the night were left just inside the tent flap. If nothing was left around then nothing could get nicked.

Maddie unlatched her seatbelt with one hand and the car door with the other. Her innards were churning as she raced to the tent and whipped up the zipper. She stuck her head in side, 'Oh, God, no,' she whispered on a stuttered breath. 'She's not here,' Maddie called louder at the footsteps behind her.

The mayor swore under his breath. Maddie felt him crouch beside her as she yanked her head out and sat back on her heels.

'Check out the ladies ablution block. If she's still feeling nauseous she could be in there. I'll get a torch and ring the station to ask where that idiot son of mine left her.' He reached out with one hand and squeezed Maddie's forearm. 'Don't worry, we'll find her.'

'But she could be dead,' Maddie wailed as she leapt to her feet, fighting back tears that were washing over her eyes.

As he followed her upright, the mayor grabbed her arm again to still her. 'If she vomited up the contents of her stomach then she purged her body of most of whatever it was those damned idiots gave her. And Liam said she was conscious.'

Maddie dragged her arm away. 'You think I'd trust what he says?' She didn't know how she felt: furious, disbelieving or what, but mostly she was downright scared. She spun around and raced for the shower block, her heart lodged somewhere in her throat making it hard to breathe. Her chest felt leaden yet ready to explode.

'Gemma,' she screeched as she yanked on the door and raced inside. The only answer was her own panicked footsteps and the echo of the door slamming behind her. She tore along the shower cubicles, shoving at each door and scanning each recess as she went.

No Gemma.

She did the same with the toilet cubicles along the opposite wall.

All were empty.

'Far out, Gemma, where are you?' Maddie whimpered as she raced outside and just to be sure, flung open the door of the men's amenities. 'Please don't let any men be in here,' she muttered as she winced at the stench from the urinals then tore up and down the aisle, checking out all the cubicles along each side. Finding them all vacant she shot back outside.

'She's not there,' she called and ran slap bang into the mayor. 'Oops, sorry,' she muttered as he steadied her. She looked up and noticed he had a torch in one hand and a mobile phone in his other.

'Liam thinks it was Rohypnol and he dropped Gemma at the entrance. Damn fool. Come, let's search the most direct route between your tent and the road,' He grasped Maddie's elbow and turned.

With a few metres between them, they began walking back the way they had come. The mayor squatted and swept the beam from his torch under vans and cars and into any dark hidden recesses. Maddie trawled one side of the road while the mayor looked behind the first row of vans on the other side. Her gut was churning so much she felt like she was going to be sick. She couldn't remember ever being this scared. The further they searched, the more intense her terror became.

They were almost at the gates when two patrol cars pulled up next to them. A window slid down.

'Find her?' came a voice from the dark interior; a voice Maddie didn't recognise.

'No.' The mayor rested one hand on the sill. 'Liam said he dropped the girl at the entrance. We've searched up this road. The tent is on the grassed area at the other end and to the right. This is the most direct route.'

'We've got searchlights,' said a different voice. 'We'll drive around the park. The girl was drugged. She could be confused.'

That was the last thing Maddie needed to hear. A new wave of moisture swept across her eyes. She squeezed them shut and willed it away as she sucked in a long slow breath then blew it out again. Keep calm. Don't panic. It's the panic that makes you do crazy things. Her mind recalled one of her father's favourite sayings. Yeah, right, Dad. Keep calm. It was certainly easy to say it and think it but trying to convince your body to obey was way too difficult. Her Dad - he would know what to do.

A blast of light hit her fair square in the face, jerking her back to the present. She blinked and turned away but red blots burned onto her retinas for a few seconds before she could regain clear focus. Both cars were moving. Just how long had she been in a daze? Not able to think what the heck she could do, Maddie turned and watched. Powerful beams mounted on the tops of the cars, swung in long slow arcs, lighting up everything in their path. One patrol car crawled along the fence-line that ran parallel to the road with the light twisting, holding still then jolting another few metres to a new position where it held for a few seconds before moving again. Lights were flicking on in vans and dishevelled people were emerging, adjusting sleepwear and hurriedly tossed on gowns. It must be the lights dragging people awake for there was very little noise except for the hums of two motors.

Spinning to her left, Maddie began following the light from the second car. It was covering the ground she'd already searched, but the strength of light reached much further than that of the torch. Each and every bush, shrub and tree to the edge of the road was highlighted. The light swung and stayed a moment then moved all around to the other side of the road. It paused, as did the car. Right, forwards then left. Left, forwards then right.

Mesmerised and still not knowing what she was supposed to do, Maddie just stood there, swinging her head from side-to-side. A rumble of voices became louder as more and more people emerged and grouped into huddles of various sizes. She felt the presence of some-one beside her so she twisted her head to look. The mayor was standing watching her. He sort of smiled as though he wasn't sure if it was appropriate. If it was supposed to give her hope and courage, it failed.

'If she's here, they'll find her.'

Maddie gulped. If she was here. 'And if she's not?' Her voice came out harsh. She coughed to clear the blockage in her throat. 'I feel so helpless,' she whispered.

The mayor moved closer and was hesitant but finally swept one arm around her shoulder and gave her a brief hug. She could tell he wasn't sure how to approach her and she wasn't sure how to react but it felt kind of good to have that human contact even though it was brief. He gave the appearance of being much nicer than his son but appearances could be deceiving. Hadn't she learnt that on this trip?

'Let's give them a chance to search before we start worrying about alternatives.' He gave her another quick hug then stepped away. She wondered if he felt guilty even though he had nothing to do with it. She sure felt guilty. It was eating away at her. She went to the loo. She stayed there way too long. She left the drinks unattended when she knew better. She let Gemma get away with her underhanded, sneaky meeting. And now all she could do was stand there like a dummy and she felt so useless just standing there.

A shout brought her head up. She searched for the source. All she could make out was that the car ahead was stationary with the light swinging ever so slightly backwards and forwards on the same spot. It was aimed through the fence, towards the road.

A car door slammed. A uniformed man began running towards the fence. Maddie's heart shot to her mouth then rammed into her stomach and then bounced like a yo-yo. Her feet began moving. She ran full pelt, leaping over smaller objects and dodging around larger ones. 'Gemma, Gemma,' she panted in rhythm with her racing heartbeat.

By the time she reached the fence, the officer had scrambled over and was on the other side with his back to her. He was on his knees crouched over something.

'Gemma!' she screamed then whispered, 'Please, please, please, be all right.' She tried to scramble over the fence but was dragged back by big hands. She fought to free herself. 'Let me go!' She twisted and turned but the hands tightened then an arm swept around the front of her shoulders and dragged her against a hard and unyielding body.

'Calm down. Let the Sarge check her over.' Maddie recognised the voice of Constable Peters. So that must be the Sergeant McKay mentioned earlier. She couldn't fathom why a complete stranger would insist on believing her but then she did mention about her father's job. Maybe it was a brotherhood thing. She wriggled to free herself but the arm tying her to the body didn't ease one iota.

'She's alive but unresponsive.' The shouted words registered through the turmoil galloping around and around in her head. The officer stood and turned. Gemma was in his arms. One of her arms was flopping downwards, her head was skewed to one side and her mouth hung open. He stepped towards them. Maddie yanked her body free and hurled herself towards the fence.

'Please, please, please. Tell me she's going to be all right.' Maddie managed to get out as the tears she'd fought back for the past few hours, began tumbling down her cheeks. She no longer cared about anyone seeing her be weak.

The officer eyed her and stepped close enough that Maddie could reach through the fence and touch Gemma. 'She's going to be all right,' he said. She's unconscious from the effects of the drug but her pulse is steady and there are no physical injuries that I can see.'

The man's voice sounded gentle as though he understood the anguish Maddie was going through. An arm went around her shoulder as she stroked Gemma's lower arm. The skin felt soft and cool on the surface from the night air but at the same time the warmth from under Gemma's skin sent a wave of relief swamping through her.

'Come we need to get young Gemma to the hospital. I can drive you if you like.'

Turning her head, Maddie became aware that the arm holding her belonged to the mayor. She sniffed then wriggled her hand back through the fence and swept her clenched fist over her face to swipe away the moisture. She felt such a fool for being so weak but all control seemed to have deserted her. 'It's okay, I can drive,' she mumbled then sniffed again: a very unladylike noise that sounded like a cross between a snort and a pig's grunt. Embarrassed at the awful noise, she grinned then added, 'Sorry.'

'A few tears to ease tension are often necessary. I'm more than thankful we found young Gemma and apart from the drug, she seems to be unharmed.' He withdrew his arm and grubbed his fingers through his hair. 'I can't tell you how relieved I am and how sorry that a son of mine was involved. He knows better – much better. He was brought up to respect women.'

Maddie used her wrist to wipe the remaining moisture from her cheeks then scrubbed the dampness down the front of her slacks. 'I think maybe you should be telling this to Gemma.'

'Liam should be on bended knee grovelling to both of you but there's no way in hell I'll be bailing him out of jail. A few days behind bars might bring him to his senses.' He turned and caught her eye. 'Do you know where the hospital is?'

With a nose that was determined to drip like a leaky tap and in the absence of a tissue, Maddie sniffed again. 'No and I need to get Gemma's bag and my jacket from your car.'

'Come then. You can follow me.'

Chapter Twenty-One

As Maddie eased into the driver's seat of Gemma's car, her foot snagged on something rope-like. A scuffing swish and plonk followed. Reaching down in the dark, she felt around, found a wire and tugged. An eerie green glow radiated from under the seat. Hooking the wire over one finger, she raised her hand then released a long puff of breath to ease the tension tightening already strung out nerves. Man, oh, man, she was a mess if something as inconsequential as Gemma's mobile phone scared the bejesus out of her. It dangled and swayed with a white square flashing – *10 missed calls*. That didn't surprise her for neither of them had even looked at their phones for days. They'd been beyond mobile coverage most of the time. Or at least Maddie hadn't looked. It was obvious Gemma had plugged her phone into the car's cigarette lighter to charge.

With a niggle of guilt for prying, Maddie pressed the arrow for she suspected she knew from whom the messages were. A number she recognised was repeated ten times. Gemma's mother would be frantic. Gemma was supposed to have called daily if she was able. But they were way behind their targeted schedule. Five days without reassurance that Gemma was unharmed had probably sent Mrs Thomas into a frenzy of worry. Since Leah's death, parental concern in the Thomas household had been smothering. They knew it, not only from Gemma's constant complaints but also from the counsellor Gemma still saw on a monthly basis. Maddie understood both sides. Mr and Mrs Thomas were terrified of losing their only other daughter and Gemma rebelled at the almost claustrophobic stranglehold they had over every minute of her life. Going to Brisbane to train in the nation-wide family business had been a compromise suggested by the counsellor. Not calling home since they left was not a good start and probably had the elder Thomas's rueing their agreement. Maddie snorted. It was a wonder Mrs Thomas hadn't sent out the entire country's police force looking for them. Maddie was only too pleased her own parents had a far more philosophical outlook after the death of a child.

But then, Paul's death hadn't been because of his careless behaviour. He'd always been the sensible and responsible person in his group of peers. They'd always looked up to him. It was something Maddie had always been grateful for, the way she and Paul had been raised to be independent thinkers from a very early age. Leah's death, on the other hand, resulted from her own stupidity and carelessness. She'd stayed out to all hours, getting drunk and frequenting seedy night spots despite her parents' pleadings. A carefree attitude of *'it will never happen to me,'* was what had ultimately caused her to take her own life. And Gemma was heading in the same direction. The unbidden thought sent a shudder through Maddie. Was it some genetic trait that made them both so impulsive?

Should she call? Maddie wavered. A glance at her watch decided her. It was way too late to call. She scoffed. A phone call at this time of night would probably give them a heart attack before they had a chance to lift the receiver. Instead she typed a text message – *Now have coverage for a while. Will ring in the morning. We're both safe.* That should allay their fears. It said enough but not too much. No way could she reveal all the little hiccoughs they'd had along the way.

Unplugging the charged phone, Maddie shoved it into the narrow recess under the radio. She slid the key into its slot, twisted and the engine rumbled to life. The car was in no way new but had been a well-maintained family classic and was always reliable. Mr Thomas wouldn't have even considered his daughter driving a car that wasn't in top mechanical condition. Shoving the gear stick into place, she released the handbrake and eased from the lawn onto the bitumen. She met up with the mayor's idling car and flashed headlights to indicate she was ready. As the mayor drove off, she followed.

The hospital was closer than she'd imagined so she'd have no problem finding her way back. For the lateness of the hour, there was a bustle of activity at the well lit entrance. Mr Faulkner was the epitome of a gentleman, holding the door open for Maddie to enter first then guiding her to the reception desk manned by a lone woman who was busy writing notes on a form. It took a few too many seconds for the woman to pause and peer up over half-moon glasses.

'Can I help you?'

'Gemma Thomas has just been brought in.' Mayor Faulkner leant against the counter.

'Ah, the O.D. girl.'

O.D.? A frisson of unease tinged with anger, snaked across Maddie's shoulders. How dare she?

'What do you mean, O.D.? She'd not a drug addict!' Maddie spat, then immediately regretted her outburst. It wasn't this woman's fault since she probably had no idea about any of the details.

A hand tugged at her shoulder. She twisted around to see the mayor shaking his head. 'Take it easy. Only the tending staff will know the true details.'

'But to make such an outlandish assumption…'

He put a finger to his lips then faced the wicked witch. 'Sylvie, her drink was spiked. Can you please tell us where Gemma is?'

Of course, he had to know the woman. He sounded so calm while Maddie's innards were still in panic mode. Despite it being after mid-night she knew she wouldn't be able to sleep with so much adrenaline still surging through her veins. Relaxing wasn't about to happen any time soon.

'Sorry,' she said to Sylvie. 'I'm a bit up-tight.' She was more than uptight. She felt as though her nerves were going to ping apart and shoot every cell of her body into outer space.

'Not a problem. I understand.' Sylvie glanced at her computer screen. 'Miss Thomas is still undergoing examination in emergency. If you sit over there.' A hand wavered to indicate a bank of seats at the far end. 'I'll let the attending physician know you are waiting.'

It was amazing how seconds felt like minutes and minutes like hours when anxiety overrode sense while you were waiting, waiting, waiting. Every smudge on the wall, word on the posters, specks on the ceiling and scuff marks on the polished linoleum had been studied assiduously and committed to memory before the mayor nudged her and stood.

Startled, Maddie shot out of her chair. 'Gemma, tell me she's okay,' Maddie stuttered to the petite woman wearing pale blue scrubs.

'She's going to be fine. She's still unconscious but her vital signs are excellent.'

Something wasn't gelling. 'Why unconscious?' Maddie asked as she wriggled from foot to foot. 'Surely since she threw up then she would have gotten rid of the drug.'

The doctor laid a hand on Maddie's arm and gave a gentle squeeze. 'It's not that simple. Rohypnol is a very fast acting drug. It's a liquid. It gets absorbed into the blood stream very quickly unlike solid food, which takes time to digest, move along the alimentary canal and be absorbed. Yes, she would have rid her system of some of the drug, but not all. Which begs the question, why did she vomit? It's not a normal reaction to Rohypnol?'

A sort of choking laugh escaped Maddie's lips. 'Crook chook.'

'Excuse me?'

'We had Indian for dinner. The chicken Gemma ate was off.' Maddie sighed then grinned. 'I feel like going back to the restaurant and thanking the poor woman. Her tainted food probably saved Gemma from…' She shuddered. She didn't want to go there.

'I have to report this incident.' The doctor gave Maddie's shoulder a friendly pat but she was facing the mayor.

'Already done. The police know who and are searching for him. Come Maddie, you need some sleep.'

'No way.' She turned to the doctor. 'Can I sit with Gemma?'

'Certainly, but we don't expect her to rouse for some time. It might be better for you to get some sleep and come back in the morning.'

Maddie set her mouth in a stubborn curve. 'Uh, uh, no way. I'm staying.'

Chapter Twenty-Two

One arm emerged from the warm cocoon, flapped around, padding the surrounds. Searching. Fingers found the cause of the obnoxious noise, grasped a firm hold and lifted.

'Far out,' growled from under the covers. It felt as though she'd only been asleep for a scant five minutes. Forcing one eye open Maddie peered at the still ringing mobile phone, fought through fuzziness for the right button, pressed and slammed the phone against her ear.

'Hello,' she mumbled then coughed to clear the rasp from her throat.

'Madison, is that you? Why are you answering Gemma's phone?'

Alert in an instant, Maddie eased up onto one elbow. Oh, heckity heck. What was she supposed to say?

'Hang on a minute. I was asleep,' she muttered to give herself a few precious seconds to think of a logical response. A glimpse at her watch and her eyes boggled. Only seven. Far out. She'd managed less than four hours' sleep. No wonder she still felt exhausted. And if it was seven here then in Perth it must be… she had to think. Two hour's difference or was it three? Far out, where was she and did they have daylight saving? Either four or five in the morning over in the west. What on earth was Mrs Thomas doing up at that hour? She snorted. Worried sick, of course.

As she struggled to free limbs from the sleeping bag, memory surged about the previous night. Most of it, well between one and three, had been spent hunched in a cold vinyl chair by Gemma's side until the nurse, who had been hovering on the other side of the bed, had made another examination of vital signs. Maddie relived the anxiety she felt as eye-lids were lifted to see how the pupils reacted. The nurse then scratched between Gemma's eyebrows and was rewarded by a groan and slight tugging to one side. With a smile shooting from her lips the nurse then knuckled Gemma's sternum. When Gemma grumbled and pulled away the nurse glanced at Maddie and grinned.

'Your friend is no longer unconscious but is sleeping. She's out of the woods.'

The sense of relief had been immense. Once she was certain Gemma was no longer seriously drug affected, Maddie had driven back to the caravan park, crawled into her sleeping bag fully dressed and must have fallen asleep in an instant for she couldn't recall anything else.

Sitting cross-legged on the thin foam excuse for a mattress, Maddie slid the phone back against her ear then sucked in a breath for courage.

'Mrs Thomas, sorry but I was sound asleep.'

'Where's Gemma? Where are you?'

Oh, man, this was going to be beyond difficult. 'We're in Broken Hill. We had a puncture yesterday and stayed here to get a new tyre.' Well, that sounded sensible; showed how mature they were being. 'We went to an Indian restaurant last night for dinner. The chicken Gemma ate was a bit off and she got a touch of food poisoning.'

'She's sick?' Mrs Thomas yelled so loud Maddie winced as she yanked the phone away from a zinging ear-drum.

'Gemma is fine but I took her to emergency just in case.' See, I'm looking after her. 'They kept her in overnight for observation.' At the loud wail blasting the same poor ear-drum, Maddie flinched then shuddered. Even though this was the type of reaction she'd been expecting, she wasn't prepared for that kind of shriek.

'Mrs Thomas, I swear, Gemma is fine. I stayed with her until just a few hours ago. She only threw up once.' That Maddie knew about so she wasn't telling porky pies. 'And at the last set of observations the nurse said that Gemma was fine and sleeping peacefully.'

'But she's in hospital?' The words sounded panicked.

'Only because it was better not to discharge her at three in the morning. I figured you would want me to let her sleep as long as she needed in the safety and warmth of a hospital rather than bring her back to the tent.' Man, oh, man, she was laying it on thick. As she crossed her fingers for luck, she prayed she wouldn't be struck by a bolt of lightning for sprouting such whoppers. Well, they really weren't lies. She just wasn't adding the bits it was better Mrs Thomas never knew about. Ever.

'You're sure she's okay?' It sounded as though Mrs Thomas was on the verge of tears.

'I swear. She's fine. I'm picking her up at nine.'

'Well, okay then. I trust you. But make sure she phones me.'

'I will. I promise.' Not wanting to talk any longer, Maddie pressed the off button then huffed and flopped back onto the mattress. Oh, boy, was she glad that was over. But now, what should she do? Going back to sleep for a couple of hours sounded so, so inviting. Of their own volition, her eyelids slid shut at the thought. Then she remembered the darn tyre. It had to be collected at eight. Gemma at nine. A shower was on the desperate list as was something to eat. They were behind schedule again and needed to get going to make up lost time. If they didn't, Maddie was going to miss her flight home. Home. Getting home sounded pretty amazing. No way did she want to miss that flight.

Groaning, she turned over and patted the pillow that was begging her head to nestle in. She sighed then shoved away all thoughts of lingering. It wasn't going to happen. Instead she began the tedious task of packing. After stowing all their camping gear, she showered, changed and was about to pack away her toiletries bag and towel when a police car drew up next to her. She recognised the sole occupant from the previous night.

'Morning, Miss Brown.' The officer looked and sounded so stern it sent a frisson of unease shooting through her.

'Good morning. Is something wrong?'

'Apart from Joshua Evans doing a runner, no. But we need both you and Miss Thomas to give us formal statements before you leave.'

A loud groan escaped Maddie's lips before she could suck it back. Of course they would. She should know that. So much for getting away. This could take forever. 'What if I come in now? No, wait, I have to collect the new tyre at eight. The nurse thought Gemma might be released after the doctor's rounds at about nine. I can bring Gemma in then.'

'The Sarge has sent an officer to interview Miss Thomas.'

That was a relief. Maybe they could get a few hundred kilometres further along after all.

'Okay, I'll be at the station as soon as I can.'

The wait for the tyre shop to open was as interminable as all the periods of waiting she'd had over the past twenty-four hours. Was it only yesterday when Gemma had almost killed them? Maddie's breath stuttered then whooshed out long and slow in disbelief. Just how much can happen in a mere twenty-four hours? She sighed. Certainly not much of it was taken up by what she needed most. Sleep. At the thought she yawned and stretched.

A sudden rumble behind her and she jerked around, sucking in her breath as still alert nerves pinged to attention. It seemed her body hadn't moved out of danger mode. She had to fight back the need to laugh at the sight of the mechanic standing there with his hands on his hips. So inappropriate to laugh but heck, it was almost like her body needed to rid itself of the past day's worth of tension.

'Something funny?' asked the man who had promised the tyre would be ready despite an already overfull workload.

She fought to school her features. 'Sorry, no, I'm just glad to see you.'

A raised eyebrow told her that her choice of words wasn't the best or had been taken the wrong way.

'Sorry, I've had a harrowing night. I was hoping our tyre is ready.'

'Last thing I did last night.'

After paying for and storing the brand spanking new tyre, Maddie returned to the police station and answered so many questions she began to wonder why they didn't want to know the colour of her knickers. They sure found out everything else about both her and Gemma. But she knew it was standard practice so they could compare both stories, looking for obvious differences. Trouble was it was unlikely Gemma would own up to anything that saw her in bad light. And since everything bad that had happened was because of Gemma's naïve stupidity maybe they would never be able to leave.

It took so long for the officers to ask their questions, record the answers, type the statement onto the computer, print it off and get Maddie to read every word before signing that she was an hour late in reaching the hospital. Her walk through the corridors would have done an Olympian walking race contestant proud. She probably looked ridiculous but Maddie was beyond caring. Getting on the road was her main concern and some food would go down well. Still striding full speed, she barged into Gemma's room.

'Where the hell have you been?'

The shrill demand brought Maddie to a sudden standstill. 'Excuse me?' Shocked, she eyed the furious face. Gemma was dressed in last night's outfit and sat perched on the edge of the bed.

'I've been waiting for ages. Why weren't you here? Why did you even leave me?' With each demand, Gemma rose and stepped closer.

Maddie held up one hand to prevent Gemma getting right into her face. 'Now just a minute!' She took one step backwards while fighting down the urge to bop Gemma on the nose. 'First, I wasn't here because I was packing up the tent then picking up the new tyre. You know – the one that had to be replaced because YOU couldn't follow basic road signs. Here's the bill. You owe me another one hundred and twenty-two dollars.' Tossing the folded paper in Gemma's lap Maddie managed another step backwards because the air between them felt tense all of a sudden. 'Second, I then had to visit the police station to give my statement. Again because of YOUR stupidity. YOU,' she reclaimed one step to close the gap she'd been keen to widen a few seconds before, 'just couldn't resist chatting up guys you knew nothing about. YOU,' she stepped even closer to invade Gemma's personal space, 'got yourself drugged. The intention was for both of us to be raped.'

Maddie didn't miss the shudder that shivered across Gemma's shoulders. 'I spent half the night searching for you and the other half sitting hunkered in that chair.' She shot her arm in the direction of the darned uncomfortable seat. 'I stayed until you were out of danger. I've had hardly any sleep while you've been in la la land for eight hours and you dare to have a go at me. Get real, Gemma!'

Anger boiled so hot, Maddie felt as though she wanted to punch the living daylights out of the ungrateful little wretch. To prevent herself from lashing out, she wheeled away and raced to the other side of the room, her chest heaving. She breathed in deep and blew out long and slow. Stay cool, Madison Brown. Stay cool.

'Leah wouldn't have left me.'

The words were so meek, Maddie wasn't sure she'd heard correctly. She spun around. 'Leah?' she yelled. 'I'm NOT Leah. She'd dead.' Stalking back towards Gemma, Maddie ignored how pale Gemma had gone. Maybe the bold statement was a bit harsh but heck it was time for a reality check. 'She's dead because she did idiotic things. Just. Like. You. Did.' She sucked in a breath. 'And last night you could have ended up exactly the same way. But who was it that realised what had happened? Who was it that searched for you and asked the right questions? Who was it that ran to the police station? Who was it that gave enough details so we could find you in time to save your ungrateful little neck? Eh?'

Maddie was so furious she didn't care when Gemma flopped onto the bed with tears streaming down her cheeks. About time she had a wake-up call, or… something. Maddie didn't care what.

'S… s… s… sorry.' stammered Gemma.

'You know what?'

'What?' Gemma sat up and swiped moisture from her face with the back of her hand.

'I don't believe you.'

'You don't? Why?'

'Because you keep saying sorry yet you follow each apology with another act of stupidity. If you were really sorry, you'd smarten up and think of consequences before you did anything. You want forgiveness from me?'

Gemma nodded timidly with downcast eyes.

'Then you need to earn it.'

There was a definite wince from Gemma as her eyes shot upwards.

'Now, one more thing.' Maddie slid Gemma's mobile phone from the back pocket of her cut-offs.

'What?' asked Gemma. It was amazing how quick her tears had dried up. Maddie felt certain they had been of the crocodile variety. Bitch, she thought to herself and really, really, really wanted to say it out aloud.

'Ring your mother. Now. She's so frantic she's thinking of coming to get you.' It was a lie but Maddie didn't care and she didn't care about the frown of worry creasing Gemma's brow.

'You rang Mum?' Gemma squealed.

'No, she rang me at some ungodly hour this morning.'

'You told her?' Gemma shrieked. 'How could you?'

Oh, boy. This was getting too much. 'I told her you were in hospital.'

'Why?'

'What else could I say when I was answering your phone and you weren't there?'

'Why didn't you tell her I was in the shower?' The wailing tone was full of condemnation.

'I'm not into lying, especially to your mother. She's worried because you haven't rung her every night when you could. Like you promised.'

'But you know what she's like. She'll never let me stay in Brisbane. And then I'll be a prisoner again. Why did you tell her everything?' Gemma dared to poke Maddie in the ribs.

Incensed, Maddie strode to the door and spun around. She'd had more than enough. 'I told her you had a touch of food poisoning, which is true. I told her that was the reason you were in hospital overnight.' She kept her voice low. 'I didn't,' she stepped forward and returned the poke to the ribs, 'tell her about the bushfire you started, or the locusts, or the three punks you encouraged in Kalgoorlie, or about almost killing us with your reckless driving, or getting yourself drugged.' She stepped closer until their noses were almost touching. 'BUT. One more stupid incident and I will. That's a promise.' She backed away. 'Now if you don't want your parents meeting us in Brisbane to take you back home, you'd better ring them right now. Then you get your selfish butt out the front entrance where the car is. You have ten minutes to the very second. If you're not there, I'm driving your car to the airport and getting on the first plane out of here.'

'B… b… but!'

'No ifs buts or anything.' She glanced at her watch. 'Ten minutes from…' she waited for the second hand to hit the twelve. 'Now.' Maddie spun on her heel and strode away, ignoring Gemma's splutters and the sound of scuffling feet chasing after her. The footsteps ceased. There were beeps of numbers being punched, then the word, 'Mum,' before hurried footsteps continued. All the way out to the car she could hear mumbled words. When she reached the car she slid into the driver's seat and waited with the door open. It was already too hot to sit stifling in the closed confines of a car. She was angry-mad but not insane-mad. All the time she stared at her watch she held up the fingers of one hand, dropping a finger as each minute passed.

Gemma slid into the passenger seat as the second last finger dropped. She was still talking. It sounded desperate, pleading, begging then promising.

'I promise I'll ring every night from now on. Love you, Mum.' The phone was then slipped into the little slot under the radio next to Maddie's own phone which she'd plugged in to be charged. Maddie had a deep need to ring her own parents. Just to hear their sane calming voices.

'Maddie?' Gemma begged.

'Do NOT say a word to me,' Maddie warned. 'I'm beyond mad at you. One word and I'm gone.' She drove and kept on driving while enjoying the sullen silence and giving her temper a chance to simmer then hopefully abate.

Chapter Twenty-Three

It took three hours to reach Cobar where they stopped only long enough to fuel up, have a bathroom break and purchase coffee and a desperately needed sandwich. It amused Maddie how Gemma was so simpering sweet in buying lunch and ensuring it was what Maddie wanted. As they drove from the copper and zinc mining town, all she had time to notice was that it was a surprisingly green and picturesque outback town. Maddie guessed it was so noticeable after all the parched scenery they'd endured so far.

Ninety minutes later they nosed through Nyngyen then turned onto the Newell Highway at Neverfire sixty kilometres further on. Silence still prevailed but only because Maddie held up a hand to stop Gemma every time she attempted to begin a conversation.

At Gilgandra an hour later, Maddie loved the appearance of the historic country town which appeared to be vibrant because it was at the junction of three major highways. She couldn't resist stopping at the Cooee heritage centre. The rammed earth walls and corrugated iron roof gave it a cute traditional aura inviting people to venture inside. Without saying a word to Gemma, she unfolded cramped legs from the driver's seat, walked to the entrance, paid the small entry fee and went inside for a quick tour. It was the name that hooked her interest. Cooee: such a strange looking and sounding word. A word that was very Australian. Many visitors from other countries wouldn't have a clue what it meant or that it originated from the Aborigines who used it to communicate with a distant person. How many times had she and Paul had cooee competitions during their bush camping trips. It was fun yelling it as loud as you could, especially when at the top of a hill or cliff and waiting for the echo to call back. Paul. Now why did she have to think of Paul? But it was a happy memory so she smiled to herself. He would like her to remember the happy times.

By the time she exited, Maddie couldn't remember much of what was inside. Her mind was full of Paul fun times. Somehow her mind had absorbed that the centre paid homage to the cultures and lifestyles, past and present, of the people of the Gilgandra district but most of the time her mind had been centred on Paul.

Gemma was leaning up against the wall outside. It must have been too hot in the car. But she could have come in if she'd wanted. Although historical things didn't really interest our Gemma so Maddie wasn't surprised.

Maddie slid into the driver's seat, shoved the key in and twisted. The engine thrummed to life. She had to stifle a grin when Gemma realised what was happening and scurried into the passenger seat just in time. Maddie was reversing onto the road before Gemma even had time to snick the door shut.

It seemed, from the farm signs and paddock sizes that they were in the centre of wool and farming country, which was pleasant after some of the bleak countryside they had driven through. An hour later they reached Coonabarabran, a modern, friendly looking town on the side of the Castlereagh River. What made it feel different were the rugged mountains to the west, north and east. Picturesque and calming was how Maddie described it and it felt peaceful despite it being the size of a small city.

Since fatigue had been clawing for too long, Maddie knew she could drive no longer and no way was she letting Gemma drive. The tension of wondering if they were going to have an accident would be too much. A glance at her watch told her it was five-thirty. They could get another hour further along but a solid night's sleep was imperative. She drove around looking for a caravan park. The first one looked inviting so she turned into the entry. It was close to the shops, which would be handy to buy food and the grounds looked clean.

'Are we staying here?' The question from Gemma sounded tentative, as though she was too scared to ask.

'I am. You can do whatever you like,' was all Maddie said before pulling to a standstill.

As soon as the car stopped Gemma shot from her seat and scurried inside, returning a few minutes later with a key for the amenities block, a receipt for payment and a map of where they were to camp. The map was held so Maddie could figure out the direction without any conversation. It amused her that, for once, Gemma had taken her words to heart. Maddie hoped that Gemma was afraid of being left behind or of having to drive the entire way by herself. Well good. About time.

The tent was set up in silence before Maddie grabbed pyjamas and toilet bag then escaped the tension to luxuriate under hot water. She washed her hair, scrubbing the day's aggravation from the roots then gave her body a vigorous scour, except around very tender dark blue bruises where she eased off to a few dabs until she felt clean and invigorated despite draining physical tiredness through lack of sleep and depleted adrenaline. How much adrenaline had she used up since leaving home? How much could the body produce?

Returning to the tent she eyed the sky and frowned. A bank of heavy clouds was forming beyond the mountains to the north-east. The direction they were headed. The way they tumbled on top of each other indicated stronger winds than the gentle wisps of air kissing her bare skin. There would be rain tomorrow. No way was she going to risk Gemma driving in stormy conditions. She couldn't handle simple road-works signs. Maddie's strung out nerves were not a match for Gemma driving through a downpour. Not going to happen.

On all fours, she crawled into the tent and was met with a look, which was a cross between mystified and hope. Gemma sat cross legged on already unfurled sleeping bags. There was an unusual gap between the two mattresses with Gemma's abutting the tent side. Was that a message to keep away? Or maybe one of regret or perhaps Gemma just didn't know what to expect. Maddie said nothing as she stowed her towel and bag then slid her legs into her bag.

'What about dinner?' Gemma whispered. Seemed she was too scared to say more. Good.

In one sense Maddie felt bad about the silent treatment but she'd been so irate earlier that she knew she'd just inflame things if she hadn't shut her mouth. In another sense she wasn't sorry, for Gemma had stepped way over the boundaries. At the same time, Maddie figured they couldn't remain silent for the rest of the trip. It would become unbearable.

'Look, Gemma, I meant what I said this morning. The only reason I'm still here is because I promised your parents I'd see you reach Brisbane in one piece. I'm really peeved with you and didn't appreciate your accusations this morning. And I sure don't appreciate all the scrapes and near death experiences I've had since leaving home. I've had it up to here.' One arm reached as high as it could, scraping the tent roof. 'You do what you want. You want dinner? Then go and get it. There are shops within walking distance that way.' The same arm swung to her right.

'But aren't you hungry?'

'I'm famished but right now I need sleep more than I need food. Now go but don't wake me when you return or I'll be even grumpier.' She slid into the sleeping bag, turned over and sank her head into the welcoming softness of the pillow. 'Goodnight.'

Chapter Twenty-Four

Startled awake, Maddie shot upright. She'd been dreaming about floating in water. Some dark force had been tugging her down under thrashing waves while she'd been fighting to keep her head above water. Struggling to breathe her chest heaved. A brilliant flash streaked through the darkness. She jumped and spun sideways to see Gemma huddled in her sleeping bag, sound asleep.

The following clap of thunder was so loud, Maddie levitated off the mattress. As she landed her hands automatically stabilised her by pressing into the ground. A very wet ground, she realised as fingers sank under water.

'What, how…?' she mumbled as one rubber thong rocked on a wave over her hand.

'Gemma!' she screamed and threw herself over Gemma's body. Dampness oozed through the thin cotton of her pyjamas.

A stifled mumble was followed by writhing. Maddie was shoved. Her foot landed with a splat in the water.

'What are you doing?' said Gemma as her head emerged.

'Getting very wet.' Maddie scrambled from her own sleeping bag and knelt on top then reached out to make a grab for the thong as it rocked back the way it had come. She dropped it on the bed, lunged and snatched her half submerged toiletries bag and shook the water from it.

A string of uncouth words slid from Gemma's mouth as she extricated wet legs from a sodden sleeping bag. Her side of the tent seemed to be a bit lower. Water was drifting that way. 'What happened?'

Lightning streaked and must have been close for there was the distinct scent of sulphur. When the thunder clapped almost immediately after, she knew the brunt of the storm was virtually overhead. She couldn't figure out why she hadn't heard it approach for there was enough water using their tent as a drain that it must have been bucketing down for ages. Yes, she'd been dead tired but with so much lightning and thunder this was ridiculous.

'Storm,' she said then winced at stating the obvious.

'But how did the water get in the tent?'

Another flash was followed by a loud clap. Not quite so close this time. Gemma whimpered and curled up tight. Gemma was afraid of thunder? Amazing what you learnt at the most inappropriate time.

The tent was supposed to be waterproof so Maddie searched for some kind of hole or tear that would allow a river to sneak in. As she searched she grabbed floating or submerged objects. Her other thong. She flicked it on her bed, a stream of splashes managing to reach both her and Gemma. It was darn freezing. Her towel was a swimming mass of tortured fabric so she left it coiled in the water. The torch. She snatched it up, gave it a shake and flicked the switch. It didn't work. Most of the other items had been rescued by Gemma. Thank goodness they only stowed overnight necessities in the tent.

Security lights outside seeped through just enough she could make things out. Finding no rips or holes she honed in on the door which she usually zippered up tight but last night she'd been first asleep. There was a gaping slash at least a quarter of the way up filled with gushing water that was streaming in. Either Gemma hadn't zipped it tight or the force of the water had levered it up. Silently she bet which but wasn't about to voice her thoughts.

'We need to get out. Quick,' Maddie said as she grabbed a hold of the zip flap and tugged upwards. Even more water flooded in. 'Oh, far out,' she muttered as she sloshed on her knees through mud, twigs, leaves and a few slimy looking blobs she didn't really want to know what they were.

She emerged and stood, stunned. 'Oh my gosh! This is unbelievable.' As far as she could see there was water: a huge lake of water. Puddling around in it were bobbing humans in various states of dress and undress, most with some attempt of covering to protect them from the deluge. Torn garbage bags made flapping hoods and ponchos. Some lucky people had managed to find parkas or coats and a few tortured umbrellas dotted the silvery lake. Everyone was scrambling in the downpour in various directions, grabbing and clutching at fold-up chairs, portable barbecues, wildly flapping clothes from make-shift clothes-lines, tables, hoses, floating shoes and all sorts of bits and pieces. Caravans were being stuffed from open doors. Tents were being torn down and bundled into untidy piles. Bits and pieces shoved into cars.

Within seconds, Maddie's pyjamas had turned into a see through second skin. The intense wind and stinging rain turned wet skin into biting cold icicles. Spinning around at a loud gasp, Maddie hauled Gemma from the tent.

'Where did all this water come from?' Looking stunned, Gemma spun on the spot as she gazed around.

'We need to find somewhere dry,' said Maddie, searching for somewhere - anywhere that looked even remotely dry, and safe, she thought as a forked flash lit everything up. They were sitting ducks standing ankle deep in water with lightning so close.

'I need to pee,' said Gemma as she squirmed.

So did Maddie. All this water seemed to bring on the urge, but then she'd been asleep for... she glanced at her watch. Twenty past two. She'd already had eight hours. 'Better put our thongs on.'

'Why?'

'Because all sorts of nasties could be lurking under this water.' Kneeling, Maddie leant into the quagmire that had been their tent floor. In that brief time her bed had become as wet as Gemma's. What they were going to do about it was beyond thinking about. All four thongs were sitting like beacons on sodden fabric. She grabbed them along with her toiletries bag and reversed out.

With their thongs on, it was difficult wading through the ankle-deep eddying water that was doing its best to suck rubber from their feet. Dripping wet, Maddie felt as though she was in some time warp as they waded through goodness knew what towards the amenities block. The entire situation was so bizarre it was beyond ludicrous. A gurgling sound erupted from Gemma's mouth. It turned into a giggle then out-and-out laughter. She began prancing about and spinning around.

Laughter bubbled up Maddie's throat. She just couldn't keep it suppressed. She broke out into a run and grabbed Gemma's hand. Locked together they splashed their way to the building. Being on slightly higher ground and on a concrete slab, water had only just begun skimming across the tiles. But it was slippery, Maddie soon discovered when she skidded then staggered to regain her balance.

'Careful,' said Gemma as she tightened her grip.

They entered separate cubicles. Maddie was so wet the water dripped from soaked clothes and hair and streamed down limbs onto the tiles.

'What are we going to do?' Gemma called over the partition.

'Not much we can do but wait it out.'

'I'm frozen. Do you think we could have a hot shower?'

Maddie's body shivered in response. 'Can't see why not. The car keys are in the tent. Under my pillow. But my towel is soaked.'

'Mine's in the car. We can both use that.'

They flushed and exited at the same time. Standing in the building doorway, Maddie eyed the sky. She really didn't want to be ankle deep in water if lightning came too close. Even rubber thongs wouldn't insulate them. Peering through the haze of sheeting rain, she waited for the next flash and noticed it had moved to the south-west. Feeling more at ease she splashed her way to the tent, dived in and snatched keys from their hiding place, trying very hard to ignore the sludge she was kneeling in. Within minutes they had managed to find clean clothes and were standing under tepid water. It wasn't surprising that whatever method the park used to heat water, wasn't working. By the time she'd soaped off grunge and unfrozen her skin from icicles to barely warm, the water ran cold. She grabbed the towel slung over the cubicle wall and rubbed briskly.

'Towel,' Gemma called.

Maddie tossed it back and pulled on underwear, the only track pants she had with her and a tee-shirt. Then she collected her toiletries and dropped them in the bag she'd had sitting upside down to drain out unwanted moisture.

While waiting for Gemma to dress, she stood just inside the building doorway. The storm seemed to be moving on. Rain was easing, the wind was half the strength but the park was still a lake. Their tent was in a sorry sagging state with bits of swirling flotsam caught against the side. Not so many people were about. She figured the caravanners were inside drying off. Where the other campers were was a mystery. Certainly not in capsized tent city. Could be in the communal kitchen or television room.

'What should we do now?' Gemma brushed against her.

'The car is probably best. You can lie across the back seat. I'll recline the front seat as far back as possible. We might manage another couple of hours' sleep.'

'What about the tent?'

'Not a lot we can do until the rain stops and water subsides.'

It wasn't a cold night, just wet. But without the sleeping bag it wasn't warm enough to be comfortable even wearing a hoodie. Gemma lay folded on her side along the rear seat, a bundle of clothes to cushion her head. From the groans and sighs every time she moved, it was obvious Gemma was in as much discomfort as Maddie. It was only so long one could be comfortable wedged into an inclined seat. Pressure points soon turned numb or ached. Wriggling didn't bring relief. It reminded her of trying to sleep crammed into too small spaces on a plane.

Unusual clicks and whines came from the rear. Then a chuckle.

'What are you doing?' Maddie asked as she tried to look around.

'Looking at the photos we've taken so far.'

'Can't sleep?'

'No way. Didn't we take a photo of Mick?'

'Umm,' she had to think. 'Yes, at the border. Why?'

'It's not here.'

'Maybe I didn't take it right.' But she had because she recalled looking at it and admiring the man.

'He was a scary dude.'

'Scary, how?'

'I don't know. Just scary. That gun. Those gloves and cable ties. Secretive.'

'The gun was licensed. Bad guys don't have licensed weapons.' Maddie managed to set the seat upright and twisted around.

'Says Mick. Didn't have to be true. Crooks lie all the time. I think he was up to no good.' Gemma was still flicking through photographs, smiling or frowning at each.

'Really? I though he was okay. He saved our necks, looked out for us, called the police. A crook wouldn't call the police. He even had the truckies keep an eye out for us.'

'Yeah, I suppose, but he had the hots for you.' Gemma grinned as she lifted her eyes.

'You think?' A blush crept up Maddie's neck and face. It surprised her but the thought sent a wave of pleasure sweeping through her. Yes, he kept things to himself. Yes, there was something dark about him but she hadn't had a creepy sensation about Mick. Not like those three crazies from Kalgoorlie. She'd been right about them. She'd liked Mick. There was something about him that had drawn her. But Gemma was right about the gun. And there was something mysterious about him. She shrugged. It didn't matter. Mick had helped them and was gone. So no point even thinking about him. Yet, how many times had his image centred in her brain since parting? Too many to count. Somehow she couldn't get him out of her mind and every time she though about him all her innards felt squishy and warm.

The next hour was spent chatting about anything and everything while munching the last four muesli bars and sipping water. All the while, Maddie kept an eye on the weather. The rain eased then vanished. Ever so slowly the lake began draining away leaving a layer of slimy looking sludge. Not long after four, people began emerging from wherever they'd been hiding. They began inspecting the damage with couples and small groups homing in on their own pile of destruction. Maddie and Gemma joined them, picking there way between strewn shredded branches, litter and escaped objects from various campsites.

Their own tent was a limp bedraggled piece of nylon wearing a large branch as adornment. The torn wood had pierced through the side Maddie had been sleeping. If she had been inside - she shuddered at the thought. Dragging the legs of her pants to her knees, Maddie hunkered down next to the door, eased one hand inside, grappled around then tugged. Gemma's sodden sleeping bag emerged. Gemma swore under her breath.

'Oh, yuck!' Gemma added. 'It's ruined.'

Next came the mattress, followed by her own gear. Maddie eyed the mess. 'I suppose a good wash might get rid of most of the yuck but personally, I'm going to dump mine in the bin. It will take a good day to get everything washed and dried. A day we don't have. If my calculations are right, then we've only got one more overnight stay before reaching Brisbane. I vote to spend it in a motel. I don't want to miss my flight home.'

'We could shove it all in the back of the car and wash it when we reach Brisbane.'

Maddie straightened and examined the shambles, then toed through the items, turning them over. It was inconceivable to think how so much foreign matter had trespassed and used their tent as a hidey hole.

'You really want this stuff in your car? It'll stink. Do what you want with your things but my bedding is fairly old so is going in the bin.' With that Maddie bent, grabbed the end of her bag, rolled it then stood on it. It squelched and belched in protest as sloppy mud oozed and trickled.

'Oh, gross,' said Gemma then did the same.

After finding the park's big steel waste bin, they wrestled the sleeping bags, mattresses and tent through the park and heaved them into the bin, tossing pillows in on top. It made packing up the car easy for once.

Chapter Twenty-Five

Sunlight streaked mystical beams through tiny gaps between still heavy clouds by the time they reached Gunnedah. Rain had stopped and for the past forty kilometres there was little evidence of the storm. It must have come from another direction. Tale end of a cyclone, someone had mentioned while they were cleaning up the aftermath. They just didn't mention exactly where the cyclone had hit.

With a growling stomach telling her it was in desperate need of nourishment, Maddie nosed down the main street hoping some eating establishment would be open for early risers. The only sign of life was a murder of crows hopping around the top of huge grain silos towering over the town. She loved the collective noun for a group of such sombre-sounding birds. A murder: could have been called that because the pesky carrion made such a soul wrenching noise in the desolate heat of putrid hot days. People wanted to go and murder them so they would shut up. She grinned at the thought. With the big bins it was easy to figure out they were still in grain growing country.

As the sky lightened to dove-grey with salmon tinges, Maddie could make out a mural adorning the other high point of the large town: the water tank. Reaching a park, she turned into the entry and pulled into a parking bay, praying the public conveniences were open. As they wandered towards the tree shrouded building that look ominous, they came across a statue. Always curious about such things, Maddie stooped and squinted to make out the words then straightened in surprise.

'Dorothea Mackellar!'

'Who?'

'The lady who wrote the words to *My Country.*'

'Never heard of it.' Gemma turned away, showing her disinterest.

Maddie hurried to catch up. 'Sure you have. *I love a sunburnt country, a land of sweeping plains.* Every school kid learns it.' As they walked Maddie sang the first verse.

'Oh, yes. I remember the tune. We sang it at ANZAC Day ceremonies.'

They reached the door with half a modernistic figure of a female. It was padlocked. 'Fabulous,' Maddie groaned and turned away.

'There must be a twenty-four hour service station some-where,' said Gemma as they retraced their steps.

Edge of town, Maddie thought. There's always one either going in or leaving a town. She tried to recall if there'd been one as they drove in but she'd been thinking about the ridiculous night they'd experienced. After dumping the remains of their camping gear there was not a lot they could do so they'd decided to get going. Maddie had studied the map, calculating distances. A thousand kilometres didn't sound all that far compared to what they'd already covered but with more built up areas having slower legal speed limits she doubted they could do it in a day. It would mean reaching their destination late in the evening.

A further kilometre down the highway yielded the answer to desperation. Lit up like a welcoming beacon, the service station was bustling. Most petrol pumps were occupied but by reversing, Maddie was able to wedge close to the needed pump. It surprised her when Gemma alighted as soon as they came to a standstill then began filling the thirsty tank. It appeared she was still a bit uptight about Maddie's mood. Not that she'd had the energy to think about staying angry.

'I'm starving so ordering a full breakfast. What would you like?' Maddie called across the car roof.

'Sounds good. Plus juice and coffee. Add it to the fuel bill and I'll pay the lot.'

Well that was a first, Maddie thought as she wove between four rows of vehicles. Maybe the comment about earning forgiveness had sunk in. Maybe she should lose her cool more often if this was going to be the result. Her mouth turned up into a wry grin. For someone who rarely lost her temper, she'd certainly made up for it over the past week.

The plate of gooey fried eggs, crispy bacon, grilled tomato, hash browns, toast and baked beans smelt spectacular and was more than Maddie ever ate for breakfast but she enjoyed every last bite. Sopping up the yolk remains with the last crust, she popped it into her mouth, savoured as she chewed then swallowed, washing it down with the last two mouthfuls of rich coffee. Yum. Maybe she'd enjoyed it so much because she'd barely eaten a thing the previous day.

'Are you still mad at me?' Gemma's words were barely audible.

Not sure what to say, Maddie took her time in placing the knife and fork together, pushing the empty plate to one side then dabbing her mouth with the paper serviette. As she dropped it onto the plate she lifted her eyes to study Gemma's face. She looked scared.

'Not so much mad but not in a forgiving space yet.'

'Oh.' The word wasn't so significant but every feature of Gemma's face sagged: a face that was make-up free, Maddie realised. And the hair was without gelled spikes. But the clothes had gone back to weird mode with odd socks and clashing colours. Now what message was Gemma giving today? Insecure with the clothes but freshly washed, smooth shiny hair and no outlandish make-up? Hmm. Was she trying to make a good impression? Was this her way of making amends? Sometimes Maddie just couldn't make Gemma out and right now was one of those times.

With a full belly and empty bladder, Maddie had renewed energy. Determined to cover as many kilometres as possible, they set off towards Tamworth, well known as the Country and Western centre of Australia. Less than fifteen minutes later her phone rang. Guessing it would be her parents, she flicked a hand in Gemma's direction.

'Can you answer that for me? I'll pull over.' She indicated, glanced in all the mirrors, eased onto the gravel then braked to a standstill. When she reached for her phone there was a frown on Gemma's brow. 'What's wrong?' Those nerves she thought she'd put to rest, twanged alive again.

'It's the police.'

Far out, what now? She sniggered. After all their little adventures it could be the police from at least three different states. All of a sudden she felt like a criminal listed on Australia's most wanted list. 'Which police?'

'Didn't say.' Gemma held out the phone.

Her heart began to hammer as she said hello then listened, jabbing in a question whenever she got a chance. Seemed the officer was hell bent on getting out all the information in one breath. For once it was good news. She slid the phone back into the slot and turned to Gemma.

'They caught Josh Evans half-way to Adelaide. He denied any involvement but Liam Faulkner 'fessed up after the other one…'

'Matt,' piped up Gemma.

'Yes, Matt. The police hauled him in for questioning and he spilled the beans. Said he walked away when he knew what Josh was planning. He's being held as an accessory because he didn't put a stop to it. They found a large amount of Rohypnol in Josh's garbage bin. Stupid idiot. Fancy dumping the evidence in your own bin. Got his fingerprints all over the container.'

'What about Liam?'

The tone of Gemma's voice had Maddie examining Gemma's face again. Coy. So he was the one who had snagged Gemma's interest.

'He's in gaol along with the others. Although he wasn't the one who slipped the drug into the drinks, he's guilty of being a party to the whole thing. But apparently he was the one who insisted on calling a halt and driving you back to the caravan park after you threw up. Josh Evans has a black eye and a few bruises. It appears Liam decked him and shoved him out of the car before driving you back to the park.'

'So they're not all that bad.'

Maddie couldn't believe what she'd heard. She grabbed Gemma's hand and yanked. 'How can you say that?' The intent was to drug both of us, rape us then more than likely either kill us or leave us for dead. How can you possibly say that they're not all that bad? Are you out of your mind?'

'Matt walked away.' Gemma tugged her arm free and leant towards Maddie, her eyes spitting sharp jagged icicles in Maddie's direction.

'Are you really so naïve as to believe that by walking away he did the right thing?' Her voice took on a mind of its own and rose. 'He didn't stop them,' she yelled. 'He didn't tell the police or anyone what was about to happen.' She stabbed a finger in Gemma's chest. 'He just walked away and allowed a criminal act to happen. If anyone is the better out of all three it would be Liam Faulkner. Even though he went along with it at first, at least he put a stop to it. But they are all as guilty as hell.' Her chest heaved. 'If your sister was as dumb as you then no wonder she's dead.'

As soon as she'd said the last bit, Maddie regretted it. Gemma gasped then punched Maddie so hard on the arm that Maddie knew she'd have a whopping bruise there to match those across her torso. 'I'm sorry, I shouldn't have said that.'

'Bitch,' Gemma hissed then turned away to stare out the side window but not before Maddie noticed the rush of tears.

'That's the third time you've called me that and it's not appreciated. I apologise for being so harsh but get real. What they did was downright wrong. It wasn't only illegal, it was abuse of the worst kind and if you don't realise that then maybe your parents should come and get you.'

A loud hiss came from the other side of the car. 'Don't you dare say that,' Gemma yelled.

'I've said it and meant it.' Furious, Maddie twisted back in her seat and turned the key. 'Twice now in the space of a week you've encouraged scum of the male variety and both times we've almost ended up raped. I can't wait to reach Brisbane and end this hell. After that, I don't care. Keep doing what you do and end up dead like Leah. I. Don't. Care!' With that she yanked on the steering wheel and planted her foot on the accelerator.

Anger boiled as she drove. Past paddocks of cotton, wheat and cattle. Past two dead koalas. Past signs that otherwise would have snagged her interest and a detour to explore. *Diprotodon – largest marsupial to have ever lived.* Even slowing when they reached Tamworth, she didn't stop. It had been on the 'to do' list to explore. But she was way too angry so ignored Gemma's demands to stop. She was so mad she almost missed the turn-off onto the New England Highway. A sharp turn at the last minute when the sign nudged her memory bank, had horns honking and Gemma swearing as she was tossed to the side. Maddie didn't care.

An hour later they were drifting through the large university city of Armidale. It was really pretty with what looked like birch, poplar and ash trees lining the streets and bestowing dappled shade that gave the impression of the summer heat not being so bad. It was so pretty Maddie was tempted to stop but didn't. Normally she would have explored but she wanted this horror journey over.

Another hour of deathly silence, another large town. This time they were in rolling hills on the north tableland. Glen Innes was beautiful and the only reason she pulled into a service station was because she was desperate for the bathroom. Gemma tailed her inside but said nothing. For that Maddie was beyond glad. One word from Gemma and Maddie figured she'd bop her on the nose. The big breakfast had filled her belly but the need for a caffeine fix had her detouring to the counter. She ordered two, paid for them, waited for her order to be filled. She might be mad but she wasn't mean. After picking up both take-away cups, she headed outside. Gemma was standing by the driver's door.

'I'll drive,' she dared to say.

'Not going to happen.' Maddie handed over one cup and used her hip to nudge Gemma out of the way.

'Why not?'

Maddie really, really didn't like the whine. It just re-ignited her level of mad. 'Figure it out yourself.' She unlocked the car and plonked into the seat, easing the coffee into the round recess in the console. Without waiting for the grump, she started the engine, clipped her seatbelt into place and began drifting forward, suffocating her grin at the mad scramble to scoot around the other side and get in.

'Why can't I drive? It's my car.'

Oh, boy, that sulky tone was doing Maddie's head in. 'Last time you drove you almost killed us. No way am I going to let that happen again.' She planted her foot and eased onto the concourse then to the edge of the highway, waiting with her temper simmering for the stream of traffic to pass before pulling onto the road.

She barely noticed the scenery as she drove, intent on getting to their destination as soon as possible without any more drama and hopefully without having to converse with whingeing Willy. The atmosphere in the car was so intense Maddie turned on the CD player then winced at the loud blast of heavy metal. 'Far out,' she muttered under her breath, pressed the eject button then searched for one of her own more soothing discs. Since they were in the centre for Country and Western, she chose a CD she was certain would get up Gemma's nose: golden oldies from Dolly Parton. She grinned at the groan from Grumpy then relaxed into the seat, huffed out her frustration and decided to enjoy the scenery of yellow rolling hills dotted with cattle, a few sheep and strips of green vegetation.

Halfway to Tenterfield she came upon a mob of cattle either being shifted from one farm to another or they were grazing in the long paddock – the strip of pasture along the sides of the highway. Maddie knew that in times of drought the cattle were allowed to graze roadsides as long as they were tended by stockmen on horseback. The herd was so thick, she was forced to stop.

'What's going on?' Gemma asked.

It was a dumb question deserving of an equally dumb answer. 'There are animals blocking the way.'

'Smart ass,' slid from the corner of Gemma's mouth as she wound down the window. All of a sudden she jerked up from her seat and half hung out the window. 'Scram,' she yelled.

'God, no,' Maddie croaked out as she unlatched her seat belt, threw herself sideways and grabbed a hold of Gemma's tee-shirt then yanked her back inside. All the while she kept an eye on the nearest beasts. Thankfully they just raised their heads and stared.

'What's wrong,' Gemma whined as she made to repeat her actions.

'Don't!' Maddie warned as she tugged her back.

'Why not?'

'Don't you have any brains in that skull of yours? If you startle the cattle they might stampede then we'll be in all sorts of trouble.'

'Huh? What do you mean?'

'Each one of those animals weighs well over half a tonne. If they stampede they'll use your car as a battering ram. Just have patience and sit it out. They'll move on soon enough.'

'Doesn't look like they're moving.'

'Look over there.' Maddie pointed to the group of three horsemen. Two cattle dogs were with them. 'They know we are here and will move the cattle so we can get through. Watch.'

It only took ten minutes and the mob had been urged to one side, giving them a clear passage.

At Tenterfield thirty minutes later, Maddie pulled into a parking space right in front of a run down looking weatherboard cottage. This was one place she was determined to see. The town was dinky, lined with many deciduous trees.'

'What are we doing here?' asked Gemma.

Maddie sorted through her CD's, found what she was looking for and slid it into the player. She flicked through until she found the right tune. Peter Allen began singing a song he was famous for – *The Tenterfield Sadler*. 'This song is about Peter Allen's grandfather.' She pointed at the building. 'That little building is where his grandfather made his saddles. It's now a bit of a museum but by the looks of things, it's closed. I just wanted to have a look.'

'I thought he was a Yankee film star.'

Maddie laughed. 'Are you serious? He was very much an Aussie.'

'Oh. Are we going to have lunch here?'

Maddie glanced at her watch. Not quite one. 'No. Stanthorpe is only about fifty kilometres further on. We'll stop there.'

Stanthorpe was a large town close to the border of Queensland and New South Wales. It was certainly much bigger than Wallangarra, where they'd stopped to take the obligatory photo under the humungous sign depicting the border. While they lunched in a cute little country bakery, Maddie studied the map. It delighted her when she figured they could reach Brisbane that day. It would give her a whole twenty-four hours to sight-see. Alone.

Chapter Twenty-Six

Maddie was already regretting her decision. Even though nothing untoward had happened she felt jittery with Gemma driving. Why, oh, why had she relented when Gemma had promised faithfully, crossing her heart and hoping to die, that she would drive with utmost care and obey every single road sign? So far she'd kept her promise. Gemma's driving was impeccable but still Maddie's innards were tensed so tight she figured if something did happen she'd ping apart into millions of atoms. The salad sandwich she'd eaten was doing tumble-turns in her stomach and fighting with the apple juice. At least it was more built up with tiny towns breaking the monotony and giving her something to concentrate on. Vineyards were a welcome change of scenery around Ballandean. The tiny town, population 467 according to the sign, was in a spectacular picturesque setting. An empty railway line accompanied them into town. What she hadn't expected was the huge model dinosaur making its home at the disused station. They crossed a pretty but swirling muddy river on the northern side of town as they left. Run-off from the rain bearing depression was making its mark.

Settling back into her seat, Maddie focussed on relaxing, determined to quit worrying as they headed for Glen Alpin. Surely they'd had enough traumas for a single journey. What else could possibly happen? There'd been fire, flood and even famine if she counted her lack of food on a couple of occasions. Then they'd had everything else in between.

Vineyards were soon joined by orchards, making the scenery even more interesting. Everything seemed to glisten despite the summer heat. Sparkling pools and puddles nestled in roadside ditches and low spots in paddocks, so it had rained but not with the same intensity. There was no resulting devastation of torn trees and layers of sticky mud. Here there was just a welcome life-renewing drink for the vegetation, which gleamed after summer dust had been washed from the leaves. With the tension easing, Maddie closed her eyes but they shot open when the car decelerated all of a sudden.

'What's wrong?'

'Nothing.'

'Then why are we…?' She didn't have to finish the question when she spied jean-clad legs under a large tatty backpack. A raised thumb peeked out the side and hoicked forwards. Whether it was a male or female hidden behind the filthy rolled bedding strapped to the top of the navy pack, was indiscernible. It didn't matter. No way were they going to pick up a stranger.

'Do not stop,' Maddie growled.

'Why not?' Gemma glanced at her. A determined pout gave her a sulky demeanour. The car was still moving but crawling like a wounded animal gasping for its last breath.

'If you need me to tell you then your I.Q. must be at imbecile level. If that person gets in this car then I'm getting out and you can deal with the results. Think druggie. Think weapon. Think bashed. Think rape. Oh, sorry, you haven't got the brains to think.' Sarcasm was strong but boy, Gemma deserved it. 'I can't believe that after Broken Hill you would even contemplate picking up a hitchhiker.' From the corner of her eye, Maddie noticed the unknown person had stopped and turned around. He was the scruffiest looking guy she'd ever seen. He was lowering his backpack. 'Oh, God, he looks like real bad news. Drive on,' she yelled.

Gemma glanced at the man then paled before swearing under her breath. She planted her foot. The car kangaroo hopped then wheels spun before finding grip and taking off with a screech just as the man reached for the door handle. Up close he looked like a thug from the worst ever criminal gang. Matted long hair looked like it had never seen shampoo or even water. A recent bloodied cut ran down one cheek under a blackened eye. There were so many scary tattoos fighting for space amongst seriously fierce piercings, Maddie couldn't recall ever seeing anyone so creepy and downright sinister. As the car pulled away there was a loud thud on the door.

'Go, go, go,' Maddie yelled.

'I'm going,' Gemma croaked.

Somehow, Maddie knew Gemma was as scared of the apparition as Maddie was.

'I'm sorry, Maddie. I didn't realise,' Gemma added as the car picked up so much speed Maddie was pressed back into the seat.

Maddie's eyes slid shut as she sucked in a long slow breath. Her heart was campaigning to escape her chest. Adrenaline was spurting through her system and her fists were so tight that her nails were cutting into her palms. She was too stunned to say a thing.

'I'm sorry,' Gemma whimpered.

With a desperate need to thump some sense into Gemma's thick skull, Maddie willed her fists to stay in her lap. She forced her eyes to open then searched the side rear vision mirror. A raised hand was giving them a rude two-finger salute and it looked as though obscenities were being hurled at them.

'I know what you are going to say,' came from her side. A loud sniff followed.

'Really?' Maddie twisted around. Tears were streaming down cheeks that had taken on a definite grey tinge. Gemma looked stricken. No words were needed.

'Just drive.'

'Okay.' Gemma swiped her wrist under her nose then grappled for a tissue from the pocket pack in the console and dabbed away moisture before blowing her nose.

The sign announcing Severnlea loomed then passed.

'You want to stop here?' Gemma whispered.

'No way. Just keep driving. I don't want to be around when that scary creep comes into town.'

Gemma kept driving, only slowing enough to keep within the lower limit as they drifted through what was no more than a little hamlet surrounded by orchards. It wasn't long before they were fighting built up traffic in the much larger centre of Stanthorpe and still Gemma didn't stop. Nor did she utter a word. The tears had ceased but every now and again she shuddered. A few whimpers escaped then she blew her nose again, breaking the tense silence.

'Are you all right?' Maddie finally asked. Gemma neither looked nor sounded all right. She looked as though she was only just holding it together.

'Yes.' There was a long sucked in breath. 'He looked so evil,' she added after a pause.

'You ever going to stop for a hitchhiker again?'

'No way. I'm really, really sorry.'

'This time I believe you. Now relax and drive.' She settled back to follow her own suggestion but the atmosphere was acute. She did her best to ease tense muscles but couldn't seem to get her body to obey.

'Have you ever seen anyone so creepy?' asked Gemma after another lengthy pause.

It appeared Gemma was having as much trouble as Maddie in getting rid of the vision. 'No and to be quite honest, I never want to again.' She scoffed. She had never been one to pass judgement on looks alone, well, not as long as she could remember. She probably did in the early years of primary school before she learnt better. The guy could have been quite innocent and an upstanding citizen but gee whiz, if anyone ever looked the epitome of evil it was that guy.

A whisper of blown out breath came from Gemma. 'Did you see those huge spikes in his ears?'

'I couldn't get past the bone through his septum.'

'What's a septum?'

'The piece of cartilage separating your nostrils.'

'How do you know these things?'

'Learning all the parts of your body is essential with physiotherapy.'

'Oh, yes, of course. But how would you blow your nose?'

'Don't want to even think about it.'

'What if you had a serious cold?'

Maddie groaned, the vision of thick globules of green snot hanging from the ends of the bone being seriously gross. Then she couldn't help it but a giggle escaped with an indelicate snort. 'Might have to shove cotton buds up each nostril.'

Gemma laughed. 'Then he'd look like a vampire.'

'Would go with those tats. Talk about spooky. I can't believe anyone would want to disfigure their face so badly.'

'He probably had them all over. Even his… you know.'

Maddie shuddered. 'Ooh, ouch, that would hurt. But I suppose you might be right. Anyone who has a chain threaded through his eyebrow has probably got weird things pierced in unmentionable places.'

'And that huge ring through a cheek. How would you wash your face and keep it clean?'

'Outside wouldn't be so bad, but the inside? It must get in the way when he eats. All that masticated food.'

Gemma laughed. 'How about kissing him? Must be kind of awkward with so many shafts and rings through your lip.'

'I'd never get close enough to find out.'

Within seconds they were both laughing as each threw out more and more gross suggestions. The easy chatter continued as they wound along the highway headed for Warwick. It wasn't the straightest of roads with lots of bends and ups and downs, but the scenery was fascinating. To fill in time, Maddie studied the map, making calculations. She suggested they stop in Warwick to fill the fuel tank, have a bathroom break and get some refreshments. Then she snuggled to get more comfortable and slid her eyes closed for a nap.

The next thing she knew was being shoved.

'Wake up, we're here.'

'Where?' Her eyes stuttered apart and she straightened then glanced around. The car was parked next to a petrol pump at a bustling service station. The sting of fuel stench tickled her nose.

'Come on, I've already filled the tank. Let's get something to eat.'

'Oh, all right but we'd better shift the car first.' Maddie twisted as she searched for somewhere to park. 'What about over there? There's a bit of shade.' She pointed to an area next to the side fence that was shadowed by a large willow.

Feeling a bit peckish, Maddie opted for a sausage roll and sauce to go with her large coffee while Gemma devoured a hot dog. She then disappeared down the far end of the service station for a while. When she returned, Gemma dropped some folded money in front of Maddie.

'What's this?'

'Money to cover the new tyre and the jeans I wrecked.'

Stunned, Maddie took her time in separating the five fifty dollar notes. 'This is a bit too much. I owe you thirty.'

'No, you don't. Don't forget the swearing fines and I owe you heaps more than just money. I owe you my life. More than once.'

'Huh, I don't understand.' It was stupid but she felt embarrassed as she stacked the notes on top of each other, folded them in three then slipped them into the back of her purse.

'Not only this past week but three years ago. You saved my life by becoming my friend.' Gemma reached across the table and grasped both of Maddie's hands. 'You are the best friend anyone could ever have and I'm sorry. Really sorry. About everything. I'm sorry I called you a bitch because you're not. You are the nicest person I know. I'm the one who has been the bitch and I'm sorry about that too.'

Already gob-smacked by Gemma's actions, Maddie reeled back as tears began flowing down Gemma's face. They were genuine tears of remorse. She didn't understand how she could tell but deep inside she just knew.

'I don't know what to say, but thank you. I can tell you really mean that.' She moved around the table and gave Gemma a long hard hug. Even though she felt overwhelmed there was something Gemma said that suddenly twigged. 'Are you trying to tell me that you were contemplating suicide three years ago?'

A bright red blush swept up Gemma's damp cheeks. 'Yes. I didn't know how to cope. I was messed up. Until you came along. You were the only one who understood how I felt inside.'

'Heavens, I never knew that's what you were thinking. You never said.'

'I know but after those first few counselling sessions together I never thought about it again.'

'Have you ever thought about it since?' She just had to know how fragile Gemma was.

Gemma laughed as she swept the moisture from her face with a clenched fist. 'No, never.'

'Well, that's a relief. Now what say we get out of here? But before we go, I want to say how much I appreciate what you just said. This is what I call earning someone's forgiveness.'

'Really? You forgive me? Oh, wow!' The look of wonderment of Gemma's face was amazing and so openly genuine.

'Yes, so let's go.'

After freshening up in the rest rooms, they hurried back to the car and buckled up.

'We've only got about two hundred kilometres to go. Why don't you phone your uncle and let him know we'll arrive at about…' Maddie glanced at her watch, studied the map then added half an hour to the time she'd calculated. 'I'm guessing about seven.' We'll be going through major built up areas. Do you want me to drive? You can navigate.'

'Okay.'

The instant agreement without any argument was a real surprise but at least her nerves wouldn't be strung so tight and she'd be able to relax more and enjoy the end of the journey. After swapping seats, Maddie pointed out the route on the map. 'We're here and we need to get there. And don't forget we have to turn onto the Century Highway which is…' she searched and jabbed a finger on the spot. 'Look out for the road sign.'

Just out of town they turned onto the Cunningham Highway. The road was busy as they rose through hills to Cunningham's Gap, which would sneak them between two high peaks and was supposed to have spectacular scenery. Maintaining a steady pace up the steep rise was easy most of the time. A few caravans slowed things down on the steeper sections and it was obvious by trails of gravel, rocks and torn foliage that the mountains had received a severe dumping of water overnight. In a few places she had to steer around larger rocks and thick piles of debris that had been collected as the water had run down the steep sides. Road clean-up crews were going to be busy.

They'd just passed through the peak when it began to rain again. Not the sheeting rain of the previous night but it was heavy and steady, requiring Maddie's full concentration. The road was going to be slippery, especially if all the debris began sliding across the road again. Through the rain haze she could just make out a winding road way, way down in the valley. A gasp escaped when she realised just how high they were. Spectacular the scenery might be to some but to Maddie it was downright scary.

'Oh, my God!' Gemma exclaimed as she cringed back into her seat. 'Is that where we're going?' She pointed to the far off narrow ribbon of denuded vegetation that indicated a road.

'I think so. I didn't realise we'd driven so high. It feels kind of scary. So you want to drive?'

'Uh, uh, no way. How about keeping to the middle?'

Maddie laughed. 'There's a double white line. I can't go over it, especially in this rain. Are you afraid of heights?'

'Not normally, no but this is really scary.'

They came to a sign indicating a right angle turn to the right. Maddie dropped to a lower gear. Her heart shot to her mouth when the wheels lost traction in streaming mud and the rear end did a little skip sideways before she regained control. Gemma's little squeal didn't help. Braking slowly, Maddie crept around the sharp bend only to see the road disappear in the opposite direction at an equally sharp angle. Far out, she sure hadn't been expecting this. Then there was bend after bend after bend with most covered in slime and debris. Who even dared take a peek at the scenery to see if it was indeed spectacular?

Ever so slow, they crept downwards. Maddie didn't care if she was holding up traffic. No way was she taking any risks. The strain of driving was much easier when high vegetation blocked the view on the down side when they couldn't see the sheer drop but when the trees disappeared and there was nothing but a treacherous looking sheer cliff that seemed to go down forever, it was petrifying. Gemma spent the entire downwards journey huddled close to Maddie and away from the side window as she squealed and gasped while Maddie was hunched over the steering wheel keeping her eyes on the guard rail and praying it would hold the car in place if they skidded and she got too close. It was especially harrowing when a car came from the other direction, crossing over the double line as it cut the corner. Maddie had never experienced such a nerve-wracking drive and wasn't all that keen on ever repeating the ordeal.

It was such a relief when they levelled out near the bottom. After that it was a piece of cake driving, even through the suburbs of Ipswich, despite having to negotiate heavy traffic, flooded kerbs and intersections and the obstacle course of severe storm damage.

It was easier still once they turned onto the Century Highway. From there they had written instructions on how to get to Indooroopilly. Gemma turned out to be an efficient navigator, giving Maddie plenty of warning when she had to turn and getting them to the fabulous looking revamped Queenslander style house. Set high up on stilts with a wide veranda wearing traditional wood shutters, the house appeared to be luxurious. It was set in a lush tropical garden.

Maddie released a long sigh as she turned off the motor and slumped over the steering wheel in sheer relief. The drive to hell and back had finally come to an end.

Chapter Twenty-Seven

Even after being home for two weeks, Maddie still couldn't get over how wonderful it felt to be on her own bed in her own room. She circled another job prospect in the local paper as she lay on her stomach with her feet swinging in the air behind her. Somehow she doubted she'd be able to find a job for the two months before she went back for her final year at university. Most summer jobs would have been well and truly filled by now. But the money would come in handy. Even though she knew her parents would support her if her funds became too depleted, she felt much better supporting herself. Every year she'd managed to find part time jobs that fitted in with her study regimen. It had given her enough to buy her study requirements, the occasional new outfit, a modicum of leisure activities and she'd even been able to save a modest amount. If she was really frugal, she would have enough to last her the final year, but it would mean no treats and virtually no social life.

She circled another position then tossed the paper onto the floor. Turning over, she closed her eyes as she wondered how Gemma was coping. There had only been one email from Gemma since Maddie had flown out of Brisbane. No phone calls, no emails, no texts, no nothing. She wondered what that meant. Was Gemma so engrossed in her new job that she didn't have time to contact? Or now that Maddie had served her purpose, had she been given the flick. Gemma would make a heap of new friends easily. She always did.

If she was really honest, Maddie was overjoyed about no longer being at Gemma's beck and call every time she was on a downer. It still gave her the creeps at the thought of being treated as a replacement sister. That felt a bit sick. Maybe with Gemma having to be more independent away from her parent's smothering, she would grow up a bit. Become more sensible, more mature.

The more she thought about it the more she realised that under normal circumstances she and Gemma would never have been friends. They had very little in common. It felt wrong to be glad that Gemma was out of her life but she was.

'Maddie!'

She sat up at her mother's voice. 'In here!'

Her mother appeared in the doorway. 'There's someone her to see you. A police officer.'

Her innards tightened. 'Police officer? Why would? Oh, no! Gemma! What's she done now?' Maddie flew off the bed, pounded down the passage and swung into the lounge-room. 'Gemma, what happened?' she yelled to the back of a large man clad in his dress uniform, which was a surprise. Why wasn't he in his work uniform?'

'As far as I know, Gemma is fine,' he said as he began turning.

That voice, she knew that voice then he turned and her mouth gaped. 'Mick? But…'

'Actually, Michael is my middle name. Dylan Michael McKay. Sergeant. Australian Federal Police. At your service.' Then he grinned.

'But you were…'

'Undercover. Chasing a gang of drug barons who owned the large shipment of cocaine being transported in both my and Bud's trucks. We've been after this particular gang for quite some time. Sorry, but I couldn't tell you. My life and the entire operation depended on keeping my identity under wraps. For a while I thought it might have been those three idiots from Kalgoorlie.' He stepped closer then held out a gorgeous bouquet of mixed blooms. 'These are for you. Happy birthday.'

'But… thank you. It was two days ago.' Mystified, she eyed him. 'How did you know?'

'Your dad.'

'Excuse me? You spoke to my dad?'

'How else was I going to find you? It was easy tracking down a police officer by the name of Brown who worked in accident investigations. And it was legal. Using official resources to track you on a personal level – probably not so legal. Besides I figured I should do the gentlemanly thing and ask if he minded me pursuing his daughter.'

He was standing so close she could feel his body heat and smell the yummy scent of him she'd dreamt about. It was doing strange things to her innards: amazing things that felt so darn good. 'Pursuing?' She felt like an idiot for not being able to string together enough words for a full sentence but suddenly her brain had turned to soggy spaghetti.

'Yes, pursuing. When we met yesterday I assured your dad I was one of the good guys while he assured me I wouldn't have to fight off any steady boyfriend, which surprised me.'

'Surprised you? Why? And why are you wearing your dress uniform?' She folded her arms and took a step back so she wouldn't fling herself onto his chest to see if he felt as good as he did in her dream last night. 'Trying to impress me?'

He laughed. 'Do I need to? No. I was on official guard duty at Government House. Some big-wigs in town. My posting is at the airport. Can we sit down? I've been standing guard for the past four hours and would love to give my feet a rest.'

'Oh, sorry, of course.' With her innards having a yoyo competition she perched on the sofa arm while Mick settled back in the cushions – a little too close for he sanity. She couldn't understand why it felt so amazing to see him again.

'I was surprised that a beautiful young lady like you hasn't got a bevy of admirers chasing after you.'

Far out, she knew she had turned bright red by the incinerator burning in her cheeks. 'I date.'

He dared to laugh again. 'There's a difference between occasional dates with various guys and a serious relationship. Your dad mentioned the first.'

'I'm going to kill him.'

He leant towards her. 'Then I'll have the pleasure of arresting you and keeping you locked up all to myself.'

Affronted, yet delighted, she glared at him. Then he reached out and grasped one hand.

'It's never happened to me before, but by the time we parted I was falling for you.'

'Falling for me?'

'Yes, more like smitten. I haven't been able to get you out of my mind, which played havoc with my concentration while taking down a gang of seriously bad crooks.' He winked. 'Especially since truckies and police officers kept ringing me to relate your latest escapade.'

All of a sudden something dropped into place. 'McKay. Sergeant McKay. Broken Hill. They rang you. You were the one who said to believe everything I said. But how did they know?'

A seriously wicked grin split his face. He was such a hunk when he smiled. 'I told you how I put your details on the truckie grapevine. Well, I did the same with the police stations. Told them you were my girl and I was concerned about your welfare.'

'Your girl?'

'It was one way they would take me seriously. I couldn't tell you without compromising my operation. Seems I was right to be concerned. You do manage to get your self into some awkward and mighty dangerous situations.'

'Gemma gets me into the situations. It was a road trip to hell and back. And you don't know the half of it.'

'There was more?' His faced turned serious as he straightened and tightened his grip.

She tried to tug her hand back because he was creating havoc with his thumb running circles around the inside of her wrist.

He tugged back. 'No. I like the feel of your hand in mine. It feels right. So maybe we should spend time together so you can tell me everything and we can get to know each other better and see if my feelings for you are the real thing. How about now? I have the rest of the day off duty.'

'Feelings? You have feelings for me?'

He grinned. 'I do, and I'm hoping they might be reciprocated.' Cocking his head to one side his eyes questioned her.

'I haven't been able to forget you either. So maybe. I don't know.'

His face split into a wide grin. 'Maybe we should find out. Have you got anything planned for today?'

'Umm, no.'

'How about we go for a drive, find somewhere to explore on foot while we talk and maybe find a nice casual eating establishment to share a meal?'

Oh, boy! She couldn't believe this was happening. 'How about we do just that? Do I have to dress up to match your formal attire?' She stood and he followed her up.

'No, we can drop by my place and I can change into more comfortable civvies. But before we go.' He tugged her close and wrapped his arms around her. 'I just want to see if you fit against me in real life, as well as you do in my dreams.' Putting his arms in various positions he made exaggerated noises of approval. 'Perfect fit and there's something else.'

'What?' she managed to stutter out before he dropped his head, settled his mouth over hers and kissed her. It was no meek little peck. Oh, my! She felt as though she'd turned into a puddle of hot jelly. And her innards turned to hot mush.

He dragged his mouth away and stared into her eyes. He looked shaken but not as shaken as she felt.

'Much, much better than my imagination. Let's go. I'm looking forward to getting to know you better. Much better.'